**Raves for the
Murder A-Go-Go Series
by Rosemary Martin**

Twist and Shout Murder

"Another . . . sixties retro-cozy from Martin, whose charming Murder A-Go-Go mystery series stars endlessly perky and naive Bebe Bennett. . . . All supercute cozy aficionados are sure to find this offering as intoxicating as an extra-dry martini." —*Publishers Weekly*

"Another groovy entry into a very mod series that will win new fans and keep readers anxious for the next Bebe and Bradley adventure."
—The Mystery Reader

"A truly enjoyable read. Rosemary Martin has got under the skin of the early sixties, which come to vibrant life. . . . This is one series I will make sure I don't miss out on—great stuff!" —MyShelf.com

"Ms. Martin has the sixties down perfectly and blends the pop-cultural elements seamlessly into the story. Bebe's the mystery genre's *That Girl!* . . . . If you want a fun blast from the past or just a riveting good mystery, then dance your way to a copy of *Twist and Shout Murder*."—The Romance Reader's Connection

"A kicky and kooky read. It'll keep you turning the pages." —*Rendezvous*

continued . . .

Other Books in the
Murder A-Go-Go Series
by Rosemary Martin

It's a Mod, Mod, Mod, Mod Murder

Twist and Shout Murder

Secret Agent Girl

A MURDER A-GO-GO MYSTERY

Rosemary Martin

A SIGNET BOOK

SIGNET
Published by New American Library, a division of
Penguin Group (USA) Inc., 375 Hudson Street,
New York, New York 10014, USA
Penguin Group (Canada), 90 Eglinton Avenue East, Suite 700, Toronto,
Ontario M4P 2Y3, Canada (a division of Pearson Penguin Canada Inc.)
Penguin Books Ltd., 80 Strand, London WC2R 0RL, England
Penguin Ireland, 25 St. Stephen's Green, Dublin 2,
Ireland (a division of Penguin Books Ltd.)
Penguin Group (Australia), 250 Camberwell Road, Camberwell, Victoria 3124,
Australia (a division of Pearson Australia Group Pty. Ltd.)
Penguin Books India Pvt. Ltd., 11 Community Centre, Panchsheel Park,
New Delhi - 110 017, India
Penguin Group (NZ), 67 Apollo Drive, Rosedale, North Shore,
Auckland 1311, New Zealand (a division of Pearson New Zealand Ltd.)
Penguin Books (South Africa) (Pty.) Ltd., 24 Sturdee Avenue,
Rosebank, Johannesburg 2196, South Africa

Penguin Books Ltd., Registered Offices:
80 Strand, London WC2R 0RL, England

First published by Signet, an imprint of New American Library,
a division of Penguin Group (USA) Inc.

First Printing, June 2007
10 9 8 7 6 5 4 3 2 1

In loving memory of a beautiful soul,
Amanda Joy Crawford,
September 10, 1982–September 21, 2006.

Acknowledgments

With thanks to my editor, Ellen Edwards. Ellen, I've learned so much from working with you. I can never thank you enough.

Thanks to Harvey Klinger, aka the Wonder Agent. Here's to the future.

Thanks to WBP for the inspiration. Bradley thanks you too.

With love and thanks to HAL for sharing his endless talent. Your work kept me somewhat sane while I wrote this book. May you always have peace and happiness.

Thank you to every author's friend, award-winning author Doug Lyle, M.D., who never hesitates with his generosity.

Thanks to Sam Roy for encouraging me and sharing life lessons.

With warmest thanks to my dear Cynthia, who never lets me down and always builds me up. I love you and forgive you for that last shopping spree.

As always, I want to thank my family, Tommy, Rachel, and Alana for their love. I love you more than I can properly express.

Chapter One

October 1964

The TV camera closed in on Hugh Downs's amiable face. "Please welcome our next guest, Bradley Williams. Mr. Williams is the corporate manager of Merryweathers' Toy Shoppe and he has some exciting news for us this morning."

The studio audience, peppered with small children, clapped politely.

Mr. Downs turned toward Bradley. "It's nice to have you on the *Today* show, Mr. Williams. What's your plan for Merryweathers'?"

Watching from the greenroom along with the store's characters, who were in full costume, I smiled when the camera shifted to my dreamy boss, Bradley.

"Thanks, Hugh. Your viewers may know that Mr. and Mrs. Merryweather decided to retire to Florida and sell the city's favorite toy store. Our company offered the elderly couple something others didn't. We agreed to keep their store as they originally envisioned it, complete with all the store characters New York families have come to love. And not only that—but today marks the opening of Merryweathers' Toy Shoppes in Chicago and Los Angeles!"

Bradley's words were met with hearty applause. I nodded to myself. Bradley's business sense was admirable. His strategy had worked. He'd said the company would lose customers and money if the old store were modernized. Instead it should be kept just as everyone loved it.

And Bradley's legendary charm could work a crowd—or a girl's dress off her back. I should know. He'd almost done it to me.

"Viewers in Los Angeles and Chicago, you're in for a treat," Hugh said to the camera before it swung back to Bradley.

He nodded modestly. I almost dropped the bagel I had snagged from the catered breakfast I'd ordered for everyone. Modest? Bradley? Confident, man-about-town, never-missed-the-cocktail-hour Bradley?

"I plan to do everything in my power to see that Merryweathers' maintains its fun, friendly traditions. In fact, all of our customers are invited to the store today for a special celebration. We're holding a fortieth birthday party—"

At that moment, the store clown raced onto the set. The tall man crouched on his little tricycle, pedaling around in mad circles. He honked the tricycle's red horn, tossed out candy to the audience, and paused to strum a snippet of music on his ukulele.

Boys and girls in the studio audience erupted into cries of joy. "Mr. Skidoo! Mr. Skidoo!" they screamed. Parents halfheartedly tried to control their shouting and jumping children.

Dressed with an Edwardian flair, the clown wore the same costume all the store's Mr. Skidoos had worn since 1924: white face paint with an ornately drawn black mustache curling over red lips, a black top hat, black tails over bright blue-and-green striped pants, a red shirt, white bowtie, white gloves, and white spats over highly polished black shoes. Everyone loved Mr. Skidoo.

Except me.

With a flick of my wrist, I threw my half-eaten bagel into the trash can. Behind me the store characters waited for their turn to go on air. Although I didn't know them particularly well yet, I couldn't help but notice that they had all turned their attention away from the TV monitor when Mr. Skidoo appeared.

The clown reveled in the adoration he received, throwing kisses and bowing to the audience. Onstage with Mr. Downs and Bradley, Mr. Skidoo steered his tricycle over to Bradley, disembarked with a flourish of his coattails, and sat down in the next chair.

"I hope Mr. Skidoo doesn't try any of his tricks on your boss while they're on air, Miss Bennett," grunted the store Pirate, Mr. Geedunk.

I turned to the beefy Pirate and gently petted the large green, red, and yellow parrot perched on his shoulder. "Surely Mr. Skidoo wouldn't do something like that on national television." Privately, I was thinking that was exactly what he *would* do.

The parrot squawked. "Kill the clown!"

Muffled laughter filled the greenroom.

I raised a puzzled brow at the Pirate, hoping for an explanation, but none was forthcoming.

The store manager, Mr. Mallory, dressed in a chalk-striped dark blue suit and bowler hat, pointed his walking stick to the room in general. In a stiff English accent he said, "I won't tolerate any public rudeness toward Mr. Skidoo. He has been the store's mascot for forty years. You must respect the clown currently representing him."

Respect is earned, I thought, but kept quiet and turned back to the TV monitor.

Bradley smiled with good nature when Mr. Skidoo squirted water in his face from a flower pin. Whisking a crisp white handkerchief from his suit jacket pocket, Bradley made a swipe at his face, then spoke. "We'll have birthday cake, punch, and the first one hundred girls under ten years old will receive a Raggedy Ann doll. The first one hundred boys under ten years old will get their own die-cast police car."

The studio audience yelled its approval.

Mr. Skidoo squirted Hugh Downs.

The anchorman laughed and said, "We'll be right back after these words from our sponsor."

That served as a cue to the rest of the store characters, who began to file out of the greenroom.

"Break a leg, everyone," I called.

They passed by me: the Cowboy, the Princess, the Pirate and his parrot, the Train Conductor, Raggedy Ann, the Toymaker, the Teddy Bear—who served as the store greeter—and finally, Mr. Mallory, his nose in the air.

Everyone gathered behind Mr. Downs and Bradley except Mr. Skidoo. The clown was front and center, playing a miniature white tuba.

I stood off camera to one side of the stage.

After the commercial break, the camera focused on the group shot. The store characters smiled and waved to the crowd.

"Thanks for watching, everyone. Please be sure to tune in tomorrow." Mr. Downs could barely close the show over the noise from the children and Mr. Skidoo's tuba.

The lights on the set dimmed as Bradley shook hands with Mr. Downs, exited his chair, and strolled over to me. "Everyone happy backstage, Miss Bennett?"

I looked into the bluest blue of all—Bradley's

eyes—crossed my fingers behind my back, and fibbed. "Yes, Mr. Williams. The catered breakfast went over especially well."

We had returned to formal address over the summer, after I had almost lost my virginity to him last spring.

He walked back with me to the greenroom. "Good. You're a superb executive secretary. I wouldn't have asked you to come with me from Ryan Modeling if I didn't think so. Thank you for saying yes."

A tidal wave couldn't have stopped me. "Of course."

Deliberately, I raised my right hand to waist level and pretended to examine my Tiffany gold charm bracelet, the typewriter charm sparkling in the light. Bradley had given it to me one sunny day before he'd turned into Mr. Strict Boss.

My mind flashed back to the end of spring. While I had thought Bradley was on the brink of selecting that perfect diamond engagement ring from Tiffany, he'd spent the summer locked in his all-business attitude, disabusing me of any such notion. Now the leaves on the trees were red and gold and he still wore the shield of a professional relationship. I wondered if I were destined to play Miss Moneypenny to his James Bond forever. Come to think of it, though, with my record of solving murder cases, I was more of a secret agent than Bradley was.

My pride demanded that I behave in a similar professional and aloof manner, but it didn't stop me from wearing the perfume that drove Bradley crazy, My Sin.

We moved into the greenroom. "You're certain you can handle your secretarial duties and keep an eye on the sales floor?" Bradley asked sternly.

I stood as tall as my five feet seven inches could stretch next to his lean six-foot build. "I'm perfectly capable of balancing my duties. I'm pleased you approved my plan to bring Danielle with us when we left Ryan Modeling. She can take over for me when I'm downstairs and help out when I'm at my desk."

"Good. I want someone I know and trust to report what our employees are like and spot any potential problems." Bradley tugged his starched white cuff and glanced at his watch. "We have less than two hours before the birthday party begins."

"Won't it be groovy? Who can resist a party with lots of children?"

He closed his eyes briefly and inhaled a deep breath. "At least no one will be murdered," he said, his handsome face stern.

I blushed, a bad, if involuntary, habit of mine. Bradley knew I had an uncanny knack for getting involved in murder investigations. He'd forgotten the last one in which *he'd* been the prime suspect and *I* had found the killer.

"Why on earth would anyone at a children's toy store be murdered? I don't know how you can even say such a thing," I said and sighed.

He shrugged one broad shoulder. "Gather the troops and meet me at the store. We have to get ready for the little devils."

The street door to the greenroom swung closed after him. I stood for a moment, twirling a strand of my hair, another bad habit. At least I didn't frown. Mama had long ago warned me how frowning led to wrinkles, something no woman wanted.

Bradley's attitude toward children was new to me and I didn't think it was cool. When we got married, I wanted at least two children, first a boy, then a girl.

The whole plan was written in my secret notebook, along with my goals of fun things to accomplish in New York City. Hmmm. Maybe Bradley didn't want to ruin his reputation as a man-about-town by ruffling a little boy's hair or curling a girl's ringlets around his finger. Yes, that was it. He would feel differently about his own children. I chewed my thumbnail.

Lost in thought, I didn't hear the door open from the studio.

Suddenly I felt my skirt being lifted from behind. I whirled around to see a leering Mr. Skidoo on his tricycle, one hand grasping the hem of my black-and-white-checked skirt. I jerked the material out of his gloved hand. This wasn't the first time he'd been unspeakably rude to me.

He grinned and tooted his horn. He had a certain way of tweaking that horn so it managed to sound dirty. "Come on. Don't be a spoil sport," Mr. Skidoo said in a singsong voice. He spoke to everyone, adults and children alike, as if they were five years old. "How about it, baby? I think you'd dig what's under this face paint . . . and the clothes."

I shuddered, totally creeped out. His hand reached for the horn again, but I placed mine over it and glared down at him. "Do not speak to me that way ever again, Mr. Skidoo. I've made it clear that I'm not interested in anything other than a business relationship with you."

The store characters filed into the room.

Mr. Skidoo gave me the once-over and said, "I'm a star. You'll come around."

"Don't bet your ukulele on it," I whispered fiercely.

"Hey, betting's not my bag, but I get turned on by the thrill of the chase. It's gonna be fun in the *swing set* for us, if you know what I mean!" He winked.

I turned on my heel and marched over to wrap up the leftover food. The only swing set I'd get on with Mr. Skidoo would be one where I could swing him off the Empire State Building.

Located on Forty-seventh Street near Fifth Avenue, Merryweathers' Toy Shoppe gleamed with a floor-to-ceiling glass front that had been the Merryweathers' last modern change to the store they built in 1924. When I arrived, there was already a crowd gathered out front, even though we had an hour until opening. I struggled to get to the front door, saying, "Store employee, please excuse me!"

The Teddy Bear was out front—what was his name? I had trouble remembering everyone's names. Complicating the problem, on the job everyone called each other by their character names.

Mr. Bob Runion—that was it—in furry brown bear costume, silently gestured to two workmen who hung a white banner underneath the Merryweathers' Toy Shoppe sign. The banner read HAPPY FORTIETH BIRTHDAY! in red letters. The Teddy Bear entertained the crowd by indicating to the workmen to move the sign a little to the left, then a little to the right. The workmen shook their fists at the Teddy Bear in mock anger. The crowd laughed at the antics.

Mr. Mallory, a few steps ahead of me, paused and nodded to the Teddy Bear. I watched a white envelope pass from the Teddy Bear's furry pocket to the store manager, who quickly slid it inside his jacket.

When he saw me approach, the Teddy Bear hurried to grab one polished brass handle and open the door for me. I smiled my thanks—so far the Teddy Bear had not broken character and spoken to me—entered the store, and looked around the sales floor. Hidden speakers issued instrumental arrangements of popular songs. I recognized an acoustic version of "We'll Sing in the Sunshine" and suppressed a giggle. Most of the store characters had returned and were busy tying red, white, and blue balloons in their respective sections.

The Merryweathers' Helpers, or salespeople, fussed over a five-tiered chocolate cake displayed on a red-, white-, and blue-topped table in the center of the first floor. Representations of each of the store's famous characters had been created in colorful frosting. Party hats and horns were piled high next to the confection, ready for the children. A large crystal punch bowl filled with red liquid was set up on a separate table, along with Dixie cups, plastic forks, napkins, and small paper plates.

Two more Helpers rode the elevator down from the upstairs Reading Corner, each carrying a big cardboard box. The Helpers were all female and wore blue uniform dresses with tan smocks decorated with an embroidered likeness of Mr. Skidoo's smiling face.

I saw Bradley talking to Betty Winston, our Raggedy Ann. Betty's domain included the dolls, dollhouses, dollhouse furniture, a child-size English tea table set for two, doll buggies, and more. Even in her red yarn wig and painted face complete with red triangle nose, Betty was a pretty girl with an excellent figure. But although Betty flirted with her long black eyelashes, Bradley wore his pleasant, cool-but-unapproachable look. I was glad to see that the Strict Boss attitude he'd mastered over the summer appeared to apply to everyone.

I looked over at the two Helpers carrying the boxes, Linda and Jane, as they struggled to reach the front door without spilling the contents. I put my purse and folder on the floor and hurried over to help. "Let's put one on either side of the open doors. Will you be able to manage handing out the dolls and police cars by yourselves? I could find you some help," I offered.

Both women smiled at me, but before either could answer, Mr. Mallory appeared at my side. He looked down his nose at me and spoke in his clipped English accent. "Miss Bennett, I am indebted to you for being so, er, helpful, but I've already given Linda and Jane their instructions."

Just a spoonful of sugar . . . I wanted to say, having seen the new movie *Mary Poppins* in August. Instead I inclined my head at Mr. Mallory, retrieved my black purse and folder, then made tracks for the escalator that led upstairs.

I stepped onto the moving stairs, saw Mr. Skidoo watching me from below, and averted my gaze, looking up—and who should be six steps above me but Bradley! With one hand over my mouth, I suppressed a giggle at the sexy view he presented from behind as I almost lost my balance on the escalator. Bradley must have heard me, because when I reached the elevator on the second floor that led to our third-floor offices, he stood waiting.

"Why are you coming upstairs, Miss Bennett?"

"I need to put my purse in my desk drawer, and I thought you'd want coffee since you wait for a cup every day."

"Give me your purse. I'll put it away and make my own coffee. I want you downstairs."

I want you to relax, I said silently to myself. "Very well." I passed him the items. "Would you be so kind as to place this folder on my desk? It contains clippings and notes on our advertisement in today's *Times*."

He accepted purse and folder and let his arm drop

dramatically. "Good Lord, what have you got in this bag? A boulder? Part of Fort Knox? An entire Lindy's cheesecake?"

"That's none of your business." I choked back a laugh at the sight of masculine Bradley carrying a purse.

"Okay, kid. I'll be on the phone most of the day with the managers of the other two stores, so have Danielle come up."

"Yes, Mr. Williams."

Kid, kid, kid. Would he ever stop using that stupid nickname for me? I'd be twenty-three in December. So what if he was nine years older than me?

Grasping the handrail of the down escalator, I thought again of Bradley carrying my purse and chuckled all the way to the first floor, until I noticed that Mr. Skidoo was still watching me.

By three o'clock, I wanted to tear my dark brown hair out by its roots. Having eaten only a tiny piece of cake washed down with punch, I heard my stomach growl, and my ears rang from the constant noise of hordes of children with cake-smeared faces. Their parents, many of whom knew each another, saw the event as a social occasion and chatted while their little girls slathered "makeup" on their faces in the Princess's area, tried on sparkly costumes, left the dressing rooms a mess, pushed one another out of the way to sit at the tea table, and scattered dolls in Raggedy Ann's section.

The boys ran around, tripped over blue trucks, silver airplanes, and red fire engines dropped in the aisles, shouted for the harried Train Conductor to make the trains run faster around the track, fought with each other for a good place in front of the Toymaker's workbench, and had mock dagger fights in the Pirate's area.

The parrot, having eaten the treats supplied by Mr. Geedunk's loving black-gloved hands, then promptly did his business on the navy and red patterned carpet. The Pirate, busy telling tales of the high seas to a group of enthralled boys, didn't notice the bird's misbehavior.

As I made my way to fetch some paper towels from the back room, I stopped dead and turned toward a familiar voice.

"Miss Bennett, I heard you and Williams had taken over here, and I raised a bottle of Bud in relief. Even you two couldn't find trouble in a toy store," Detective Finelli said.

"Bud is a beer, right, Daddy?" asked a five-year-old boy with a crew cut that matched Detective Finelli's.

"Of course it is, stupid," answered his brother, wise at the age of seven and sporting a similar crew cut.

Both boys were dark-haired like their father, dressed alike in rust-colored sweaters over white collared shirts and tan corduroy pants.

The detective butted their heads together in what seemed a habitual, roughhouse gesture of affection. "Beer is for grown-ups. Both of you say hello to Miss Bennett, then go get some cake."

"Hello, Miss Bennett."

"Hello, Miss Bennett."

They raced off before I could answer or ask their names. I knew their ages from a previous adventure that involved the detective, but I'd never met them. I smiled at Finelli and he half smiled back. Though he'd been madder than a cat in a bathtub full of water when I'd "interfered in police business" during prior murder investigations, all that was in the past. Heck, when I had almost died during the last case, and was in the hospital, he'd even brought me chocolates.

"Truce, Detective?"

"Gotta say yeah. Jeff and Robbie love this place and that clown. Costs me a fortune every time I come in here with them."

"I'm sure you enjoy it as much as they do. There's a little boy in every man."

He raised an eyebrow. "All I know is if I let the wife bring the kids, she finds her way up Fifth Avenue and shops."

"I'm sure she deserves to shop, what with the anxiety of having you as a husband and two boys to watch over," I said and laughed.

I was cut off by Mr. Skidoo, winding his way around my ankles on his tricycle. The clown handed out candy from his enormous trouser pockets to nearby children, then looked at me with a twisted grin. "Now I know your secret! Maybe I'll tell everyone!" he sang, giving my skirt hem a tug with each word. He beeped his horn three times and drove toward the Pirate.

The parrot's head turned to one side, one beady black eye on Mr. Skidoo. He squawked, "Kill the clown!"

Mr. Skidoo whipped out a small air gun and shot the parrot, causing the bird to reel backward on the Pirate's shoulder.

Mr. Geedunk noticeably refrained from yelling at the clown in front of the children, but I saw him bristle and give Mr. Skidoo a look that promised he'd deal with him later.

Detective Finelli looked at me in the inquisitive way I knew too well: his eyes narrowed slightly, his expression stoic. "What secret, Miss Bennett?"

I avoided his gaze. What did Mr. Skidoo think he

knew about me? In a flash, I remembered him watching me watching Bradley on the escalator. He may have even seen us on the floor above. There was only a glass wall on the second floor so that people downstairs could clearly see the Reading Corner. I grimaced. My facial expressions were usually easy to interpret unless I made a point of covering them, something I had begun working on over the summer when Bradley turned chilly.

Had my personal feelings for Bradley been obvious as I ogled him on the escalator? Had the leering clown clued in to my attraction to my boss?

Darn Mr. Skidoo!

"Miss Bennett?"

Detective Finelli had been waiting for my answer, but rescue arrived in the form of his boys. They ran to him, each with an armload of toys, cake crumbs on their mouths and sweaters.

"Happy shopping!" I exclaimed and, face warm, escaped.

I paused beside the Jungle, a grouping of tall, expensive stuffed animals, some of them life-sized—a giraffe, grizzly bear, tiger, lion, zebra, and even an elephant. The cutest monkey I'd ever seen hung suspended between two leafy trees, giving the impression he was jumping from one to another.

I bent over to push straw around the animals' feet, listening to the soft recording of jungle sounds that played constantly in the area. I told myself I was not hiding from Finelli, though as I saw the detective leave the store, boys in tow, I breathed a sigh of relief.

Beyond the Pirate's area, a door marked "Employees Only" led to a storeroom, where I grabbed some paper towels and a bottle of Mr. Clean. I returned to

Mr. Geedunk's area intending to wipe up the parrot's mess.

In character, the Pirate bellowed, "Ahoy, matey, swab the deck!"

I saluted him and made quick work of my task.

The children laughed and one young voice rang out, filled with contempt, "She's a girl! Girls can't be on pirate ships. They're bad luck!"

The Pirate roared, "Then she'll walk the plank if she doesn't leave our ship." For my ears alone, Mr. Geedunk said, "That clown isn't bothering you, is he?"

"Well . . ." I rolled my eyes. "I hope your parrot is okay."

The Pirate petted the bird as he spoke. "Junior is fine. Be on your guard with Skidoo. He's a bad one."

I nodded and returned to the back room, throwing away the dirty paper towels and using the ladies' room to wash my hands. Trying not to think about the irritating clown, I smiled at Mr. Geedunk's name for the bird: Junior. The Pirate certainly did treat the bird like a spoiled child.

Finally it was five o'clock, closing time, though it was another half hour before all the customers left.

"I know Mr. Williams will be impressed with the store's profits today, Mr. Mallory," I said, trying to thaw the manager out a little.

Mr. Skidoo, high from all the love and attention that had been lavished on him during the day, was still on his tricycle, riding around like a madman. He overheard my words, looked at the puffed-up Mr. Mallory, and said, "Would you bet on it, Mr. Mallory?"

Mr. Mallory was busy closing out the old-fashioned

cash registers and spoke without looking at the clown or me. "In the seven months I've been here, Merryweathers' has always done well. I expect nothing less for today."

What a crab! Then I looked around and realized that all the employees appeared to be exhausted. The Helpers disappeared out the front door first, their job done. The Teddy Bear came inside and locked the door, leaving the keys in the lock so employees could exit. Trying to give Mr. Mallory the benefit of the doubt, I figured he must be tired too. Heck, I was more than ready to flop down on my bed at home and groove to one of my Beatles albums.

Mr. Mallory, finished with the four cash registers, stepped into the center of the sales floor and addressed the store characters. "Thank you for your efforts today. I know everyone wants to go home, put their feet up, and have a cup of tea. Please do so. Report at eight thirty in the morning."

A chorus of "Thank you, Mr. Mallory!" greeted his words.

The Train Conductor, an older man with bushy white sideburns, wearing the traditional blue-and-white-striped overalls, matching cap, and white shirt, said, "I won't leave my display until it's exactly the way I want it. Those children knocked my trees over, upset my bridge—"

Mr. Skidoo rode to the elaborate display and picked up a female figure. Looking at me sideways, he addressed the Conductor. "I'll take this lady home with me tonight, unless I get a better offer, Mr. Kirchhoff."

I gritted my teeth and picked a few dolls off the floor. What would it take to stop the clown's unwanted attentions?

"You are to call me Conductor," the train man

hissed at Mr. Skidoo. He ripped the figure from the clown's hand. Mr. Skidoo laughed and pedaled away.

"You can fix everything to your liking in the morning, Conductor," Mr. Mallory said. "I'm turning the main lights out for the evening."

The Conductor's gaze ran over his small world and he wrung his hands.

Eager to get away from Mr. Skidoo, I took the escalator, then the elevator up to the executive offices. Danielle was gone. There was no sign of Bradley either, though his light was on. Disappointed, I sat at my desk—a heavy wooden piece, surely dating from 1924—and scanned the messages Danielle had taken. Twenty minutes later, I retrieved my purse from one of the squeaky drawers and turned out all the lights except one rose-patterned china lamp on a side table.

I stepped off the elevator on the second floor, spared a glance for the scattered books in the Reading Corner, and walked over to the escalator. The machine had been turned off for the day, so I grasped the handrail and began to walk down the steel steps, my heels clacking noisily.

All the lights were off except for the faint night bulbs that lined the bottom of the big glass front window, bathing the store in an eerie glow. I pulled my store keys out of my purse in case someone had removed the ones from the front door.

About halfway to the bottom of the escalator, a flood of uneasiness came over me as my eyes fixed on the dolls, especially the ones of Mr. Skidoo. They seemed to glare right back at me. Scolding myself for being childish, I nevertheless moved my gaze to my Jungle friends.

The giraffe had toppled over onto its side.

The tiger lay on top of the lion.

The cute monkey had disappeared. One tree leaned against the other.

What had happened to them? Hadn't the Jungle been tidy before I went upstairs?

I reached the first floor and hesitated. The music was off. The store was completely silent. A tingle went up my spine as if a ghost had touched me, not that I believed in ghosts. Except Casper, the Friendly Ghost.

I hastened my steps, then stopped just shy of the front door. I reminded myself that I was a strong, independent city woman who would not be intimidated by, of all things, dolls.

Disgusted with myself, I placed my purse on the floor and went over to the Jungle. I would prove I wasn't afraid by taking the time to straighten the animals.

I found the monkey and propped him next to the tree that was still standing. On tiptoe, I pushed the fallen tree back into position.

"Poor Mr. Giraffe," I whispered, righting him to his great height.

Great, now you're talking to stuffed animals.

I made swift work of putting the tiger on his feet, then grabbed the lion by either side of his fluffy mane, glanced beneath him, and screamed.

Mr. Skidoo lay sprawled on the floor with one of the Pirate's toy knives stuck in his chest, his eyes staring blankly at the ceiling.

Chapter Two

I clutched the lion's head, shaking. My thoughts raced before my brain grabbed onto an idea.

Mr. Skidoo couldn't be dead. The Pirate's knife was a *toy* made of painted gray rubber. That was fake blood around the wound in his chest. The clown must have stayed behind and played a cruel trick on me.

"Get up, Mr. Skidoo," I demanded, tossing the lion to one side. "I know you're pretending."

No response.

What a creep!

"All right, I'll call your bluff." Anger rose in me, and I grabbed the pirate knife by its tin handle, gasping when I felt the blade pull through the clown's body, blood seeping from the wound and dripping from a very real knife.

Dear God, this was not a trick. I stood in shock, unable to move, my gaze fixed on the clown's dead face, gripping the knife in my right hand.

"Miss Bennett! What are you doing down here in the dark? And did you turn out the lights upstairs?"

Bradley flipped a switch and the room was flooded with a brightness that made me blink.

I couldn't find my voice. I stood motionless.

"What the hell?" Bradley crossed the room quickly,

bent, and placed his slim fingers at Mr. Skidoo's neck, feeling for a pulse.

He rose and with one finger gently turned my face to his. In a low voice he said, "Bebe, Mr. Skidoo is dead and you're holding a knife. What happened?"

Incapable of speech, I stared into his blue eyes.

The sound of the storeroom door opening and closing drew our attention. The Pirate walked toward us, saw Mr. Skidoo on the floor and the bloody knife in my hand, and his brown eyes bulged beneath his black eyebrows. "Miss Bennett, did you murder the clown?"

My voice scraped out in a whisper. "I didn't—"

Bradley interrupted. "Miss Bennett didn't kill anyone."

Mr. Geedunk pointed one gloved finger at me. "Man, she's holding the bloody knife."

"What are *you* still doing here, Geedunk?" Bradley asked.

"I always cage Junior in the storeroom before I go home. The parrot sleeps here. I didn't know I had to report my bird's sleeping arrangements to you, Mr. Williams."

"Now you know you do. Don't leave the store, Mr. Geedunk," Bradley ordered.

"Are you implying that *I* killed Mr. Skidoo?" The Pirate stood with his black-booted feet planted wide. He glared at Bradley, who did not answer.

With shaking fingers, I turned the knife handle and saw the painted image of a pirate dressed in black, standing on the deck of a ship, skull and crossbones on the ship's flag. My hand jerked and the knife fell to the carpet, bounced once, and landed between Mr. Skidoo's spat-covered shoes.

My body temperature dropped as I felt a strange, fluttery sensation in my head.

"You'd better sit down, Miss Bennett, before you faint," Bradley said, leading me to the Toymaker's workbench. I sat slumped over, my hands pressed to my forehead.

Vaguely, I heard Bradley phone the police. Then he was at my side, a Dixie cup filled with water in his hands. "Here, drink this."

The cool liquid slid down my throat, reviving me. "Thank you. It's not the first time I've seen a dead body. I'm okay."

The Pirate stood rooted to the spot, staring at the dead clown.

The sound of sirens blared from outside, but it was the man who walked through the front door that had me swaying on the bench and wishing for a bottle of my roommate Darlene's Old Rose Whiskey.

Bradley's muscles tensed at the sight of him. "Are you the *only* detective in New York City, Finelli?"

Uniformed NYPD officers flowed through the doorway along with a man in a white coat. Finelli paid no attention to them, and shot an annoyed look at Bradley. "The *only* one who knows the two of you. A senior detective is on the way. My boss knows that I'm acquainted with you and Miss Bennett." Finelli sounded like he'd been diagnosed with a terminal disease. "He's decided that I might not be objective in this case. I'm just here to assist."

He rubbed a hand across his crew cut in a gesture I knew to be one of acute frustration. Holding his small notepad in one hand and the stub of a pencil in the other, Finelli consulted with the doctor who was examining Mr. Skidoo.

A heavyset man with black hair strode through the door, his hard dark gaze running over the scene. Dressed in a brown suit and wearing a fedora, he

walked wordlessly past Bradley and me, his focus on
Finelli. He took a long look at Mr. Skidoo, then began
speaking to Finelli and the doctor.

When they finished talking, the two men joined us,
the senior detective sizing me up with what seemed
like seasoned practice.

"Detective Snyder, NYPD," he barked. "You, Williams, gimme the name of the deceased."

"Mel Kinker," Bradley replied.

"And how long had Mel Kinker worked here at
cheerful little Merryweathers'?"

"I've known him for three days," Bradley answered.

"So have I," I said before Detective Snyder could
ask.

Mr. Geedunk came forward. "Mel Kinker is Mr.
Skidoo's real name. He's been at Merryweathers'
about six months, I think. The clowns here don't last
long."

The Pirate's unfortunate choice of words hung in
the air.

"They quit when they can't take the kids crawling
over them anymore," Mr. Geedunk elaborated.

Snyder lit a cigarette and pinned his gaze on the
Pirate. "Who are you?"

"Name's Geedunk. Bill Geedunk. I've been the Pirate character here for nine years. The Merryweathers
can vouch for my reputation."

"Reputations don't matter much to me. Anyone can
be a killer. Even innocent-looking young women."
Snyder blew smoke out through his nostrils, his eyes
now on me.

Finelli took notes, but at the senior detective's
words, he slid me a warning look.

Snyder ignored the ashtray on the counter at his
elbow and tipped cigarette ash onto the floor. He di-

rected his attention to Bradley. "You're saying you only knew Kinker for three days, yet Geedunk here says the clown worked here for six months."

"That's right. My uncle, Herman Shires, closed the deal with the Merryweathers months ago, but Miss Bennett and I only physically moved into our offices here three days ago."

"When you took over, did you plan to fire Kinker? You and the clown have an argument?"

"I plan to keep everyone on provided they do their jobs," Bradley said. In the same somber voice, he added, "Mr. Skidoo did spray water in my face from his flower pin on national television. You think that's a motive for murder, Mr. Snyder?"

"That's Detective Snyder to you, pretty boy. Don't get sarcastic with me. I know who you are, Williams— one of the city's best-known rich playboys. Though I noticed your name's been absent from the gossip columns lately, making me cry," he said with a malicious look.

Bradley's full lips folded into a thin line.

Snyder turned to Mr. Geedunk. "What about you? What was your relationship with the deceased?"

Tiny beads of sweat formed on the Pirate's forehead. "Can't say I liked him, but I had no reason to kill him."

"Did the two of you argue?" Snyder pressed.

The barrel-chested Mr. Geedunk looked off to the right, appearing to think about the question. "The man had a talent for grating on people's nerves. We scrapped like any coworkers scrap every now and then."

Kill the clown. The parrot's voice sounded loud and clear in my head, but I said nothing. I remembered the Pirate telling me that the clown was a "bad one."

Just how many enemies did Mr. Skidoo have? One of them had been deadly. Had he or she been one of the store employees? Mr. Geedunk was still in the store at the time of the clown's death, a death caused by a modified version of one of the Pirate's toys.

"Girly, I asked you a question," Snyder said.

He startled me out of my thoughts.

"My name is Miss Bennett. What was your question?"

"I'd advise you to pay attention, *girly*. You found the body, correct?"

If Snyder weren't so intimidating, and I wasn't so afraid of the mess I'd landed myself in, I would have slapped his face. "Yes, I did."

The police had propped open the store door and a cool autumn breeze drifted in, making me shiver.

Bradley stepped closer to me.

Finelli said, "Why don't you take us through it step by step, and don't leave anything out. Not that I think you would withhold information from us, Miss Bennett."

Snyder's head whipped around to face his colleague. "Take notes, Finelli. I'm the detective in charge here."

"If you don't mind, Detective Snyder, I'd rather speak to Detective Finelli," I said.

"I'm sure you would, girly, but it ain't gonna happen."

What a Neanderthal.

I concentrated on giving an accurate account of what had happened. "I thought everyone had gone home for the night. I came downstairs ready to leave the store when I saw my Jungle friends in a mess."

"Your jungle friends?" Snyder mocked me.

I felt myself blush. "The large stuffed jungle animals

across the aisle from Mr. Geedunk's area are particular favorites of mine."

Snyder's lips spread in a smirk. "Ain't that sweet."

Finelli gave a little shake of his head.

"As a store employee, I felt it my duty to correct the situation. When I picked up the lion, I saw Mr. Skidoo."

"What was the clown doing?"

An incredulous noise came out of my mouth. "He was dead!" I paused before I went on. "Although at first I didn't think he was dead. I thought it was just another of his pranks. He played a lot of pranks."

Finelli let out an exasperated breath.

"Miss Bennett, I don't think—" Bradley began.

Snyder's gaze swung to Bradley. "Williams, you want to shut up unless you're ready to move this party to the stationhouse."

Bradley let out a sigh of frustration and thrust his hands into his pockets.

The word *stationhouse* caused words to burst from my lips. "Mr. Skidoo played tricks. That was his job as a clown. But in the short time I knew him it seemed that sometimes he went too far. He squirted water in Hugh Downs's face on national television. He did it to Mr. Williams too and he's his boss. Even Mr. Geedunk's parrot was a victim. Mr. Skidoo shot Junior with an air gun and the bird almost fell off Mr. Geedunk's shoulder."

Snyder turned to the Pirate for a reaction. "Why are you still in the store anyway?"

"I was bedding Junior down for the night. Mr. Skidoo never hurt my Junior. The parrot is fine. It was a silly joke, nothing more."

"Is it safe to say you are protective of the bird, Mr.

Geedunk?" Snyder asked, his gaze sliding from a row of pirate knives in the Pirate's area back to the man himself.

Sweat ran down Mr. Geedunk's temples. "The clown annoyed people, that's all, and some couldn't take it," he ended with a pointed glance at me.

Feeling betrayed and panicky, I said, "So why did your parrot say 'kill the clown' all the time, Mr. Geedunk?"

The Pirate, red-faced, answered the question, increasing his insinuations. "All parrots talk nonsense. On the other hand, Miss Bennett was angry at the clown for pestering her."

Snyder's eyes, which reminded me of a snake's, bore through me. "Now, what exactly did the clown do to you, girly?"

"Nothing, really," I managed, my throat dry.

"It won't do any good to lie to the police, Miss Bennett," Mr. Geedunk said. "You know how upset you were when Mr. Skidoo kept leering at you, lifting your skirt, flirting with you."

"What?" Bradley exclaimed.

"Silence, Williams!" Finelli commanded and held my gaze. I knew he was remembering what had happened while he was in the store with his boys. I could feel my heart beating fast. Despite any truce, any cordial relationship between us, Finelli was a detective first and foremost. He took his duties seriously; his primary loyalty was to his job.

To his credit, Finelli hesitated before he spoke. "I saw it myself. When I was in the store earlier with my sons, the clown rode up behind you on his tricycle, Miss Bennett, grabbed your skirt, and said he knew your secret. He said he might tell. What was the secret?"

Trembling, I looked at the swirls of red and blue in the carpet. My head felt like it was swirling in tandem. I couldn't blurt out that my secret was that I loved Bradley and the clown had guessed it. Not here in front of Bradley. I'd die of embarrassment. Besides, Mama always said that men like to think that they're the ones doing the chasing. I'd never get Bradley to the altar if he knew I was in love with him.

"Can we talk about this later in private, Detective Finelli?" I said, my eyes pleading. Finelli knew about my feelings for Bradley. If I could just get him aside . . .

"No, girly," Snyder said. "You'll tell me and you'll tell me *now*."

I reached up and twisted a piece of my hair. All eyes were on me. I looked at Bradley, then quickly slid my gaze back to Finelli. "The secret i-is that Mr. Skidoo, I m-mean Mel, and I went out together socially a couple of times," I said, making the story up as I went along. "He, um, got the wrong idea about me and I ended it."

I couldn't look at Bradley.

"Persistent, was he?" Finelli asked.

"I suppose."

Snyder stared at me. "Are your fingerprints on that knife?"

I swallowed. "Well, yes, because when I found the body, I thought Mr.—um, Mel—was playing a practical joke on me, as I've told you. I didn't think it was a real knife because it's exactly like all the play ones hanging in packages against Mr. Geedunk's wall. So, I pulled it out."

Finelli wrote furiously. When he looked at me, there was an expression of pity in his eyes. "Williams, did you see Miss Bennett with the knife in her hand?"

Bradley shrugged. "The place was dark. I remember seeing the knife on the floor."

My eyes met his for a moment. Bradley had just lied for me. My head swam.

"Or maybe, Williams, you're protecting this little piece of fluff. Sounds to me like we got a witness to girly's statement that she held the knife." Snyder dropped his cigarette on the carpet and rubbed it in with the point of his shoe.

Piece of fluff!

"I saw Miss Bennett with the knife in her hand," Mr. Geedunk said.

I felt a burning sensation behind my eyes.

"A definite witness." Snyder looked at me. "And your excuse is that it wasn't until you pulled the knife out of the clown's body that you recognized the weapon as being real. That your boyfriend was dead."

"He wasn't my boyfriend!"

Snyder motioned to one of the police officers. Taking a pair of handcuffs from him, the senior detective gave a sharp nod of his head, and the officer went to stand with the others.

"Girly, you've admitted that you and the victim were having a fling that soured. I've got you at the murder scene, murder weapon in hand. The case is clear-cut: a lovers' quarrel with a deadly ending. Turn around so I can snap the bracelets on you."

"Don't you touch her," Bradley snarled. "Despite your bluster and cheap tactics, Snyder, you don't have a shred of proof against Miss Bennett. All you have is circumstantial evidence. Last I knew, that's not enough for a grand jury to indict anyone. I'm certain my lawyer would agree, just as I'm certainly not going to allow you to railroad Miss Bennett with these trumped-up charges. She is not going to jail."

I almost swooned.

"Christ," Finelli muttered.

Unfortunately, it was crystal clear that Bradley had made a dangerous enemy in Snyder. The detective's eyes betrayed his fury as he spat out his words. "For now, no one employed in your kids' store is to leave town. I'm gonna be on this case like your father was on your mother nine months before you waltzed out of her."

Snyder turned and stormed out the door, Finelli behind him.

Outside, police and ambulance lights lit Forty-seventh Street in a red glow. I shivered, coatless, since I had sworn I would not wear the old-fashioned one Daddy had bought me two years ago.

Mr. Geedunk hurried out of the store without a single word to Bradley or me.

Policemen began leaving. The ambulance crew carried out the tall body of the clown, mostly covered by a blanket. Reporters were already on the scene, their flashbulbs going off. A male voice yelled, "Hey, I know those shoes! That's Mr. Skidoo, the store's clown. Everybody, Mr. Skidoo is dead!"

One officer shouted for them to clear away, unwisely letting it slip that they were trespassing on a crime scene.

The reporters ran off in different directions, probably to call in the stories to their bosses. In the morning, everyone would know that Merryweathers' Toy Shoppe's mascot had been murdered.

Chapter Three

Bradley closed the door and turned off the main lights, leaving us standing in the shadows.

I silently counted the small lightbulbs that lit the front window, unsure of what he was going to say. Would he comfort me? Hold me in his arms?

I cleared my throat. "Thank you for your help. Without it, I believe I'd be in jail right now."

Bradley walked past me and leaned against the counter, studying his fingernails. "They couldn't have kept you. I know you didn't kill Kinker."

But he didn't sound convinced.

"I didn't kill him, no matter how much it looks like I did."

"Didn't I just say as much?" He sighed, pressed two fingers against the bridge of his nose, and said, "I guess you'll be investigating the murder. Any way I can talk you out of that?"

"Are you joking? Snyder wants me behind bars. I have to defend myself."

"You could defend yourself by hiring a good lawyer. The company will pay for it."

"I appreciate that very much, but I still have to—"

Bradley waved a hand. "I can't stop you. I've learned that much, among other things."

Was that last part about my dating Mr. Skidoo? If so, why didn't he come right out and ask me? *Sure, Bebe. Like he cares who you date.*

"Miss Bennett, I hate to point out the obvious, but news of the clown's death will be all over the city tomorrow," Bradley said, biting out the words. "We'll lose customers, children will be crying themselves to sleep—hell, we'll probably make tomorrow's news."

Huh? All he could talk about was business now?

"I'll find another clown to play Mr. Skidoo immediately, Mr. Williams."

"I expect nothing less. And no drunks. A professional. You can be too kindhearted sometimes," he said in a disapproving tone.

My chin rose. "The moment the new Mr. Skidoo is in the store, I think we should take out a carefully worded ad in the *Times*. Maybe we could have a sale—"

"Merryweathers' never holds sales. You should know that from the store policies booklet I gave you."

Darn him! "How about a special thank-you to our customers for helping us celebrate the store's birthday? In it, we could invite all the children to come in and visit Mr. Skidoo again soon."

Bradley rubbed his chin. "That would help. I'll put out a press release as well. I think you'd better go now. We've had enough for one day."

No offer of a taxi ride home, much less any comfort in the form of a relaxing drink at his town house. Even a dead body wasn't thawing him out.

I found my purse and went out onto the dark street. I could walk home, but it was a distance. I usually walked in the mornings and took the bus in the evenings. As I reached the corner, I turned toward Madison Avenue. The wind gusting between the tall

skyscrapers chilled my Virginia bones. Absently, I
thought about the ugly coat hanging in my closet.
Mama always said a woman had to suffer for beauty.
She was right.

I kept my thoughts on trivial matters while I took
the bus up Madison to East Sixty-fifth Street, fearing
I would burst into tears in front of a crowd of strang-
ers if I thought of the murder, how that nasty Detective Snyder wanted me in jail, how Bradley kept his
distance from me. Heck, the way he acted, an entire
ocean rose and fell between us.

When the bus passed the back of St. Patrick's Cathe-
dral, I glanced at the building with a guilty feeling. I
dug out the little notebook I kept in my purse, turned
to the "Confessions" section, and wrote in the lies I'd
told about dating Mel Kinker. I added a line about my
lust for Bradley, then chewed my bottom lip and crossed
it off. My priest had heard it so often, he might suggest
something awful, like quitting my job.

Exiting the bus, I walked two blocks over to my
apartment and found Harry the wino on my front
stoop. Harry slept across the street behind the Catho-
lic high school, though I couldn't be certain he did so
every night. Tonight he sported a worn green army
jacket and his hands shook.

"Here's Miss Sweet Face. How was the big bash?
Any booze left over? I'm kinda in a bad way."

Smoothing the back of my skirt, I sat on the step
next to him, trying not to wonder when Harry had
last bathed. "My friend, I'm working in a children's
store, remember? No liquor there." Although I'd
wished there had been.

"Yeah, I remember now. Damn. Hey, you don't
look too happy. Hate kids?" he asked, scratching his
thick gray beard.

"No, I don't hate children. I want some of my own one day."

"What's got you all ruffled? Is it that guy you're in love with? I tell you, love hurts forever."

Love hurts forever. This was more than I'd heard about Harry's personal feelings in the entire eight months I'd known him. He had clammed up every time I asked him why he lived on the streets. In a casual voice, I said, "Did you used to have a special woman in your life? Did she leave you?"

Instantly Harry got up. "I've got to be somewhere."

"Harry," I said, rising to my feet and putting a hand on his arm, "wait just a minute."

I extracted my Buxton wallet and pulled out three quarters. When I pressed them into his hand, he took them, but for the first time I noticed he grimaced as he accepted the handout.

I held his palm. "I'm a good listener if you ever want to talk. You can trust me."

Harry looked down at the pavement as if it held all the answers. "Yeah, okay."

Then he turned and hurried toward Lexington. I knew he wouldn't buy food with the money I had given him.

I sighed. Would I ever be able to help Harry? I wanted to very much. My roommate, Darlene, always said Harry didn't want help, and she fussed at me every time she saw me give him money. But Harry's words tonight only served to encourage me in my quest to get him off the streets. I couldn't help but be concerned for him, since Harry had been a fixture in the neighborhood since I'd moved here. He'd even helped me out of a tight spot once.

I walked up the three flights of stairs to my apartment and unlocked the four locks on the door. Once inside, I didn't even bother to take off my suit. The events of the day flooded over me. I flung myself onto the pink sectional and cried until I thought my mascara would leave a black stain on my favorite piece of furniture.

I didn't want to be alone. I needed Darlene. She and I were best friends as well as roommates and had seen each other through prior murder investigations.

And here I was again, mixed up in another murder, now as the prime suspect.

Darlene, a top stewardess, had been on a brutal work schedule all summer. Air travel was growing as more and more families felt comfortable flying, and Darlene was in high demand. I missed her. Maybe I could find a way to talk with her, though I had no idea where she was.

In my bedroom, I took off my suit and hung it on the extra clothes rack I'd had to buy when I moved to New York from Richmond, Virginia. The rack made the room seem even smaller, yet I still managed to have my bed, a dresser with a turntable on it, my Beatles albums, and a bright yellow vinyl chair in the shape of a banana. The banana chair, which I had picked up via "curbside" shopping, was where I often curled up and wrote in my special steno pad, the one that had my list of fun things to do in New York and the serious goals I wanted to accomplish over the next few years. So far, I hadn't reached many of them, but I promised myself I would.

I pulled on a pair of soft cotton pajamas—I didn't see the need for sexy lingerie like Darlene did—and padded over to the wall phone in our miniscule green-and-white kitchen.

Knowing my trouble with numbers, Darlene had taped the main telephone number for Skyway Airlines on the fridge. The problem was, how on earth could I convince whoever I talked to at the airline that I needed to get in touch with Darlene immediately? Family emergency? Darlene's mother hadn't spoken to her daughter in years. Darlene's father had taken off when she was a little girl. Could I pretend to be her sister? No, they probably had records that would reveal she was an only child.

An idea popped into my head. I dialed the number.

"Skyway Airlines, Mr. Rentell speaking."

"Mr. Rentell, this is Mrs. . . . Lanson. I rent an apartment to one of your stewardesses, a Miss Darlene Roland, and I'm very worried," I said in my best elderly lady voice.

"Ah, yes, I know Miss Roland," he said, his voice full of admiration.

And I'd bet it wasn't just for her hard work. Darlene was a flame-haired bombshell whom men found irresistible. She was also a first-class flirt.

"Is there something wrong?" he asked.

"Dear Mr. Rentell," I said, "I'm afraid there is. I only hope you can help me. I don't know what to do."

"I assure you, I'll do my best."

"I don't want to alarm dear Miss Roland, but there's been a fire here in the building that spread to her apartment. I think she should know." I managed a sniffle. There, that sounded good.

"That's terrible. She'll get the message tonight. What number should I give her to call?"

"Goodness, I couldn't bear to break the news to her myself. Could you possibly have her call her roommate? I've forgotten the girl's name. I know she's been trying to salvage what she can."

"Should I simply have Miss Roland call home then?"

"What a good idea, Mr. Rentell! Thank you so much. You've lifted a great weight off my shoulders. The worrying isn't helping my heart condition—"

"I'll take care of it personally. You can depend on that. Good night, Mrs. Lanson."

He hung up, clearly unwilling to hear an old lady's complaints, just as I'd thought. I allowed myself a smile. If only I could charm Bradley that easily.

My smile faded as it dawned on me that Darlene might be genuinely alarmed by the news of a fire in her apartment. Hopefully Mr. Rentell would give "Mrs. Lanson's" name as the building owner. Darlene would know it was a fake name and call me.

Washing my makeup off in the tiny bathroom, I looked in the oval mirror and said, "Bebe Bennett, you know what you have to do. Find the person who murdered Mel Kinker before Snyder hauls you in for the crime."

A shudder went through me as the image of the dead clown flashed in my brain. I patted my face dry. Blowing air into my bangs, I concentrated on the rude Detective Snyder. I pegged him for the lazy sort, confident in his position, with no real passion for the job. His only enjoyment probably came from the sense of power he had. And from being a moron.

Finelli, on the other hand, was different. A nononsense kind of guy, the detective had been friendly in a gruff sort of way when I'd solved two other murder cases. He cared about the truth, and he was highly dedicated to his job. Nothing would stand in his way when it came to bringing a criminal—or the person who he thought was a criminal—to justice.

I'd be lucky if I didn't find myself in jail soon.

Lord, what if Daddy found out there'd been a murder at the store! He'd been trying to drag me home since the day I left Virginia, and while he and Mama still lived in Richmond, Daddy had an uncanny knack for gathering news from New York. My hands trembled.

Grabbing a steno pad from the supply I kept in my dresser, I plopped down on my stomach on the black, white, and yellow daisy bedspread that covered my bed. My feet waved in the air as I wrote steadily. I described everything I knew about Mr. Skidoo, which wasn't much, a summary of the birthday party, and then the details of how I came to find the body. Feeling shaky again, I dashed into the kitchen for a glass of milk and a bar of Hershey's chocolate, chocolate being my cure for all anxiety.

I wrote about Mr. Geedunk and Junior, especially the way the Pirate had thrown the heat on me when being questioned. That made me mad. And suspicious.

The sad truth was that I didn't know any of the store characters. I'd have to change that and do my sleuthing along the way. One of the employees had wanted Mr. Skidoo dead. The murderer had to be among them, as no customer would have had access to the store after it closed.

I must have dozed off because the phone woke me. My pencil was stuck to the side of my face where I'd laid on it. Flinging it to the bed, I dashed into the kitchen, noting it was after midnight, and picked up the receiver.

"Hello?"

"Where's the fire, honey? Did you and Bradley finally do the deed?" Darlene asked in her Texas accent.

"Darlene! Thank God you called. I'm in trouble."

"Didn't you read about condoms in that Helen Gurley Brown book I loaned you?"

"This is serious, Darlene. Stop joking."

"Well, if you're not pregnant, what's the problem? Was there really a fire?" she asked, voice rising.

"No. I'm sorry if I scared you."

"You didn't really. I knew you just needed me to get in touch right away."

"Okay, good. I need to talk to you, Darlene. You're my best friend and I need your advice."

"Honey, you know I'm always full of advice . . . or something."

I rubbed the mark the pencil had left on my cheek. "We had our big birthday party at the toy store today and the clown was murdered."

Darlene let out a gurgle of laughter. "Bebe, have you been drinking?"

"I'm not kidding! The clown acted like a complete jerk to me, and the Pirate and Detective Finelli knew it, and then when I found Mr. Skidoo's body and pulled the knife out of his heart, Bradley called the police and this horrible Detective Snyder was assigned the case because Finelli knows me too well and Snyder is positive I'm the murderer," I said, and took a deep breath.

Silence.

"Darlene? Did you hear me?"

"Yes, much as I wish I hadn't. Don't say anything else to Snyder or Finelli. Not a word, Bebe. I'm in Los Angeles. I'll be home tomorrow night."

"No! I don't want you to mess up your schedule at Skyway. I'm going to find the killer," I announced.

"That's exactly what I'm worried about. Bebe, I'm coming home."

Chapter Four

Despite my exhaustion, and even with Darlene's assurance that she'd come home, I slept poorly. Mr. Skidoo's dead body haunted me. In one nightmare, his corpse rode around me on his tricycle while I stood in the middle of a jail cell.

Deciding I might as well get up, shower, and dress, I found I had plenty of time to walk to work. I loved walking through the city early in the day, feeling it awaken like the living, breathing thing I felt it was. People strolled with their dogs, pedestrians hailed yellow cabs, trucks delivered goods, and an intangible energy charged the air.

A cool wind reminded me I had to choose a new coat, something suitable for a young professional woman. The breeze made strands of my long hair catch on my lip gloss. I reached up and pulled my hair away from my face. Sometimes I still couldn't get over the fact that I was really in New York, in the city of my dreams, though it had been over eight months since my move from Virginia. I never wanted to live anywhere else. Well, that wasn't exactly true. One of my goals was to have a house with the man I'd marry. I'd always thought that meant moving outside the city. It wasn't until I'd been here for a while that I realized

Bradley and I could raise our children in a Manhattan neighborhood.

Bradley. I sighed loudly. I crossed briskly over to Fifth Avenue, Central Park in front of me, grass turning to brown, leaves red and yellow. One tree in particular caught my eye. I stepped to the curb, entranced by the golden leaves shaking and shimmering as if they were dancing to nature's tune. Autumn was my favorite time of year, and being in the city made it more intoxicating. Reluctantly, I moved on.

Usually, if I had time while walking down Fifth, I did a little window-shopping. The stores were like nothing I'd ever seen, full of tempting, glittering, luscious, expensive goods. What I truly wanted—Bradley's love—cost nothing, but seemed as out of reach as the emerald and diamond necklace in the window at Cartier.

I thought back to last night. Bradley hadn't seemed convinced that I was innocent of Mel Kinker's murder. Maybe I had misread him all along. Maybe everything I thought was between us was a product of my imagination, and I needed to take off my rose-colored glasses. A plan formed in my mind. I'd talk it over with Darlene when she came home. She was the love expert.

Right now I had to focus on finding a replacement for Mr. Skidoo. Bradley had put me in charge of the job and I didn't look forward to the interview process. Maybe we had applications on file and I could call those people. I'd have to check references, wait until the new clown gave notice wherever he was working now, train him, and hope he did a good job.

All that could take weeks. Bradley would be pacing the floor.

By the time I reached the store, I had an idea that brought a smile to my face.

Pulling the door open—the silent Teddy Bear wouldn't be outside until quarter to ten and it was only nine—I went directly to my desk. The executive office area was dingy at best, dark paneled walls, beige linoleum floor, and tan file cabinets. Two big wooden desks occupied my area, which suited me perfectly since I could sit at the one closest to Bradley's office and Danielle could take the other. Not that my desk was close to Bradley's office. A whole row of those icky tan file cabinets separated us.

On the wall opposite was a narrow table holding a china lamp, a coffee machine, coffee, mugs, sugar, and napkins. As I'd done each day since I began working for Bradley last April, I started the morning by making a pot of coffee.

While it brewed, filling the air with its comforting scent, I pulled out the massive New York City telephone book, hoping the guy I had in mind to play Mr. Skidoo had a phone.

He did, and I dialed the number.

"Hello," a deep male voice greeted me sleepily.

"Tom? Is this Tom Stevens?"

"Yes," he answered, sounding more awake. "Who's calling?"

"Bebe Bennett. I don't know if you remember me or not, but we met at Pierre Benoit's photo showing last May. I was the brunette you talked with about a shot of Miss Bardot. You were with Lauren Bacall."

A deep chuckle came across the line. "I wasn't *with* Miss Bacall. She was just being nice to a starving actor. I do remember you, though I never got a chance to get your name. Or your phone number."

Remembering that Tom was at least six feet two and bore a slight resemblance to Bradley, I blushed. "How are you doing in the theater?"

"Bit parts mostly, but I've got a play lined up that I hope will garner some attention. What are you doing?"

"I'm the executive secretary at Merryweathers' Toy Shoppe. Do you know it?"

That deep chuckle again. "Know it? My parents took me there as a kid. I used to love the place. Haven't been there in years."

"So you're familiar with the store clown, Mr. Skidoo?"

"Yeah, he could always make me laugh with his tricks. It wasn't until I got into theater that I figured out how much work the guy put into his performance."

"Well, actually, Tom, Mr. Skidoo is the reason I'm calling. You see, the current Mr. Skidoo has, uh, well, you'll read it in the morning paper. He was murdered yesterday."

"You're putting me on. Who'd want to kill a toy store clown?"

"I honestly don't know. The guy was practically a stranger to me since I started here just this week. The police are working on it."

"Kids all over the city are going to flip out, you know that, right?"

"I sure do. I need to find a replacement immediately. I hope you won't think I'm crazy, but I thought of you. If you aren't busy, maybe you could play him for a while?" I closed my eyes and sent up a prayer that Tom would say yes.

"Hey, I could definitely do that until we start rehearsals. In fact, you'd be helping me out, Bebe. I need the dough."

A big grin spread across my face. First problem solved!

"Perfect! Tom, could you come in the store today so we can settle all the details?"

"Sure. Is one o'clock okay?"

"Sounds groovy. I'll be waiting for you."

"Thanks for remembering me, Bebe. Playing Mr. Skidoo will be a blast, as will seeing you again. Later." He hung up on those words.

The coffeepot gurgled, indicating that it had completed brewing. I turned on my transistor radio and heard the Beatles singing "Do You Want to Know a Secret." Thinking there were lots of secrets I'd like to know—such as who killed Mel Kinker—I walked over and poured myself a cup, feeling I deserved it. Adding a tiny amount of sugar from the jar, I thought of what I needed to do next. I'd have to find the store employment application for Tom to fill out. Then there was the matter of his costume. I'd have to dig around and see if the Merryweathers had kept a supply.

Placing the spoon I'd used to stir my coffee on a paper towel, I jumped when I felt Bradley brush past me, his blue suit making contact with my forest green A-line minidress.

"Good morning, Miss Bennett," he said, dropping a file in the in-box on my desk. "Coffee ready?"

Had he lost his sense of smell? "I'll be right in with it."

I filled his St. Louis Cardinals mug and followed him into his office. Whereas my area was narrow, Bradley's office encompassed a large part of the third floor. He'd brought all his personal furniture with him, including *that* sofa. The one where we'd kissed so passionately, where his shirt had been unbuttoned, revealing velvety soft skin over hard muscles, where—

"Here's your coffee," I said, placing the mug on his mission-style desk, pushing the memory aside for the moment.

I wouldn't tell him about Tom Stevens yet, just in case the actor backed out on the deal.

Bradley took off his suit jacket, hung it on a coatrack, and sat down in his blue leather chair. "We dodged the evening news, but have you seen the morning paper?"

"Not yet."

Bradley raised his eyebrows. "I think you'd better." He reached into his briefcase, extracted a copy, and slid it to my end of the desk. "That's all for now. I expect to be tied up on the phone all day again today and you've got your work cut out for you."

"Yes, Mr. Williams," I said, my tone polite and distant.

He glanced at me, a hint of surprise on his face.

I smiled to myself—maybe this new tactic would work—picked up the newspaper, and glided out of his office, proud of myself. Then my brain nibbled on an idea that had crossed my mind—only to be pushed firmly back—that the reason Bradley had turned chilly, had turned into Mr. Strict Boss, was another woman. Someone he kept secret from me. The society section of the newspaper rarely mentioned his name nowadays, and when it did the writer always referred to Bradley Williams and "date"—but that could mean it was always the same date. No, that couldn't be it. Bradley had told me he wasn't ready to settle down with one woman. But that was last May and now it was October. Maybe he'd met someone over the summer and changed his mind. If that was the case, I hated her! I'd find out who she was and . . .

I sighed and sat in my desk chair, radio playing low in the background, the newspaper open in front of me.

Sipping my coffee, I read the article, noting with no small amount of dismay that it was on page two and above the fold.

POPULAR CLOWN MURDERED

by Todd Simmons

Merryweathers' Toy Shoppe, a New York City institution since 1924, was the scene of a shocking murder last night at the close of the store's fortieth birthday party. Mel Kinker, 29, who was employed as the store's popular clown, Mr. Skidoo, was found stabbed to death after the store closed for the evening sometime after five thirty.

Police are withholding further information as they aggressively pursue the victim's killer.

This reporter was able to reach Mr. Merryweather in Florida, where the previous owners of the famous store retired recently. When told of the news, Mr. Merryweather expressed his sympathy and stated that he would be consulting his lawyers regarding a possible nullification of the store's recent sale to Herman Shires of Palm Beach. As of press time, neither Mr. Shires nor Bradley Williams, corporate manager of Merryweathers', could be reached for comment.

Mr. Kinker will be buried in his hometown in Ohio.

By the time I reached the middle of the article, my coffee sat forgotten and my stomach was queasy. Bradley's name was in the newspaper again. The Merryweathers were considering legal action against Bradley's uncle. Would Herman Shires continue to trust and believe in Bradley? Mr. Shires had to name someone in his will to take over his conglomeration of companies when he died. He had no sons, so the prime inheritance would go to one of his three nephews: Bradley, Drew, or Alfred.

Alfred ran a movie studio in Hollywood. While I'd never met Alfred, Bradley assured me his cousin was happy with his life just as it was, and had no desire for further responsibilities.

I made a face, thinking of Drew, whom I had unfortunately met on more than one occasion. Drew wanted the inheritance and went after it like a hound after a fox. I smirked. Actually, Drew reminded me of a fox with his auburn hair, triangle-shaped face, and constant sneer. Currently, he ran a chain of department stores based out of Chicago. I hoped he stayed there, but wouldn't bet on it with this latest murder happening on Bradley's watch.

Without my permission, my mind flashed back again to that never-to-be-forgotten day when Bradley had laid me down on his sofa. I groaned, thinking of his hand making its way up my thigh. Drew had been the one to interrupt us. No, Drew was not my favorite person in the world.

My elbow on the desk, right hand propped against my chin, I thought about what had happened after Drew's laughter had announced his arrival. To be fair, Bradley hadn't continued the proceedings. He could have if he'd wanted to. I had been incapable of stopping him at the time. But he hadn't. Not one to seduce virgins, my Bradley. Darn him.

Danielle crept in and said, "Not a good morning, is it? I can barely hear your radio."

I reached over and turned up the volume. The little

radio was permanently set to WABC. The Beatles sang "A Hard Day's Night."

"The Beatles!" Danielle said. "Our favorite."

"Second song they've played this morning. Oh, and John belongs to me," I said.

"Good, because I'd fight you for Paul. Oh, and have you seen that new TV show, *The Man from U.N.C.L.E.*? What a couple of hunks those guys are."

I tilted my head. "Yes, I've checked it out. Not only are they good-looking, but they sure know how to investigate, almost as well as James Bond. Did you read about the murder?"

Danielle, a tiny woman with short, glossy dark hair, was a godsend. While we were at Ryan, I'd found her in the typing pool and discovered that she made a fine secretary and a good friend. She'd recently been going steady with a nice guy named Herb. I knew she hoped to marry him, settle down, and have a family.

She nodded, taking a seat at the desk behind me. "Is there anything I can do, Bebe?"

I thought for a moment. There was no need yet to tell Danielle that I was the main suspect. "Thank you, hon. I haven't had much time to get a good look around the store's back rooms. Do you know if there are extra costumes for the store characters?"

"Mr. Skidoo costumes?"

"Yes."

"I've seen some moldy boxes in the first-floor store-room labeled with the different store characters' names. There are more costumes on hangers in there too."

"Good. I'll go down there after I finish these invoices and see if I can find a couple. I've got a guy coming in this afternoon who might be a temporary Mr. Skidoo."

Danielle's eyes widened. "You found someone already, Bebe? You're amazing."

"Don't congratulate me yet. The deal's not final. And don't say anything to Mr. Williams. Would you mind answering the phone when I go downstairs?"

"Not at all. I guess I know what to tell the reporters."

In unison, we said, "Merryweathers' has no comment at this time."

We exchanged grim smiles and began the day's work. After a while I pushed my chair back and headed downstairs.

I reached the first floor, looked around, and had to glance at my watch. Ten thirty and not a customer in sight. Though the store characters appeared to be busy fussing over their areas, I had the strangest feeling that there was a festive air about the place. Shouldn't everyone be mourning the brutal loss of a coworker?

Calls of "Good morning, Miss Bennett" met my ears. Even the crusty Train Conductor tore his gaze from his beloved trains and tiny villages and saluted me.

"Good morning," I repeated several times, completely confused, before reaching the storeroom marked EMPLOYEES ONLY.

Closing the door behind me, I found myself staring into the eyes of the Pirate, Junior on his shoulder. He tried to pass me without a word but I blocked his way. "Mr. Geedunk, why did you turn on me that way in front of Detectives Snyder and Finelli?"

The Pirate fed his bird a treat, then said, "I didn't kill Mel Kinker and I'd be damned if I'd let myself be bullied by that detective fella."

"But you made *me* look guilty," I said, arms

crossed. "By the way, why does Junior say 'Kill the clown'? What's the real reason?"

The Pirate turned away. "I said last night that the bird talks nonsense."

"Odd that he would repeat that one bit of nonsense over and over, almost as if he was voicing someone's thoughts."

Mr. Geedunk stiffened. "The entire staff thinks you did it. Congratulations, you've won instant approval here."

He walked around me to leave and closed the door to the sales floor behind him.

I blinked. Was that why everyone was chipper instead of grieving? They thought I had killed Mr. Skidoo and that made them happy? What had Mr. Skidoo done to draw such animosity from his coworkers?

I didn't know, but I would find out—even if I had to question Junior.

Chapter Five

Half an hour later, I swiped at the dust that clung to my dress. The storeroom was anything but organized, and I'd had to go through box after box of Mr. Skidoo costumes. Most of them were torn and moldy with age. Then I discovered a door next to the employee restrooms. I turned the handle and found myself in a room about the size of Darlene's and my kitchen.

About a dozen character costumes hung against the walls, including four sets of Mr. Skidoo's outfit. The second my hand touched the brim of the top hat, the image of the clown lying dead in the Jungle flashed in my brain. I squeezed my eyes tight and mentally erased the picture.

I studied each costume against what I remembered of Tom's height and weight. I set two possibilities aside. When Tom came in, he could try them on. If necessary the garments could be adjusted, though that would take another day or two, delaying the placement of the ad in the newspaper inviting children to come see Mr. Skidoo.

With an hour until noon, I returned to the sales floor, wondering what the day's gossip was about me. Did the store characters really believe I had killed Mr.

Skidoo, making me a heroine in their eyes? Or would they guess I was investigating the murder and close ranks?

Mr. Geedunk stood on a step stool dusting off plastic skull heads. He didn't acknowledge me. Junior was perched on the crossbar of a tall wooden stand. "You bet the clown's dead!" squawked the parrot.

The Pirate turned around. "That's enough, Junior."

The Cowboy chuckled. "Been sayin' that all mornin', hasn't he?"

"Mind your own business, Larabee," the Pirate grunted as he smoothed out a black flag with white skull and crossbones with a sharp snap.

"No need to get worked up."

I approached the Cowboy with a friendly smile on my face. Since the Pirate was close by, I doubted I'd have a chance to question the Cowboy about him. Still, since I wanted to get to know all the store characters, I might as well take this opportunity with the Cowboy. He wore a brown fringed shirt, blue jeans, a brown cowboy hat, and boots with spurs. "Hi there, I'm Bebe Bennett. I don't think we've had time to chat. Since Mr. Williams took over the store we've all been so busy. How long have you been with Merryweathers'?"

"Four years, I reckon." He tipped his hat. "Pleased to meet you, miss. My real name is Dave Larabee. You can call me Dave or Cowboy. Makes no difference to me, though it's store policy for us to call each other by our character names."

The Cowboy was handsome in a rugged way, perfect for his role. He had dark blue eyes, a strong jaw that ended in a square chin, and a muscled build that would charm the mothers buying toys for their children. His big, strong hands had been busy arranging a fight scene between small cowboy and Indian figures, but he had stopped to give me his full attention.

"Please call me Bebe. That's quite a display you're making. Between all the cowboys and Indians, and that collection of guns, the boys must flock to your area."

He smiled. "You've got that right. The Red Ryder BB gun is real popular. So is the Johnny Eagle Skeet-Shooter. I have to keep that one up on a high shelf to make sure none of the kids gets hurt."

"Mr. Williams will appreciate that." I ran my index finger along one of the miniature gray boulders in the fight scene. Then, giving Dave a wide-eyed and innocent expression, I said, "Someone definitely got hurt in our store last night."

The Cowboy's rough gaze shot over to Raggedy Ann. It was quick, perhaps an unconscious gesture, and if I'd blinked just then I would never have seen it. He answered in a stiff voice. "Mel Kinker won't be missed. I think you of all people know that, Bebe."

Exactly what did he mean by that? Did Dave think I'd killed Mel Kinker? "To be honest, Dave, I've picked up an air of relief in the store this morning. Am I imagining it?"

He pulled his hat down lower on his head. "Don't think so."

"Why is that?"

He fidgeted. "Can't speak for anyone but myself. Didn't like the man. It wasn't right the way he treated the ladies here. Think *you* know what I'm talkin' about," he said, staring at me.

Darn it, was everyone aware that the clown had leered at me? I chose my words carefully. "Mel Kinker could be aggressive about what he wanted."

A furrow appeared between the Cowboy's eyes as once again he looked over at Raggedy Ann. "I'm just happy he's not around anymore. I'd like to shake the killer's hand. Not that I condone murder, make no mistake, but sometimes people need killin'. It's over and done with now."

"Who do you think murdered the clown?"

The Cowboy looked at me from under the brim of his hat. Seconds passed before he said, "If you'll excuse me now, I want to take advantage of the store being quiet and put things in order here."

The dismissal was kind and polite, but a dismissal just the same. "Sure. I'll talk to you later."

He tipped his hat, then his big hands returned to arranging the mock fight scene.

I walked toward the escalator with the intention of returning to my desk. The Cowboy hadn't answered my question in so many words, but he had looked at me in a certain way. He thought I'd killed the clown, or at least he was acting like I had. I wanted to pull out my notebook and write down what the Cowboy had said. The man did not like the clown—big surprise—but what interested me was the way he kept glancing over at Raggedy Ann. I caught her eye as I rode up the escalator. She smiled and waved at me. I returned the gesture.

Were Dave and Betty friends? Dating? Had the clown done something to Betty? The Cowboy struck me as the honorable, protective type. Could he have killed Mel Kinker over the way the clown treated women, Betty in particular? The opinion he expressed about how some people needed killing sent a shiver down my spine. I decided that Betty would be the next person I'd question.

Danielle sat at her desk, Dictaphone earpieces in

her ear, typing away. We exchanged smiles, then I pulled out the steno pad and wrote down my conversation with the Cowboy. I had finished that and was almost done writing a draft of an ad for the *Times,* inviting the children to come visit Mr. Skidoo, when the phone rang.

"Merryweathers' Toy Shoppe, Bebe Bennett speaking."

"Finelli here."

I lowered my voice. "I'm glad you called. I need to talk to you, clear up some things I said last night. Can you meet me somewhere? Not here at the store, please."

The sound of a heavy sigh came from the other end of the line. "I'm near the corner of Madison and Fifty-ninth Street."

"Is there a hot-dog stand nearby?"

"What?"

"It's almost lunchtime and I always have a hot dog and a Tab."

"Yeah, there's one near this phone booth."

"I'll be there as quick as I can."

Grabbing my purse from the desk drawer, I told Danielle I'd be back in time to meet Tom Stevens at one o'clock and that she could take a lunch break then.

I stood waiting for the elevator, nerves jangling, when Bradley walked up.

"Going out, Miss Bennett?"

"I'm meeting someone for lunch." That sounded good. Honest, but vague.

The elevator door opened and we walked in. "What progress have you made finding another clown?"

"I have a candidate coming in this afternoon."

He raised an eyebrow. "That was fast."

I shrugged. "He's a friend, an actor between jobs."

Bradley's blue eyes bore into me. "A friend, you say?"

"Yes." The elevator stopped on the second floor and we exited into the Children's Book Section with its Reading Corner and a wide, plastic tree house where the children could sit and look at books. I quickened my pace and walked ahead of Bradley down the escalator steps. Let him think I was in a hurry. Actually, I was.

He stopped to speak to Mr. Mallory and I fled through the front door, and remembered to smile at the Teddy Bear greeter.

The chilly air hit me, reminding me again that I had to buy a coat that went with my fashionable new clothes.

I walked fast through the crowd, having mastered the art of navigating through the packed sidewalks. Finelli would help me. He'd get me out from under Detective Snyder's grimy magnifying glass. All I had to do was tell Finelli the truth.

The detective came into view, leaning on his Pontiac Tempest, dressed in a dark gray suit and tie. I practically ran into his arms, ignoring the nearby hot-dog stand.

I caught my breath and managed a smile. "I'm happy to see you."

Finelli grunted. "What did you want to tell me?"

"Many things. First, you must know what the 'secret' was that Mr. Skidoo—I mean Mel Kinker—found out about me."

The detective raised his eyebrows and tilted his head to one side. "Miss Bennett, I think you're a woman of many secrets. Which one are we talking about?"

I looked around, rubbing my arms.

"Here, come into my office," Finelli said, opening the passenger door to his car.

I stepped in gratefully, noting the scattered papers on top of the dashboard and the police radio.

He got behind the wheel and pulled out his notepad, pencil poised. "Ready now?"

I nodded. "See, it's all very simple. The clown was trying to get me to go out with him, not that I ever did, despite what I said last night. The man was creepy. I only said I'd dated him because Bradley was standing there. I couldn't let him know the truth, you know, how I . . . care for him deeply. I believe what my mama says about men wanting to do the chasing. In fact I've been chilly with Bradley with that very goal in mind. It might be working because he gave me the strangest look when I told him I was meeting someone for lunch and that I already had a candidate for a new Mr. Skidoo coming in today. What you need to do is explain all this to that awful Detective Snyder and ask him to keep it under his hat. Then he'll realize that I didn't kill the clown." I took a deep breath and waited for Finelli to agree with me.

The detective rubbed a hand over his crew cut. "I can't give details about something unless I understand it myself."

"But I just explained it all to you with perfect logic!"

"Let's start over. I'll ask the questions and you try your hardest to give simple, uncomplicated answers. Agreed?"

I nodded.

"What was the secret Mel Kinker thought he knew?"

"That I-I have, well, *warm* feelings toward Bradley.

I just told you that, even though from past experience you already knew—"

Finelli raised a hand. "Step by step now. I'm aware of your feelings toward your boss."

I twirled a piece of my hair. "Do you think Bradley returns my . . . admiration?"

"Oh no. There's no way you're going to draw me into that conversation, Miss Bennett. Let's stay on track. Kinker wanted to date you, but realized that you have a crush on your boss. How did the clown find out?"

I let out an indignant breath. "I don't have a 'crush' on Bradley. I love him!"

"Okay, okay. Just answer the question. How did the clown know?"

"I think he figured it out when he saw me staring at Bradley while riding the escalator. He may have even watched Bradley and me talking on the second floor. My face gives me away, I guess."

"Most of the time."

I crossed my arms. "I'm working on it."

"Don't. It's part of your charm."

"Why, thank you."

"And it helps me understand what's going on in that brain of yours."

I frowned, but remembered the possibility of wrinkles and composed my face.

"When I was in the store with my boys, the clown rode up to you and tugged your skirt. He said he knew your secret and that he might tell what it was. We've established that the secret was your cru— love for Williams. Got it. Did it upset you that the clown threatened to tell everyone? Don't deny that he did, because I was right there when Kinker said it."

My fingers twirled my hair faster. "Yes."

"Now let's return to last night's questioning," he said, flipping back through the notepad. "You stated you had been out socially with Kinker, and that he got the wrong idea about you and you ended it."

"Right, but you know I made that up, for heaven's sake." I rolled my eyes. "Like I'd really date that annoying, leering creep. What's wrong? You look mad."

"You *lied* to the police."

"Just a tiny white lie and I'll confess it at church. I did have a good reason—Bradley—and I'm telling you the truth now. I wanted to tell you last night but Snyder wouldn't let me talk to you alone."

"Christ! You lied about your relationship to Kinker, you were discovered with the dead body, you had the murder weapon in your hand. You might as well have put the noose around your own neck! Snyder will be more convinced than ever that you're the killer."

I trembled. "Does he have to find out? What purpose would that serve? I mean, you don't think I killed the clown, do you, Detective Finelli?"

The pencil he had been writing with snapped in two. "You've put me in one hell of a situation, Miss Bennett. You know how I feel about my job. I worked hard to become a detective and have a wife and two boys to support. How can I not inform Snyder that you lied to us?"

Tears stung my eyes. "I'm sorry. Although we've had our differences, I've always thought you were on my side."

He let out a snort, then mumbled, "Tried to save you from yourself is more like it."

"I do respect you," I continued. "I won't ask you not to tell Snyder. I'll leave the decision up to you."

Finelli looked out the window and shook his head.

"I hope you know by now that I would never take another human being's life. Even if I were such a person, though the clown was a pest, I had no motive to kill him—"

"The case could be made that Kinker threatened to expose your intimate regard for Williams."

"That's a motive? I promise you that I've already started investigating—"

"Dear God! That's the last thing you should be doing. You always get yourself in trouble."

"I'm already in hot water, Detective."

"You're right about that. Don't you want to know why I called you in the first place?"

I started to feel very cold. Suddenly Darlene's warning that I not speak to Snyder or Finelli came back to me. "What?"

"I called to tell you that Snyder is waiting for the coroner's report. If the coroner agrees the knife you were holding caused the clown's death, then he plans to bring the case before a grand jury."

"With me as the accused killer," I whispered.

Finelli nodded. "I think you'd better take Williams's offer of getting a good lawyer, Miss Bennett. You're going to need one. Fast."

Chapter Six

"Go ahead and take your lunch hour, Danielle."

"You sure you don't want me here to cover the phones while you're doing your interview?"

"That's okay, I can handle it."

Once Danielle had gone, I glanced at my watch. I had ten minutes to compose myself before Tom Stevens came in. I took a sip of Tab. My stomach had recoiled at the idea of eating after my meeting with Finelli.

I flinched at the thought of going into Bradley's office and asking him to have the company pay for a lawyer for me. That would put me right back into the weak role that I was trying to shed. He'd probably pat me on the head, tell me he'd take care of everything, and add a stern lecture against doing any personal investigating.

I didn't want that, but I didn't want to go to jail either, and there was no way I could possibly afford a lawyer. I would have to swallow my pride and accept Bradley's offer. I looked down the hall. His door was closed. Good. Maybe after I met with Tom I could show Bradley how I had replaced Mel Kinker and then, while he was marveling at my efficiency, I would ask him about the lawyer.

Precisely at one o' clock, the elevator dinged and

Tom Stevens walked out, saw me, and grinned. He looked mod in dark, narrow-cut trousers, a paisley jacket, and boots. "Bebe, so groovy to see you."

I smiled when he kissed me on the cheek, then he pulled a chair next to my desk and sat down. He was every bit as tall and handsome as I remembered. I especially admired the sexy curve of his lips and his tousled sandy brown hair. "I'm glad you could make it."

"Hey, like I told you, playing Mr. Skidoo would be a great temporary gig for me," he said, and pulled three small yellow balls from his pocket and began juggling them.

I laughed. "You came prepared!"

"Am I impressing you yet?"

"Yes!"

"Are you sure?" He placed the plastic balls on my desk, reached into his sleeve, and out sprang a bouquet of plastic pink flowers.

I bent over in my chair, laughing and laughing, Tom joining in. Then I looked up and saw Bradley staring at us, coffeepot in one hand, mug in the other. The coffee splashed over the top of the mug, burning his hand. He cursed, stalked back to his office, and shut the door. Bradley, jealous? Better and better.

I quickly went over the store hours with Tom, had him fill out the employment application, and told him about the Mr. Skidoo costumes I'd put away for him to try on in the storeroom.

"What about face paint?" I asked.

He waved a careless hand. "I have an entire supply of all sorts of makeup for the stage."

"That's great," I said, accepting his completed application. "Can you go downstairs and try on those costumes now? I hope one of them fits."

"No problem." He rose and my traitorous eyes slid to the slim-fitting pants he wore.

I chewed on the end of my pen after he'd gotten on the elevator. Some intuition told me that Tom was going to ask me out. Would I accept if he did? Mama always told me not to get involved with actors. In her opinion they were all immoral and broke unless they were big Hollywood stars, in which case they were immoral and rich. But what harm could there be in my spending time with Tom? He was funny, charming, handsome, and I doubted he was ready for a serious relationship, since he was young and concentrating on building his career.

Tom returned in about twenty minutes, a box in hand. "Luck is on our side, Bebe. I found a costume that fits pretty well and, more important, a pair of shoes in my size."

"Wow, things have really fallen into place. When can you start?"

"The sooner the better. Like I said, I need the dough."

I breathed a sigh of relief. "How about tomorrow?"

He grinned. "Tell you what. I'll start tomorrow morning on the condition that you let me take you dancing tomorrow night. You know, to ease the tension of my first day."

I rolled my eyes, secretly pleased that my intuition had been on target. "Dancing? I can't claim to be a very good dancer."

"This is a swinging club, Bebe. It's called the Orb and plays all the hits. You can dance any way you want, nobody cares. Just put on another of those cute minidresses like the one you're wearing now and we'll have a blast."

I made like I was thinking it over carefully, then blurted, "Yes!"

He favored me with a wide grin.

After I gave him my address, we agreed that he'd pick me up at eight tomorrow night, though I'd see him in the store tomorrow.

When Danielle returned from lunch, I proudly told her we had a new Mr. Skidoo and then made my way to the sales floor, putting off my meeting with Bradley. Looking around, I saw that business was still slow, with maybe a dozen customers in the store. Mr. Mallory had a pinched look on his face as he spoke in hushed tones with the girls running the cash registers.

Recalling my mission to question Betty, I strolled over to the doll section, ignoring the Mr. Skidoo dolls. My gaze lingered over the baby dolls. On a high shelf that couldn't be reached by little hands, one of the dolls, a little boy dressed in a soft cotton outfit, caught my eye. He was so lifelike that I picked him up and cradled him in my arms. Allowing my imagination to take hold, I wondered what it would be like to hold my own baby boy, Bradley's baby, the three of us a family. Would it ever happen, or should I move on, look for another job and another man? Was I a fool, loving someone who didn't love me back? I supposed the question would be answered for me if I were tried and convicted of killing Mel Kinker.

Betty, in her Raggedy Ann costume, came up to me and stood by my side. "You have good taste, Bebe. He's our most expensive newborn doll. Notice the hand smocking on his pale blue outfit and the detail of his tiny fingers."

Snapping out of my thoughts, I remembered my purpose was to question Betty, see if I could find out why the Cowboy had looked at her repeatedly while he and I had talked about Kinker.

"He is adorable, Betty. Trust me to pick the costly one," I said with a rueful smile. "Here, you'd better take him." I transferred the doll to her arms just as one would hand a real baby over to another person. "I was thinking about how I'd like to have a baby someday. How about you? Do you want children in your future?"

Betty returned the doll to his place then wrinkled her red triangle nose and sighed. "Like most girls, I guess I do."

I chuckled. "You don't sound too enthusiastic."

She fussed with the already neat child's tea table, moving the flowered ceramic pot an inch, fluttering her hands over the matching teacups. Then she straightened. "I don't have much luck when it comes to men," she finally answered in a clipped voice.

"Oh, come on. I can't believe that a pretty girl like you with a great figure would have the slightest bit of trouble getting dates," I said truthfully. Betty had a body like Ann-Margret's and strawberry blond hair peeked out from her red-yarn wig. I whispered, "At least you don't have to suffer with thirty-four-As like me."

Instead of laughing, like I'd intended her to do, a hard look came into Betty's brown eyes. "Sometimes a girl's body is all certain men are interested in, even when they sweet-talk you and pretend to be genuinely interested in you as a person."

I reached out a hand and touched her arm. "I'm sorry, Betty. Did a man treat you that way?"

She stiffened under my fingers, so I dropped them. I took a quick glance at the Cowboy's section, only to find him staring at us.

"I'm sure you know the drill, Bebe. We girls have to weed out the good guys from the bad, unless you're like Mary, the Ice Princess, as I call her over there. She never dates, at least that's what she says."

I slid my eyes over to the Princess. Young and beautiful, with honey-colored hair and almond-shaped blue eyes, she looked ethereal in her fitted silver gown and small, glowing tiara.

"Do you have reason to think otherwise?" I asked.

Betty shrugged. "I don't know anything for sure except that she's a former Miss Connecticut and Kinker was always making passes at her."

I thought she seemed more of a Shy Princess than an Ice Princess, playing with a jewelry box that opened to a tiny dancing ballerina and tinkling music. Yes, I could imagine that Kinker had pressed his attentions on the Princess.

"What was her reaction to the clown's flirting?"

"Hmpf. She didn't want to have anything to do with him, which made him try even harder. He was like that, always relishing the chase. You should know, Bebe."

Darn it, everyone in that store knew about the clown's leering and picking on me. If he treated the Princess the same way, maybe it was how he treated all women, including Betty. Was that why the Cowboy seemed protective of her? Did that mean he was also looking after the Princess?

Betty looked around to make sure we were not overheard, then gazed into my eyes. "I'm glad Mel Kinker is gone. I'm thinking one woman wasn't going to put up with his slimy passes and took action." She nodded at me in a knowing way.

Betty thought I'd killed him too! "No one deserves to be murdered," I said in my most serious tone.

"Well, I don't know how we got on the subject. I'd much rather talk about our sexy new corporate manager, Mr. Williams. Just the sight of him makes me weak in the knees. You've been working with him for a while, I hear, Bebe. What does he find attractive in a woman? Is he really as notorious as the Society section of the paper makes him out to be?"

My brown eyes surely matched my green dress. I remembered seeing Betty flirting with Bradley on the day of the birthday party. "I couldn't tell you. Our relationship is strictly professional," I fibbed.

"You're his secretary. Don't you know if he's dating anyone seriously?"

"I honestly don't have a clue." Which was the absolute truth.

Betty and I talked for a few more minutes—she demonstrated the Chatty Cathy doll for me—and then I told her I needed to return to my desk.

Once there, I wrote notes about our conversation in my steno pad. Chewing the tip of my Bic pen, I thought about Betty's comment regarding not having luck with men, and how she had avoided answering my question about whether she had been treated badly by a guy.

On my transistor radio, the Supremes sang "Where Did Our Love Go?" I realized that Betty had not said anything about Mel Kinker flirting with *her*. He must have, so why was she keeping mum on the subject? I marked her down as yet another person who was glad to see him dead. I refrained from writing about Betty's interest in Bradley. That piece of information would stay lodged in my head without my having to record it. I bit my lip. Where were the store personnel files? I'd like to have a look at those. Were they in Mallory's office? Bradley's office? I'd find out.

Around four o'clock, I decided to gather my dignity

and talk to Bradley about his offer of a company lawyer. The light on his private phone line was not lit, so
I had no excuse to delay the matter.

"Danielle, can you cover the phones for a few minutes? I have to speak with Mr. Williams."

"Sure, go ahead. I'm just doing some filing."

"Thanks."

I pulled my purse out of the squeaky wooden
drawer, found my Mary Quant pale pink lip gloss,
applied a fresh coat, and returned the items. Taking
a deep breath, I straightened my posture, walked
down the short hallway to Bradley's closed door,
and knocked.

"Come in."

I opened the door and saw him sitting in his blue
leather chair. I noticed his suit jacket was on a hanger
by his private restroom and that the sleeves of his
white shirt were rolled up, revealing his muscular fore-
arms. *Strong, Bebe, you have to be strong.*

He raised one eyebrow. "What is it, Miss Bennett?"

"I have two issues to discuss with you," I said in
my most professional, distant voice.

Some emotion flashed across his face. Instinct told
me that it was disappointment, but the look was gone
so fast there was no way to be sure.

He motioned toward a chair. "Have a seat."

I sat down and allowed my minidress to ride up to
a dangerous level. The new Businesslike Bebe would
match the new Strict Boss Bradley measure for measure verbally, but I'd keep showing off my legs.

Bradley's gaze went slowly from the top of my head
to my toes. My heart pounded in my chest. Could he
be thinking dirty thoughts about me? How yummy.
His blue eyes had kinda clouded over. I managed to
restrain myself from running a hand up my thigh.

"Thank you, this won't take long," I said.

"Fine," he said, with a touch of irritation that warmed my heart. Then he leaned back in his chair, holding the ends of a pencil between two fingers, looking adorable.

I wished I'd sprayed on a bit of My Sin before entering his office.

"First, I'm happy to report that we have a new Mr. Skidoo. His name is Tom Stevens and he'll be starting first thing tomorrow morning." With an effort, I kept my voice neutral.

"Is he the fellow you were giggling with at your desk earlier?"

"Why, yes. Tom and I are friends."

"Friends? I told you I wanted a professional."

"Tom *is* a professional. He's a stage actor, and as a boy he was a frequent store customer. Tom and I are confident he'll have no trouble whatsoever playing Mr. Skidoo."

"Are you sure? Look, kid, I know you try to help people out when they're down on their luck, but Merryweathers' has a reputation to maintain. I can't afford to place an ad in the newspaper inviting folks to come in and visit Mr. Skidoo only to have them find a guy dressed up in a costume with no personality or talent."

My temper rose. Bradley had told me to find someone, and now that I had, he was questioning my judgment. Keeping my voice calm, I said, "Tom has plenty of personality. You'll be able to observe his performance tomorrow. If you have any specific concerns, let me know, and I'll discuss them with him while he and I are out tomorrow night." Zing!

Bradley's pencil fell to the desk. "You're dating him?"

I tossed my hair. "That's a very personal question, Mr. Williams. I don't ask you who you date."

He sat there, seemingly at a loss for words. Then, "I think Merryweathers' has a policy of not allowing coworkers to date."

"Really? I didn't see any mention of that rule in the original employee handbook written by Mr. Merryweather."

"Well, I must trust you on that, Miss Bennett. I haven't time to read the employee handbook and assume you did before dating Mel Kinker."

Oh, God, that lie. This was the only situation where that lie worked to my benefit.

"Speaking of Mel brings me to the second issue I need to speak with you about."

"Has that blowhard Snyder given you any more trouble?"

"I haven't spoken to him. However"—I raised my chin—"what would be the terms of my taking you up on your offer of a company lawyer?"

He shot me a stern look. "What has prompted this request? Something else happened, or you wouldn't be in here asking me about a lawyer."

I crossed my fingers behind my back. "I've had time to consider my financial situation and have come to the conclusion that I can't afford to hire a lawyer on my own. I'm sure I could ask my father for the money, but frankly I'd like to keep the information that I am a suspect in a murder investigation from him as long as I can."

Bradley rubbed his forehead then returned my gaze. "No doubt he'd come up here and force his Little Magnolia to return to Richmond. Maybe that's not such a bad idea, Miss Bennett. Since you've been in

Manhattan trouble has followed you around like a devoted puppy. Besides, you're very young—"

Angry, I interrupted him, holding on to my calm demeanor by a thread. "If you check the employee records, you'll find that I'll be twenty-three in December, hardly a little girl. Many women my age have married and had a child. Others, like me, relish living in the city, enjoying their work. For the most part." Oops, those last words just slipped out. "If you don't wish to employ me, I'll simply find another job here in New York."

He sighed. "I'll find you a lawyer. Don't worry about the cost. When do you need him?"

"I'd like to meet with him tomorrow or at his earliest convenience. As for his fee, I'll begin taking a deduction from my paycheck to reimburse the company." I rose, turned on my heel, and made it to the door before he could react.

"Miss Bennett! I said that you needn't concern yourself over the money."

I swung around. "Why not? Will you be paying for the lawyer out of your own pocket? Or will it be taken from the corporate account? Picked from a secret money tree?"

He turned away and looked out his window. After a tense minute, I understood he was not going to answer me.

I turned to leave, then realized an opportunity had presented itself. "Mr. Williams, since we'll be adding a new employee, I need to know where the personnel files are so that I can update them."

"Not so fast," Bradley said. "A final decision about your friend's employment here hasn't been made."

Darn him! I wanted those files! "Where are the personnel files? I should know—"

"No, you shouldn't," Bradley replied, his tone final.

Was there a more stubborn man?

"I'll start the deduction from my paycheck right away. I'm an independent woman, you know."

This time I did make it out of his office, but not before I heard him mutter, "Stubborn female is more like it."

I mentally patted myself on the back for keeping my cool.

A short time later it was time to go home. Danielle and I covered our typewriters, I switched off my radio, and we rode the elevator and then the escalator downstairs.

"Was Mr. Williams proud of you for replacing Mr. Skidoo so quickly?" Danielle asked.

"I think he wants to wait and see how Tom works out before showering me with compliments."

Danielle giggled. "Mr. Williams has changed since Suzie Wexford was murdered last spring. I don't think it's about grieving her, but he seems to have cut himself off from other people, almost put up a barrier."

I tilted my head. "You've noticed it too?"

She nodded. "I still see his name in the Society section of the paper, but at the office he doesn't laugh very much. I think he's got something heavy on his mind."

We were standing near the Jungle. "Danielle, he's just taken on a lot more responsibility, with the other two stores opening, and then the murder."

"You're right. But his new attitude started before all that, remember?"

"I guess so."

Danielle slipped her arms into her red coat. "I think he's at his worst with you, Bebe."

"Why do you say that?" I asked, noticing the Teddy Bear entering the store and locking the door.

"I think he's fighting something he *thinks* he doesn't want to feel," she said, and winked.

"Danielle! I don't know what you're talking about." She laughed and left the store.

I stood frozen in place before I remembered I wanted to tell Mr. Mallory about Tom starting tomorrow.

Mr. Mallory's office was situated behind the cash registers. I walked up to the open door in time to see the Teddy Bear take out another one of those envelopes and toss it on the store manager's desk. This was the second time I'd observed this type of exchange between the men.

Mr. Mallory stared at me, causing the Teddy Bear to turn around. I would have liked to have seen his face, but he was still in costume. He brushed past me without a single word despite my cheery, "Good night, Mr. Runion." My curiosity about the white envelopes was stronger than ever. If I could catch the Teddy Bear alone, I would find a way to question him.

The store manager was anything but cheery. He slipped the envelope into his inside suit pocket, never taking his eyes off me. "What do you want?"

Suddenly, I felt nervous. I knew how territorial Mr. Mallory was over the store and figured he'd be mad about my going over his head to hire Tom. Mr. Mallory had treated me with nothing but contempt since Bradley had taken over the store. In fact, he treated Bradley much the same, although he masked it a little better.

"I wanted to give you the good news that we have a temporary replacement for Mr. Skidoo."

"What? *You* hired someone without my interviewing the person?"

His pale complexion had turned a mottled red.

"Look, Mr. Mallory, I'm only doing my job. Mr. Williams instructed me to find someone and hire him. I'm sure you'd agree that we needed to be quick about it. Tom Stevens is a trained actor. He's familiar with the store and the Mr. Skidoo character. I think you'll be pleased with him."

"That remains to be seen. I shall discuss this with Mr. Williams personally. The store will not thrive if we have inexperienced young girls hiring staff. Good evening, Miss Bennett."

He promptly strode out of his office. I had no choice but to step back, though I had an urge to rummage through his desk to check for the personnel files. He locked the door behind me, eliminating any snooping possibilities.

After nodding good night to the few remaining employees, I stepped outside and immediately decided I could go no longer without a groovy coat. Maybe I could buy one tomorrow during my lunch hour, unless I spent the time with my new lawyer. Finelli had warned me to get a lawyer before the coroner's report came back. Somewhere inside me I felt the clock ticking, the moment when I'd be arrested growing closer.

I caught the bus, deposited change into the machine, and took a seat. Thinking about Mr. Mallory, I decided it would be wise to introduce Tom to the store manager the moment he came in. Hopefully, Tom would arrive in full makeup and costume and be his charming self, winning Mr. Mallory's approval.

I couldn't help but be curious about that white envelope. Today was the second time I'd seen the Teddy Bear passing one to Mr. Mallory. What was in it? Maybe I could slip into the store manager's office and find out.

As I reached my building, there was no sign of

Harry. I hoped he was okay. Wearily I climbed the four flights of stairs and was turning the lock in the apartment door when the door swinging open startled me.

"It's my favorite murderer!" Darlene greeted me, grinning from ear to ear.

I threw myself into her arms.

Chapter Seven

"When did you get home?" I asked when we had finished hugging and were inside the door. "I didn't expect you until tonight, not that I'm complaining."

"I ended up taking a night flight, slept at Stu's, then came home. You wouldn't believe how happy I am to have some time without him," she said in her Texas drawl.

Bert "Stu" Daniels was the heir to the Minty-Mouth Breath Mint fortune, a former stew-bum who was now devoted to one Miss Darlene Roland.

I tossed my purse on the pink sectional. "I thought you loved Stu."

Darlene nodded, red curls bouncing. "I do, honey. It's just that he's spent the summer taking every flight I worked, stayed with me during layovers, bought me dinner every night, and followed me around like a three-year-old holding his mama's hand down a dark street. I don't dig being smothered. Now come on in the kitchen. I've made my famous tuna casserole—"

She stopped talking and listened with an amused twinkle in her blue eyes.

"Give it to me, Willie! I want it rough!" a woman's voice cried from the apartment above us.

A piece of furniture—a bed?—thumped repeatedly against a wall.

"You asked for it, Lily. You're not gonna be able to walk tomorrow once I'm finished with you tonight!" a man's voice shouted.

"Oh, God, yes! Harder! Harder!"

I stood frozen, heat creeping up my neck, my throat dry.

Darlene snickered and tugged my arm. "You can't hear them from the kitchen."

"What?" I croaked out, automatically taking my place at our tiny table in the cramped space.

"We have new neighbors upstairs. I saw the moving truck outside when I came home. Didn't catch sight of the couple, but they've been at it off and on for the last hour. Guess they're newlyweds." Darlene slid a plate of food in front of me along with a glass of milk.

"If I have to listen to that every day, I'll . . . I'll . . ."

"Be thinking sexy thoughts about Bradley," she finished for me. "Speaking of him, has he relaxed or is he keeping his distance from Temptation Bebe?"

"Temptation Bebe, that's a good one. Bradley's a block of ice where I'm concerned." I began to eat, then sipped my wholesome milk, willing myself not to think about what was going on upstairs, what could be going on between me and Bradley if only he didn't see me as a not-to-be-touched virgin. Although to be fair, I *was* a virgin, and intended to save myself for my wedding night. I shifted uncomfortably in my chair. Maybe I'd have to amend that to "save myself until the next time I found myself alone with Bradley."

Darlene slid into the seat opposite me. "I'm sure you're exaggerating. The man adores you."

"He's got an original way of showing it." I ticked off items on my fingers. "He's back to calling me 'Miss Bennett,' he doesn't chat with me in the mornings like he used to, he barks orders at me, he never takes me to lunch, and, now that I think about it, he avoids looking at me."

"Trying to keep his pants zipped around you."

"Darlene . . ."

"It's true. He's got it bad. I've been telling you so all summer during our phone calls. From what you've said, I think Bradley is struggling to come to terms with the impending end to his bachelorhood. Bless his heart."

"You've got quite an imagination, Darlene. You should write books."

"Just telling things the way I see them."

"The way I see it, Bradley is ashamed of, you know—"

"Almost going all the way with you on his sofa last spring?"

"Exactly. A big guilty sign is painted on his forehead and he's trying to let me know that . . . incident . . . meant nothing to him. He's protecting my feelings by keeping his romances to himself."

"Yeah, okay, we'll see. Now fill me in on the murder."

For the next half hour, I told her everything that had happened thus far. She listened carefully and only got up once to put a white bakery box containing a chocolate cake, forks, and plates on the table.

She almost choked when I got to the part about meeting Finelli at lunchtime.

"Bebe! I told you not to talk to the fuzz. Now Finelli knows you lied about dating Kinker the clown. When he tells Snyder, and he will tell him," she insisted, pointing her fork at me for emphasis, "your credibility goes out the window and straight into a garbage can."

I winced. "You're right. I should have listened to you, but I thought Finelli was a friend."

"He's a cop. He would lock his own wife up if he caught her shoplifting."

"One good thing came out of the conversation."

"Oh?"

"He warned me that I'd better get a lawyer quickly. Snyder is just waiting for the coroner's report to come back before he charges me with the murder."

"Damn! I'll have Stu get someone for you. Let me call him right now."

"Sit back down. Someone else is hiring a lawyer for me."

Darlene smirked. "Could that someone be Bradley?"

I sighed. "It's not what you think. He made the offer the night of the murder, probably thinking of the store's reputation, but I didn't take him up on it. I guess because I knew I hadn't killed Kinker, I thought I could go without a lawyer. After what Finelli said today, I changed my mind and went to Bradley. Before you say anything, I was very professional about it and even promised to pay the company back by taking a chunk out of my paycheck each week."

"Professional, eh? Did Bradley tell you that you needed to pay him, er, the company back?"

"Well, no, but I want to so he'll see me as an independent woman."

Darlene considered this. "Not a bad strategy. Give him a dose of his own medicine. Professional. Independent. Yeah, you might be on to something there."

"It won't do me any good if I'm in jail."

"I don't know about that. Seeing you behind bars might be just the thing that throws him over the edge. I'm kidding, I'm kidding! Wipe that scowl off your face and tell me how your investigation is going so far."

I told her what I knew of the store characters and about hiring Tom. "Remember the last James Bond movie? *From Russia with Love*?"

"How could I forget? Sean Connery is dreamy."

"Smart too. Anyway, there's a chess game near the beginning of the movie. That's how I'm thinking of the store characters: They are all pieces on the chessboard of Merryweathers'. I need to be the female version of Bond and decipher the moves of each one of the potential killers. Kinker knew my secret. He must have known secrets or personal information that the other players on the board didn't want revealed."

"I'm impressed."

"I'm desperate."

"Too bad we don't have Q around to make some gadgets for us. He could convert your purse into a deadly weapon, Miss Bond."

I smiled. "I prefer to think of myself as a secret agent girl."

"So how do I fit in? You know nothing can stop me from helping you find the killer."

"You're the best, Darlene. How much time off is Skyway giving you?"

"Two weeks. They owe me that and more, as much as I've been working flights this summer, plus what they have planned for me over the holidays."

I leaned forward. "Darlene, I was hoping I could get you a job at the store. No one needs to know that we're roommates, and I'd value your impressions of the people who work at Merryweathers', the characters on the chessboard."

"You want me to work at a children's toy store? You know how I feel about kids. They're fine when they're quiet and belong to someone else, otherwise . . ."

I hung my head. "I'm sorry. I forgot. I thought you could be one of the store's Helpers. All they do is help find toys. A few run the cash register, but you wouldn't have to be one of those, I don't think."

Darlene sighed. "I'm the one who's sorry. It's a good plan and I'm game. I'll try hard not to strangle any of the brats. Just tell me two things: How are you going to get Bradley to agree to this—he sure knows I'm your roommate—and what do I have to wear?"

I considered this. "We won't go through Bradley unless we have to. You'll show up at the store and talk to Mr. Mallory. Remember, he's the store manager and he hates that I hired Tom as the new Mr. Skidoo. He would relish making a new hire and not telling me or Bradley."

"I get your drift. Leave it to me and I'll handle Mallory. But what will Bradley do when he realizes I'm working there?"

"He won't be able to say anything, because if he did, Mr. Mallory would throw a fit. Plus, Bradley would have to give a reason why you can't work at the store. What would he say? That the two of us are investigating the murder? There's no rule forbidding roommates from working at Merryweathers'."

Darlene chuckled. "I'll pick out a sexy number to wear first thing tomorrow morning. Hey, you still haven't told me what I'd have to wear at the store as one of these Helper people."

"A blue uniform dress with a tan smock. There's an embroidered likeness of Mr. Skidoo on the front of the smock. Sorry."

Darlene pretended to shiver in horror. "I hope no one I know sees me in that getup."

"First, you've got to get the job."

She stood up to put away the bakery box. "Piece of cake."

Chapter Eight

I meant to be on time, especially since this was Tom's first day and Darlene would be coming in to meet Mr. Mallory. I was rarely late for work. Blame it all on a black trench coat and thigh-high black go-go boots.

While I was shivering down Fifth Avenue, the coat and boots screamed at me through a shop window. *Here,* they called, *you want to be a secret agent girl? You need us!* I obeyed the call, trying on the coat—I needed a coat after all—and then the shocking boots. *Oh, the boots,* a part of my brain whispered, *wait until Bradley sees you in those.*

After writing a hefty check, I wore the trench coat out of the store over my long-sleeved coral-colored mini-dress, carried the box containing the boots, and took a bus the rest of the way to work. Johnny Rivers's song "Secret Agent Man" played in my head the whole way.

The Teddy Bear silently opened the door for me and I thought again about the two times I'd seen him give Mallory a thick, white envelope. Curiosity demanded I find out what was in those envelopes, though I couldn't yet think how. Mallory guarded his office as if it were Buckingham Palace. Then I remembered my vow to question the Teddy Bear.

"Good morning, Mr. Runion," I began cheerfully.

Ever in character, the Teddy Bear remained silent. I needed to shake his tree.

"Mr. Runion, I'm going by Mr. Mallory's office. Do you have one of those white envelopes to give him? I could pass it along."

Silence.

I leaned closer and stared into his black button eyes. "You don't have to stay in character with me, you know. What are you guys exchanging? Military secrets? Girls' phone numbers? Recipes?"

Not by any indication did the Teddy Bear even acknowledge that he'd heard me. Trying to hide my frustration, I entered the store.

My heart jolted when I reached the executive offices area and found Mr. Skidoo sitting on the edge of my desk, one leg swinging idly. When he saw me, he jumped down and made a slow circle, ending with a short tap dance.

"Hey, Bebe, how do I look?" boomed Tom's deep voice.

"Good enough that you almost scared me to death," I said, putting my purse away and leaning the boot box against the wall.

"Good morning, Danielle." I managed to smile to Danielle at her desk.

"Hi, Bebe. You sure picked a good Mr. Skidoo," she said.

It was plain eerie seeing Mr. Skidoo alive again. Then I noticed that Tom was taller than Kinker had been and more slender. The face he'd painted on looked happier, maybe because of Tom's pleasant grin as opposed to Kinker's leer. I let out a breath I didn't know I was holding.

"I'm not supposed to have a scary effect on you, babe," Tom said and laughed.

"What effect are you supposed to have on her?"

Bradley! He had materialized out of nowhere and stood not five feet away, shirtsleeves rolled up, dirty blond hair neatly styled, a frown creasing his mouth.

Before I could cough up an introduction, Tom moved forward and extended his hand. "Tom Stevens, your new Mr. Skidoo. You must be Mr. Williams."

Bradley accepted Tom's hand and shook it, examining Tom from head to toe. "The costume fits and you've done your face well, but are you going to be able to handle the children?"

Tom laughed. "Sure. I love kids and I'm armed with lollipops."

A sound like a snort came from Bradley. "Mr. Mallory and I will be pleased if you are as good as Miss Bennett claims." He gave me a sharp look.

So Mallory *had* gone to Bradley and complained about my hiring Tom without his approval. Rats.

"Don't sweat it, Mr. Williams. I wouldn't disappoint Bebe."

At these words, I sat at my desk looking as innocent as the newborn doll I'd held yesterday in Raggedy Ann's section, hoping that Bradley was thinking about how *he* had disappointed me.

Tom said, "You want to introduce me to the other store characters, babe?"

Bradley narrowed his eyes at the word *babe*.

"I sure do. Let's go downstairs right now."

Ignoring Bradley's stare, secretly hoping he was good and jealous, I tried to keep up with Tom's long strides. On the sales floor, heads turned as we descended the escalator. The employees' faces reflected shock. Before I could take Tom over to them individually, he was swarmed by three girls and six boys aged five to eight. Their mothers looked on with interest, no doubt having read about Mr. Skidoo's death in the newspaper.

Tom threw out his arms and crooned, "Where have you boys and girls been? You know I miss you when you don't come to see me here at Merryweathers'. Do you still like lollipops?"

A chorus of yes's rang out. Tom's white-gloved hands pulled the colorful candies from his pocket and dropped them in eager palms. In seconds sounds of crinkling cellophane preceded clear wrappers falling to the floor.

"Where's your tricycle, Mr. Skidoo?" a boy asked, his tongue already turning green.

Tom placed one hand on his hip and another to his face in an exaggerated thinking pose. Suddenly, he seemed to remember. "It's been in the repair shop. I hit a fire hydrant while riding it down the street. You should have seen the water fly out of the hydrant. Luckily I had a bar of soap with me. Best bath I've had in a week!"

The children laughed and I smiled at Tom's improvisation. The tricycle was in the storeroom, though I had forgotten to tell Tom.

A little blond girl stepped carefully up to Tom, her hair in pigtails, her thumb in her mouth. She darted out her free hand and touched Tom's. Tears stood in her eyes. "My friend Kimmie told me you were dead."

In the silence that followed, Tom flung himself to the floor on his back. He covered his eyes with his hands and said, "You mean like this? Help! I can't see anything!" He began pounding his spat-covered shoes on the carpet like a two-year-old having a tantrum.

Everyone laughed. The children gathered around him and tugged his hands away from his eyes. This brought gales of laughter from Tom as he praised the children for helping him see again. The death subject had been deftly avoided and effectively quelled.

A movement at the top of the escalator caught my eye. Bradley stood to the side watching events unfold. I gave him an "I told you so" smile. He returned it with a slight inclination of his head and moved out of sight.

I thought of Mr. Mallory and glanced toward his office. He had been observing too, but when I smiled at him, he turned on his heel and marched into his office. Mallory was such a drag. I hoped Darlene would have better luck with him.

In the meantime, since Tom was busy, I started to make my way to the storeroom to retrieve Mr. Ski-doo's tricycle from the "repair shop." When I passed the Pirate's area, Junior squawked, "You bet the clown's dead!"

I gasped and was about to cover his beak with my hand, then I reconsidered, fearing for my fingers. I needed my ring finger especially.

"Mr. Geedunk," I hissed low at the Pirate so that not even the Cowboy in the next section could hear. The Pirate sent a boy and his mother—who gave the parrot a bewildered look—over to the cash registers armed with an eye patch, a toy ship, and a plastic sword.

"What can I do for you?" Geedunk asked, anything but joyful to see me.

"You have got to make Junior stop saying the clown is dead."

He shrugged. "I can't control what my bird says."

I arched an eyebrow at him. "If that's the case, then I'll speak to Mr. Williams about banning the parrot from the store."

"You're turning out to be as nasty as Kinker. He

must have taught you a few things on those dates you went on."

My face burned. "I mean it, Mr. Geedunk. The store cannot afford to have its customers reminded of Mr. Kinker's death. If I hear your parrot say that one more time—"

The Pirate held up a hand. "You're wasting your breath. Mallory came over here earlier and told me the same thing. If either one of you forces me to take my Junior home, you'll be looking for a new pirate," he threatened. In a low voice he added, "And I'll take what I know about everyone here with me, leaving you in the dark, Miss Bennett."

"If you have knowledge of a store employee's motive for killing Kinker, you need to share it with me or the police."

"Why should I when you tried to pin the murder on me?"

"I only said the things I did because you were making *me* look guilty and I didn't kill him. Do you want to see me arrested and tried for a murder I didn't commit?"

He considered this. "Maybe not, but you need to know that I didn't kill him either."

I wasn't sure I believed that, but I played along. "Then tell me. Who do you think did?"

"I didn't see the actual murder, but I think you'd be better off getting to know our esteemed Train Conductor. I say 'esteemed' because while he is respected at Merryweathers', I doubt he was respected in the nuthouse."

My eyes widened. "A mental institution? Mr. Kirchhoff was hospitalized for mental problems?"

"Yes, though you won't find that fact in his employee record. He kept it a secret."

"But that doesn't make him a murderer. Wait a minute. If the Conductor kept his past a secret, then how do you know?"

"You're forgetting that Kinker was a keeper of secrets. Sometimes he didn't keep his mouth shut. Why don't you go over to the train section and study the meticulous way the Conductor keeps that display. It's his life. Then think of this: Kinker was a prankster. The day before the clown was murdered, he changed the name of the Conductor's tiny warehouse to 'whorehouse.' "

I gasped. My gaze swept past the Cowboy, past the Toymaker, and rested on the Train Conductor. His body was bent in half as he worked on his display with a feverish concentration. While I couldn't see exactly what he was doing, for the first time I noticed the intensity in his eyes and his rigid posture. A scene flashed in my mind, from the night of the store's birthday party: Kinker snatching a lady figure from the Conductor's display, crowing about how he'd take the lady home that night unless he had a better offer, the anger on the Conductor's face. Then when Mallory announced they could all go home, the Conductor had dragged his feet, reluctant to leave his display looking less than perfect.

I nodded at the Pirate. "I'll think about what you said. Try to keep Junior quiet."

Entering the storeroom, I retrieved Mr. Skidoo's tricycle and parked it near the Jungle. My plan to introduce Tom around to the store characters seemed unnecessary, as I saw him dividing his time between the children and the other store characters, charming them all.

Around eleven o'clock, Tom saw me approaching from where he'd been talking with the Princess. We met in the center of the sales floor, close to the cash registers, only to be interrupted by Mr. Mallory and Darlene coming out of his office. Darlene had on a wild purple, white, and yellow short dress with a neckline that showed her ample cleavage.

"Miss Bennett, I'd like you to meet our newest Helper, Miss Darlene Roland," Mr. Mallory said smugly, his expression relaying that he was the store manager and he did the hiring. "Darlene, Miss Bennett is Mr. Williams's executive secretary."

Tom stood by watching.

I bit back a smile and held out my hand. "Welcome to Merryweathers', Miss Roland."

She shook my hand, giving it a squeeze. "Please call me Darlene. I'm just the luckiest gal today," she said, favoring Mr. Mallory with a blinding smile. "I've always wanted to work here in this darling toy store and finally worked up the courage to come in and apply."

Mr. Mallory took over the narrative. "Linda left us recently so I had an immediate opening. Perhaps, Miss Bennett, you could find a uniform for Darlene so that she can start tomorrow."

"I'd be delighted to. Mr. Mallory, have you met Tom Stevens, our new Mr. Skidoo? Tom, Mr. Mallory is our store manager and this, as you've just heard, is Darlene."

Greetings were exchanged. I gave Darlene a "he's mine" look when she dimpled at Tom.

Mr. Mallory reluctantly accepted Tom's proffered hand and gave it a brief shake. "I've observed you this morning, Tom. If you continue to ease into your role, I'll have no need to dismiss you."

Pompous stick in the mud!

Tom took it in stride, though, thanking Mr. Mallory, who used his walking stick to help him turn back toward his office. He stopped and addressed me over his shoulder. "Miss Bennett, Mr. Williams called downstairs about ten minutes ago and asked that you step up to his office."

Ten minutes ago! "Thank you, Mr. Mallory. Darlene, let me show you where our storeroom is and you can pick out a uniform. I need to get upstairs right away."

Tom said, "Um, Bebe, could I have a second of your time?"

"Okay, but we have to make it quick. Darlene, do you see the Pirate's area around the corner?"

"Yes."

"There's a door marked 'Employees Only' right beside it. Can you—"

"Don't worry, Miss Bennett. I'll find it. Bye now." She strutted away.

I turned to Tom. "Is something wrong?"

He took off his top hat and scratched his head before replacing the hat at a rakish angle. He bent to whisper in my ear, voice low. "Are you clued in to the fact that some of these store characters think *you* murdered the last clown?"

Uh-oh. I nodded. "I didn't kill him and I'm trying to find out who did. I'm playing the part of secret agent girl."

"Like the Johnny Rivers song?"

I nodded. "I'm sorry. I probably should have told you."

"Don't freak out. You're too wholesome to have done anything that evil, although as Johnny sings, 'a pretty face can hide an evil mind.' " He grinned.

I chuckled. "You still want to go out tonight even though I'm a suspected killer?"

I felt the tip of a gloved finger raise my chin and my eyes met his. "Yeah, I do, babe."

Two things happened at once.

From above, I heard Bradley's voice call, "Miss Bennett!"

A boy ran up and flung himself at Tom's leg. "Mr. Skidoo, there's your tricycle over by the big lion. Are you gonna ride it?"

"I am, by Sam, I am," Tom said, reminding me of Dr. Seuss.

I parted from Tom and hastened to the escalator. Instead of walking up the moving stairs in a hurry, though, I stood—not really posing—and rode at my leisure.

Bradley stepped into the elevator that would take us to the third floor, his posture radiating anger. I followed as if nothing was wrong. Silence prevailed until we reached his office. He closed the door behind me and indicated a chair.

Trying hard not to look at the magical sofa where Bradley had kissed me as if he'd never tasted a woman's lips before, I sat, crossed my legs, and nudged my minidress up a few inches.

He dropped into his leather chair and stared at me.

I swallowed hard at the angry look in his blue eyes, but kept my poise. "You wanted to see me, Mr. Williams?"

"Yes. Ten minutes ago."

"Mr. Mallory only just gave me your message."

"Perhaps that's because he saw you were busy flirting with your friend Tom."

Jealous! I bit my tongue so I wouldn't laugh, or worse, jump up with glee, clutch him by the collar, and sing, "You love me! You love me! Why don't you just admit it?"

Instead, in a calm tone, I replied, "Mr. Williams, I assure you that I'll restrain myself from flirting here at the store. I will, after all, be seeing Tom tonight."

Bradley picked up a silver Cross pen and began tapping it on his desk. "You've put my mind at ease. Now, let's move on to important matters."

Oooh! The beast. I'd pay him back for that one.

"I've found a lawyer for you. Jim Lincoln will be coming in to meet with us during lunch. Send Danielle out to get sandwiches."

"You mean I have to talk with him in your office?"

"Yes. I've hired him and I want to make sure I'm getting my money's worth. I plan to be present during all your meetings."

I felt heat rise to my cheeks. "While I appreciate your paying for his services, may I remind you that I'm reimbursing the company and that I can handle this myself?"

Bradley tilted his head and gave me a sarcastic look, pen tapping faster on his desk blotter. "Have you ever retained an attorney to defend yourself in a criminal matter, Miss Bennett?"

"No, but—"

Bradley shook his head. "No buts about it. You need someone older looking after you, kid, unless you want to call your daddy."

My eyes widened. "Are you joking?"

"Hardly." He glanced at his watch. "Jim will be here in about twenty minutes. Go give Danielle her instructions and think about what you're going to say to your new lawyer. Remember that you have to be honest with him."

A sliver of guilt crawled up my spine. I'd lied about dating Kinker, darn it. Now I'd have to lie again since I'd be speaking to Mr. Lincoln in Bradley's presence.

Just like with Finelli, I'd have to catch up with the lawyer later and tell him the truth. I crossed my fingers behind my back. "I am not a dishonest woman, Mr. Williams."

He straightened papers on his desk. "We won't debate your little white lies and schemes. Put on a fresh pot of coffee, please."

"By the way, where are the employee personnel files kept?" I asked.

"Why?" Suspicion was laced through the word.

I thought fast. "As your secretary, I need to record updates in the employee files."

He shook his head. "I know you. I know why you want the files and you're not getting them."

I flipped my hair back over my shoulders. "That's okay. They're here somewhere and I'm bound to stumble across them."

"They are at my house, a place you don't have access to," Bradley said flatly. He might as well have said, "Checkmate."

I rose without replying, glided out of his office, and closed his door with a gentle click. Outside, I leaned against the door for a moment, static causing my hair to spread out. I took a few calming breaths, set the coffee to brew, then moved to my desk.

I had to say Danielle's name twice before she heard me over the Dictaphone.

"Sorry, Bebe. Gosh, your face is flushed. Are you okay?"

Plopping down in my chair, I reached into a drawer and pulled out the petty cash box. "Actually, I'm a little nervous. Mr. Williams hired a lawyer for me and the three of us are meeting in about twenty minutes."

Danielle's mouth dropped open. Recovering, she said, "Oh, Bebe, you shouldn't have to go through that. Don't the cops understand that you had nothing to do with Mr. Kinker's death?"

I slid my chair across the floor mat so that I could touch Danielle's hand. "Thanks for believing in me."

"Don't be silly," she said with a smile. "Anyone who knows you couldn't possibly think you'd kill someone."

"Tell that to the cops and the store characters. I need you to run out and grab three sandwiches. Turkey should be okay. Here's the money—what's wrong?"

Danielle looked down for a moment, then raised her gaze to mine. "I did hear some gossip about one of the employees, Bebe. I don't know if it means anything to the murder case." Her face went red.

"Tell me all about it."

Danielle took the money from me, then lowered her voice to a whisper. "You know Betty, the girl who plays Raggedy Ann?"

I nodded.

"She came up here looking for Mr. Williams. I think she might be interested in him romantically," Danielle confided and waited for my reaction.

While I seethed inwardly, I tried my best to control my facial expression. "I've noticed that about Betty too."

"I don't think she'll get anywhere with him, Bebe. I think she's fast and Mr. Williams won't want a girl like that."

A snort escaped my lips.

Danielle looked around, then back at me. "The point is, she chitchatted with me about men in general. Before I could tell her I have Herb, Betty told me not to have anything to do with Mr. Frederick."

"The Toymaker?"

"Yes." Danielle's complexion went that dark red

again. "She said that Mr. Frederick is a . . . a . . . homosexual."

I blinked. "I had no idea, not that it matters. Mr. Williams told me that the Toymaker is actually over-qualified for his job. Apparently he's trained in carving Black Forest wood."

"But consider this, Bebe. According to Betty, Mr. Frederick doesn't want anyone to know that he's . . . that way. He's always been afraid that if the Merry-weathers found out, they'd fire him."

"Then how does Betty know?"

"She said Mr. Kinker told her. Betty said she'd gotten curious when the clown kept calling Mr. Frederick a sissy."

This could be important. "Thanks for telling me. If you hear anything else, I'd be grateful if you shared it."

"You know I will, Bebe. I'd better get those sand-wiches now."

After she left, I pulled out my notes on the murder and wrote down everything Danielle had told me.

I leaned back in my chair and chewed the end of my pencil.

How had Kinker found out Mr. Frederick's per-sonal business?

Had the Toymaker been angry enough to kill the clown?

I'd have to find the answers to both questions.

Chapter Nine

WABC was playing "Needles and Pins" when Jim Lincoln arrived ten minutes late, wheezing and smoking a cigarette, his clothes rumpled. "Are you Bebe Bennett?"

I stood and held out my hand. "Thank you for coming, Mr. Lincoln."

He shifted his battered briefcase and shook my hand. "Call me Jim. Otherwise I feel like a dead president. You're too pretty to be behind bars, but if there's one thing I've learned, it's that murderers come in every shape and size."

How reassuring.

"Mr. Williams is expecting us in his office. Shall we?" I grabbed the bag of sandwiches and led the way. Bradley and Jim shook hands, exchanged a few remarks about football, then seemed to remember I was standing there.

"How do you take your coffee, Jim?"

"Black, no cream or sugar." He patted his bulging middle. "Damn doctor wants me to lose weight. I told him I'd diet if he'd get off my back about smoking." He burst into a coughing fit that ended in a wheeze.

I went to get the coffee, then Jim and I drew our chairs up to Bradley's desk. The lawyer tucked into his sandwich, crumbs falling down his wrinkled, not-quite-white shirt and landing on his stomach. He reached into his briefcase and pulled out a file. "Got a copy of the police report," he said between mouthfuls.

Neither Bradley nor I touched our sandwiches. Bradley smirked and said, "Must have friends over there, Jim."

The lawyer waved his sandwich in the air. "They would have gotten around to sending it to me, but why waste time? Ed Snyder is the head detective. That's bad news for you, Miss Bennett."

"Please call me Bebe. To tell you the truth, Detective Snyder and I didn't hit it off."

He grunted. "Don't take it personally. Snyder likes to think of himself as one of the last great detectives out of some forties movie. He's hated women since his wife ran off with a truck driver."

Bradley stretched into the back of his chair, forcing my gaze to roam across his long body. He said, "That would explain why the detective treated Miss Bennett as if she were the lowest of criminals. His entire manner was insulting and threatening."

My champion!

The lawyer's eyes went from Bradley to me. For the first time, I noticed the sharp intelligence in his gray gaze. He wiped his hands on a napkin. "Bradley, why am I on a first-name basis with Bebe, while the two of you call each other by your last names?"

Bradley looked at me, then squeezed his thumb and index finger on the bridge of his nose. "I think Miss Bennett prefers it that way because she's so young."

Barely, just barely, I restrained myself from throwing my sandwich in his face.

Instead, I pitched a little Southern belle into my voice and said, "Oh, Jim, isn't that just the silliest thing you ever heard? Why, here I am, old enough to buy my own liquor, old enough to be out in the world on my own, old enough to enjoy my freedom, and Mr. Williams thinks I'm stuffy and want to call him by his last name." I leaned over to the lawyer and spoke in a stage whisper. "Maybe he's bought into the idea that everyone over thirty is *old*."

Jim laughed and I was quick to join him.

Trapped, Bradley gritted out his words. "I don't consider myself old, *Bebe*. Just experienced."

Oooooh! I felt the heat burn my face like I was in Virginia sunbathing on an August day. How I'd like to be the recipient of his "experience."

He went on. "Jim, let's talk about the freedom that Bebe prizes so highly. What are the chances the district attorney will call for a grand jury hearing?"

The lawyer settled back in his chair, brushing crumbs off his stomach and situating his briefcase on his lap. He pulled out a yellow legal pad and wrote my name at the top. "Before we address the issue of jail, I've read the whole report, but I want to go over a few details with you, Bebe. That okay by you?"

"Yes, Jim. Bradley, Detective Finelli already told me that the police are just waiting for the coroner's report before they schedule a grand jury hearing."

"When in the hell did you talk to Finelli? And why didn't you tell me?"

Uh-oh. Mentally, I saw my list of confessions grow. "I ran into him down on the corner yesterday when I was buying a Tab. We chatted a bit, and he kinda mentioned the part about the coroner's report."

By the expressions on their faces, I doubted Bradley or Jim bought my story.

Bradley took a sip of coffee, leaving the room in heavy silence for a moment. Then he said, "I've instructed you to tell me everything regarding Kinker's murder. I see you're not complying with my request. Perhaps I need to hire someone to follow you around."

I gasped. "Don't you dare! You don't have any rights where I'm concerned once I leave this building."

"Next you'll tell me you're not investigating the murder yourself."

I raised my chin and said nothing.

Jim broke the exchange. "I can't stress enough how important your cooperation and honesty are, Bebe."

"I understand." My pulse picked up speed, my mind jumping ahead to when he'd ask me about dating Kinker. "Detective Finelli is a decent man. His job comes first, but I do think he knows and likes me."

Jim nodded. "It's always good to have a friend in the police department, Bebe, but I think you should refrain from talking to Finelli about the case. Now, if we could move on, it says here in the police report that you were found standing over the victim with the murder weapon in your hand. Bill Geedunk, employed by Merryweathers' as the store Pirate, is the state's witness." Jim looked at me.

I fished out a strand of my hair and began twirling it. "Yes, that's true."

"There's more to it, Bebe. I think you need to tell Jim in your own words how you discovered Kinker's body," Bradley said.

Turning to the lawyer, I explained what had happened after the store's closing time. I'd thought I was alone in the building, went downstairs to leave, found the Jungle animals a mess, discovered the body, and believed Kinker was playing one of his pranks. "It was only when I pulled the knife out of his chest that I realized that Kinker was really dead."

Jim scribbled on his pad. "But it turned out you weren't alone in the store with the victim, correct?"

"Yes. Mr. Geedunk came out of the storeroom and saw me."

The lawyer studied Bradley. "You were in the store, too, and phoned the police. It says here that you denied seeing Bebe with the knife in her hand. Snyder's circled that and written 'covering for piece of fluff.' Excuse me, Bebe, I'm just repeating what's in the report."

I nodded. Then I remembered how Bradley had lied for me, saying it was too dark for him to see. Would he lie to Jim too?

Jim put his pen down. "Bradley, I know you understand about lawyer-client confidentiality. I consider you a client just as much as Bebe, since you're footing the bill for my services."

Bradley put his fingers together, making a steeple. "I appreciate that."

"Good. Maybe you can clear up something I don't understand. How is it that you entered the scene, called the police before Geedunk came out of the storeroom, and yet *you* did not see Bebe with the knife in her hand?"

I spoke before Bradley could. "He did see me. He just evaded Snyder's question."

"Bebe!" Bradley exclaimed, his face tight with anger.

"Jim said this was just between us!"

Bradley pointed at me. "You asked earlier why I needed to be present today. Now you have your answer."

"No, I don't have any answer. Didn't you hear Jim talk about this being confidential?"

"Yes, I did," Bradley ground out as if it were just the two of us in the room. "What you don't understand is that Jim can either accept or decline this case. If he thinks you're guilty—"

"Bradley, let me put your mind at ease," Jim interrupted. "I'm taking the case whether or not I think Bebe is guilty. My job is to defend her and make certain she receives a fair trial, *if* it comes to that."

Some of the tension left my shoulders.

Bradley looked like a little boy whose mother had scolded him for not doing his homework. He said, "I was out of line, Jim. I apologize. Yes, I saw Bebe with the knife, but I know she's not capable of murder. She told me what happened and I believe her."

I twirled my hair faster. It was either that or jump into Bradley's lap and kiss him senseless. Why was it that the man could be infuriating one minute and endearing the next? I wasn't that way. Was I?

The lawyer inquired about Kinker's employment record and asked to see his personnel file.

Bradley handed it to him. "I brought it in thinking you might need it."

"You mean you don't keep personnel files at the store?" Jim asked.

"Not since the murder. Under my uncle's advice, the files are kept at my home. Once the killer is apprehended, I'll bring the files back. He didn't think it wise, and I agree with him, to keep the employees' personal information where the killer might access privileged information even under lock and key."

Bradley and I exchanged looks. He knew I wanted those files, darn him.

"Good thinking," the lawyer said. He read through Kinker's file and took notes. Then he began the questioning I dreaded.

"Bebe, Snyder's report says that you had a personal relationship with the deceased."

"I wouldn't call it a relationship," I said, keeping my gaze fixed on the edge of Bradley's desk.

"You told Snyder that you'd gone out with Kinker on a few dates."

"Um, yes."

"How long had the two of you known each other before you dated?"

My stomach hurt and my skin felt clammy. I darted a quick look at Bradley. He appeared relaxed, his expression giving away nothing. I'd vow never to use my Aqua Net hairspray before I'd tell him that Kinker figured out my secret: my, er, high regard for Bradley. Yes, high regard sounded better than lust, or worse, love.

"Actually, we'd just met."

"Impressed you, did he?"

I held back a gag. "Mel could be charming."

"How many times did the two of you go out?"

Thinking fast, I blurted, "Twice."

"Did you sleep together?"

I bolted out of my seat, knocking my sandwich to the floor. I cleaned the mess up, certain my face was vying with my dress for color, and looked for the trash can. Bradley stretched an arm out behind him, pointing to his. With shaky steps, I dumped the sandwich inside and sat down again, wiping my fingers on a napkin.

Jim lit a cigarette. "Look, Bebe, I didn't mean to embarrass you. Sometimes I have to ask what you would consider very personal questions."

"Or insulting ones. The answer is no, I did not sleep with Mel."

The lawyer tapped his cigarette on the ashtray. "That's what I thought. Snyder's written that you told the guy no and that ended things."

"Yes."

"Was it a big argument? How angry was Kinker?"

"Uh, not very."

"But he teased you in the store," Jim persisted.

"Some."

Silence. I looked at the lawyer, only to find him watching me.

He put out his cigarette, coughed, then wheezed. "I think that's enough for today," he said and started to close his briefcase. "I want to talk with the Pirate character, see if I can find a hole in his story."

Relief swept over me.

"He should be downstairs," Bradley said. "There's a storeroom next to Geedunk's area. You can take him in there, but you might be interrupted. The store manager, Mr. Mallory, has an office behind the cash registers. He takes a late lunch. His office might be empty."

"Sounds good." Jim closed his briefcase, then slapped his forehead and reopened it, foraging through a manila envelope. "Bebe, I almost forgot to show you this. Sorry, it's a morgue shot, but it's just Kinker's face. This is him, right?"

He thrust the black-and-white photo in front of my face. I squirmed in my chair at the sight of a dark-haired man with thin lips, and wrinkles around closed eyes that would never open again. I'd never seen Kinker without his makeup. I doubted Bradley had, or for that matter, most of the store characters. Since I'd lied again about dating him, Jim would expect me to know what he looked like.

"Yes, that's him."

"That's what I thought, but I wanted to be sure," he said, putting the photo away and closing his briefcase. He stood and tapped his temple with one finger.

"I like to know what the victim looked like, and since the police have been unable to locate any family, a morgue shot was the best I could do."

We stood. Bradley shook Jim's hand while I tried to erase Kinker's face from my mind.

"I'll call you when the coroner's report comes in, Bradley. Bebe, could you show me where Mallory's office is so I can meet with Mr. Geedunk privately?"

"Of course."

We rode the elevator to the second floor without saying a word. By the time we were on the escalator heading for the first floor, I had to break the silence. "I appreciate your trying to help me, Jim."

He gave a terse nod.

Jane was the only Helper behind the cash registers. Business was still slow.

I smiled at her. "Is Mr. Mallory in his office?"

"No, Bebe, he's out to lunch."

"Is his door locked, or can I go in?"

She frowned. "I doubt it's locked. Everyone knows Mr. Mallory doesn't allow a soul in there unless they are meeting with him."

I rolled my eyes. "Thanks, Jane."

"Here you are, Jim," I said, opening the door and stepping inside. I looked around, wishing I could search the area for clues about those white envelopes the store manager and the Teddy Bear kept passing between them.

The sound of the door closing with a sharp click brought me out of my thoughts. Jim sat down in a chair opposite Mallory's desk. He glowered at me.

"Have a seat, Bebe, and tell me why you lied about dating Mel Kinker."

My breathing quickened and I fumbled for Mallory's chair, slowly lowering myself into it. "I—"

"No more lies. That wasn't Kinker in the photograph I showed you. My gut told me you were holding back from me and I tested you. You failed the test. It would be better if you confessed to the murder. I can try to arrange a plea bargain—"

To my shame, tears sprang to my eyes and ran down my cheeks. "I'm sorry. I'm sorry I lied about dating Kinker. I didn't want to. Please don't think I killed him. I promise I didn't."

The whole story spilled out of me, including the part where I'd told Finelli the truth during our not-so-accidental meeting.

"You lied to the police, then told Finelli you lied. Then you lied to me."

I nodded, wiping my face with my hands.

"You did all this because Kinker found out you're what—in love with Bradley?"

"Yes."

"And you don't want Bradley to know how you feel."

"Right. Please don't tell him. I'll never get him to the altar—"

"You're in a lot of trouble, Bebe. I wouldn't worry about getting married at this point. By telling Finelli the truth, you've handed the DA the material he needs to bring you before that grand jury. Not only can he place you at the crime scene, murder weapon in hand, but now he has another motive for you to have killed Kinker: that Kinker knew about your 'secret' feelings for your boss. The DA can paint you as a liar, and has the proof, in the form of a respected detective's testimony, to back it up."

"*If* Finelli tells the DA I lied," I said, my voice shaking.

"*If* he tells? Bebe, I've known Finelli a long time,

had him up on the witness stand back before he was made detective. He's an honest joe—you even said as much."

I shook my head. "Finelli knows me and I don't think he's going to say anything." At least I hoped he wouldn't.

Jim rose and walked to the door. "We'll soon find out. I'm going to find the Pirate. Take a few moments to compose yourself."

I sat in Mallory's chair feeling sorry for myself. How had things gotten so tangled up? Could I rely on Jim to work hard in my defense when he probably didn't even believe in my innocence?

I wiped my face and gathered my strength. I'd have to continue my investigation and count on myself to find the killer. After all, I thought, the theme from the Bond movie *From Russia with Love* running through my head, I was a secret agent girl.

Jim had closed the door behind him. Quickly I scanned the contents on top of Mallory's desk: sales reports that Danielle had typed for him. Catalogues from toy companies. The store characters' work schedules.

I opened the middle desk drawer. Nothing incriminating. Pens, pencils, a calorie counter in a little metal case—that made me snicker. More papers related to store matters and a folded racing form. Ha, so Mallory liked to bet on the horses.

Blowing air into my bangs, I shut the drawer and opened a side file drawer, but it contained only files of monthly sales reports going back several years. Frustrated, I was about to look through the credenza when I heard Jim's voice outside the door.

Slipping past the two men with a murmured "Excuse me," I fled to my desk. Danielle smiled at me, typing away while listening to the Dictaphone.

Before I could even catch my breath, Bradley walked down the hall, coffee mug in hand.

"I would have refilled your cup."

"Had you been at your desk when I buzzed you, I suppose so."

"I was only showing Jim to Mr. Mallory's office," I said, tossing my hair.

"Then can I assume you'll be at your desk for the remainder of the afternoon? Or do you plan to leave early and get ready for your big date tonight?"

"Gee, I hadn't planned on leaving early, but now that you mention it, I think I will. I want to have a nice long hot bath, shampoo my hair, take my time selecting the perfect outfit."

He stood before my desk, looking perfectly composed. Then I glanced down and saw that his fingers were almost white from clenching the handle of the mug. Hmmm. *You always did look good with that green tinge, Bradley.*

"You may leave an hour early and that's only this one time. I won't cater to your personal plans."

"Yes, Bradley," I said sweetly.

He took a sip of coffee, blue eyes staring at me over the rim of his cup.

"While I have your attention," I said, innocently, "shall I go ahead and place that ad in the *Times*? You remember, the one thanking our customers for helping us celebrate the store's fortieth birthday and inviting them to come visit Mr. Skidoo?"

"Your boyfriend is playing his part well," he replied with a smirk.

"At least Tom knows how to be a boyfriend," I

said without thinking, then held my breath waiting for Bradley's reaction.

"Unlike Mel Kinker?"

I opened my mouth to hotly deny the clown's ever being my boyfriend, then remembered my lies about dating him. "Oh, I'd say there's a big difference between the two Mr. Skidoos."

Bradley gave me a lingering once-over. He ran his tongue across his full lips, causing that deep ache in me that only he brought on.

I hoped I wasn't drooling.

The phone rang.

"Go ahead and place the ad, kid," he said, and abruptly stalked back to his office.

I picked up the phone. "Merryweathers' Toy Shoppe, Miss Bennett speaking."

"Is this Bebe Bennett?" a timid female voice asked. "I've heard my boss mention that you're Bradley Williams's secretary."

"Yes, it is. May I help you?"

"I feel so embarrassed, Miss Bennett, but I'm determined to see this through. I was hoping that you'd be easier to talk to than Mr. Williams since you're a secretary, like me."

My curiosity rose. "Okay."

"I'm Shirley Harrison and I'm calling you from Chicago. I'm, I mean *I was,* Drew Pruitt's secretary." She started crying softly.

Thoughts flew through my brain. Drew! Bradley's mean cousin who'd stop at nothing to make their uncle leave the corporation to him instead of Bradley.

"Please call me Bebe. May I call you Shirley?"

"Y-yes. I'll pull myself together in a second. This is difficult and maybe you'll think I'm cruel and vindictive, but that's a chance I have to take."

What on earth was this about? "Go ahead. I'm sure I won't think anything of the kind."

"Bebe, I have documented information in hand that shows Drew has been embezzling funds from the Sheppard's department store chain. I thought I might give it to you to handle however you want."

Drew embezzling money! If Herman Shires had proof of that, Bradley would be a shoo-in for his heir. And if I could make that happen, maybe Bradley's vision of me as a "kid" would change. Maybe he'd be so proud of me he'd fall madly in love with me and then . . . I took a deep breath. Why was she handing me this plum?

"Shirley, you must be angry at Drew. Did he fire you?"

"Y-yes. You see, he told me he loved me, not his wife. He said he was waiting until Mr. Shires named a beneficiary before leaving his wife and marrying me. We've been, we've been . . ."

"Seeing one another?" I tried.

Another sob. "For about a year. He fired me when I told him I was pregnant with his baby!"

Chapter Ten

"Come on, Darlene, what would you have done?" I asked. "I had no choice but to tell Shirley to come here and stay with us. Drew offered her money t-to st-stop the pregnancy, then he fired her when she refused. He even told her he'd have nothing to do with the baby. Her parents disowned her after she refused to give the baby up for adoption. Her grandmother refused to speak to her. No one will hire a pregnant woman so she doesn't have a job, and she had to give up her apartment and is living in a seedy hotel with no one to count on. We talked about my trying to get her a position at the new Merryweathers' in Chicago, but I realized that location probably didn't have any- thing because they just opened. Plus, Shirley doesn't want Drew to be able to find her once he knows that she has the goods on him." I took a deep breath.

We faced each other on the pink sectional sofa. Darlene had her arms folded in front of her chest. I was waiting for my pearly pink nail polish to dry.

"What would I have done? I'd have kept my knees glued together in front of that scumbag Drew."

"Really? You're always telling me to sleep with Bradley."

Darlene chuckled. "Bradley's not like this Drew varmint. Sonofa—" She was interrupted by a female voice coming through the ceiling.

"Come on, big boy, bring it over here and put it to good use!"

"Nothing about me is good, Lily, except how I do this to you!"

"Oh! Oh! Oh! Be a bad boy!"

"Take it! Take it all!"

Darlene and I looked upward.

"The newlyweds are at it again," I said. "How come their bedroom is right above our living area?"

"Damned if I know," Darlene said and chuckled. "Let's go in your room."

Darlene sat on the bed while I stood and flapped my hands in an effort to dry my nail polish. I'd already done my hair and makeup for my date with Tom, but still had to pick out what I was going to wear.

"Is this Shirley person going to live here once she has the baby? Because I'll tell you right now that I won't have any screaming, peeing, pooping baby in this apartment."

I leaned over and hugged Darlene, careful to leave my hands facing out. "Oh, I knew you'd understand. And don't worry. I'll help Shirley find a job and maybe she'll meet someone to marry. She won't be here long."

"Have you lost your mind, Bebe? No man is going to hitch himself to a woman who is pregnant by another man."

"You don't know that, Darlene. Shirley is taking the bus from Chicago and won't be here until tomorrow. Together we can figure something out. Do you think Stu knows any bachelor who wants to settle down?"

"You're trying to fix her up and you don't even know what Shirley looks like. She could be a complete dog."

"I doubt Drew would have a woman working for him who didn't look good," I said. "Besides, it's what's inside that counts."

Darlene put a hand to her chest in a dramatic fashion. "Bebe Bennett, haven't I taught you anything? A man wants a woman on his arm who makes him look like a stud."

"You think that's why Stu loves you? Because you're gorgeous?"

"I don't know," Darlene grumbled. "He's become so possessive. I spent the whole day with him after I got the job at Merryweathers' and he wanted to see me again tonight. I told him no."

"Well, I think it's normal that Stu would want to be, and even *need* to be, with the woman he loves. And I don't think he loves you just for your looks. Why are you being so hard on him?"

She picked at the daisy pattern in my bedspread. "I'm scared."

"What? Darlene Roland scared? Texas spitfire Darlene? Darlene who knows how to wrap a man around her pinky? Sophisticated, worldly Darlene?"

"That's enough. Never mind."

I sat on the edge of the bed and softened my voice. "I'm sorry. I shouldn't have been flip. Come on, tell me what you're afraid of."

"It's like I told you. Stu is smothering me, which only makes me pull away."

I thought for a moment, then said, "I know Stu is rich and handsome and could have any woman he wants. He wants you. Maybe he hasn't recovered from the big fight you had last spring. After all, you did get engaged to someone else."

Darlene rolled her eyes. "Don't remind me."

"What I'm trying to say is that Stu might be insecure about your relationship and that's why he's clinging. Why don't you give him some reassurance and see if that helps."

Darlene grinned. "I have taught you something after all, sweetie."

I smiled. "Good. Now help me pick out what to wear for Tom."

After holding up dress after dress, we agreed on an op art mini that featured small black and white triangles. If you looked at the dress too long, you'd get dizzy. Satisfied that my nails were dry, I slipped on the dress.

"I think I'll try out my new black go-go boots," I said, pulling the box out of my closet.

Darlene gasped in delight. "When did you get those?"

I smiled. "They're something, aren't they? I got them at the same place I bought my black trench coat. If you hurry, you might be able to pick up a pair."

"Honey, nothing could stop me. How boss! They come up over your knees."

I stood and twirled around. "Think I could get away with wearing them to work?"

Darlene grinned. "Sure. Wear them tomorrow. I want to be there when Bradley drags you caveman-style into that big brown tree house in the book area and totally loses control."

I put my hand over my mouth and giggled.

"Or maybe he'd push you into the elevator and then pull the stop button between floors."

"Darlene!" I said, laughing so hard I feared my mascara would run.

She lowered her voice to a whisper. "Or maybe he'd manage to control himself until he got you into his office and onto *that sofa*."

I drew in a sharp breath. "The magic sofa."

"Yeah."

The intercom buzzed.

"You better get it, Bebe. It's probably Tom and we don't want him to know we're roommates. And drink a glass of ice water before you go. Your face is as red as the silk curtain around my bed."

Minutes later I met Tom outside my building. The crisp autumn air made me grateful for my black trench coat.

Tom broke into song when he saw me. "Bebe, you're looking so fine, I'm glad you're mine tonight."

I couldn't suppress my amusement.

He wore a black sweater, scrunched up to his elbows, and gray slim-cut trousers, and he looked devilishly cute. He held out a hand, which I took. "Come on, I've got a cab waiting to transport us to that fun place I told you about."

Tom's enthusiasm was catching. While we rode, he talked and gestured with his hands. By the time we reached the Orb, I was already having a groovy time.

Inside the dimly lit dance club, I looked around and chuckled. On the silvery walls, large eyes were painted in bright colors, the lashes long on some, short on others, the eye colors impossible shades of vivid green, sunshine yellow, a startling red along with blue, brown, and green. The eyes were grouped together like large paintings. A DJ spun records—currently "You Really Got Me" by the Kinks—for a large dance floor that teemed with couples moving to the beat.

"I see an open table. Let's snag it," Tom said, grabbing my hand. We beelined over and claimed the small round table before another couple could reach it.

Tom grinned and helped me take off my coat and drape it over my chair. "Wow! That's a far-out dress, babe. And those boots are bitchin'."

I laughed. "They're part of my secret agent look. I love James Bond movies."

"Hey, me too. So you're Miss Bond, are you?"

My smile slipped. "I have to be in order to save my own neck."

Tom nodded in understanding. "Yeah, like I said, some of those funky people at the store think you're the heroine responsible for my predecessor's demise."

At that moment, a waitress wearing a tiny yellow satin mini, highly teased blond hair, and exaggerated eye makeup approached. She sat a bowl of twisty pretzels in the center of the table and asked what we wanted to drink.

I leaned over and said, "Tom, I'm not much of a drinker." The music stopped right as I said the word *drinker,* causing it to sound louder than I intended.

"You like orange juice?"

"Sure."

Tom turned to the waitress. "The groovy lady will have a screwdriver and I'll take a rum and Coke."

"Have to see your ID," the waitress said to me.

I produced it, Tom snickered, and the waitress shrugged. "Back in a minute."

He nudged me with his elbow. "Don't get bent out of shape, babe. It's always a compliment when someone thinks a woman is younger than she is."

Maybe not always, I mused, thinking of Bradley calling me "kid."

I smiled at Tom. Really, it was impossible to be in

a bad mood around him. "Thanks. Listen, what did you mean when you called some of the store characters 'funky'?"

"We're not gonna talk shop all evening, are we?"

"No, I promise. It's just that I have the unwanted title of Number One Suspect in the police's book."

"Cripes, I didn't know it was that bad. I'll keep my ears open for you, Miss Bond. You know I've only been there one day, but let's see. The Train Conductor gave me an intense lecture on never touching his display. He strikes me as the type whose whole life is centered on those trains." Tom scooted his chair closer to mine and added, "You just know his whole house has train sets in every room. They're probably set by some gadget the Conductor invented so that they all start running at the same time in the morning. Probably serves as his alarm clock."

I giggled.

He grinned. "His wallpaper is patterned with trains, his cookie jar is in the shape of a train, the soap in his bathroom rests in a freight train holder—"

"Stop! Stop!" I cried, laughing helplessly.

"Okay, I won't tell you about his train chandelier."

The waitress returned with our drinks. I took a sip of my screwdriver.

"Taste okay, Bebe?" Tom asked.

"Sure. Tell me more about your first impressions."

"Only if you dance with me."

"I told you I'm not a very good dancer."

"Look around, babe. Everyone is just groovin' to the music. It's not like you have to waltz or do the fox-trot."

He stood and again held out his hand. I took it and we headed to the dance floor, Tom guiding me toward the edge. The DJ put on "Dancing in the Street" by

Martha and the Vandellas. Tom caught the beat and stayed close.

"On with the show," he said. "I'm guessing it's gonna be a couple of weeks before everyone accepts me as Mr. Skidoo. I think that Kinker guy brought out the worst in everyone and I'm guilty by association."

"How so?"

"I can't put my finger on anything specific. It's just the vibe I'm getting. Mallory, that Pirate guy— Geedunk—and even that silly Teddy Bear have been as cold as a Popsicle toward me. Hey, you fibbed. You're a great dancer."

The thought dawned on me that I'd been so wrapped up in what Tom was saying that I'd just let my body move to the music. I smiled my thanks, the song ended, and we went back to our table.

I took a gulp of my drink.

"Easy there, Bebe. You can't taste the vodka in there but that won't prevent it from making you drunk."

"You really are a sweet guy."

"Aww, shucks, ma'am," he said in a fantastic Western accent. "That reminds me of our resident Cowboy. He doesn't say much with his vocal cords, but those eyes of his were talking up a storm every time I went near Raggedy Ann."

I felt a tremor of triumph. Tom had also noticed how protective the Cowboy was of Betty. What did it mean? "Do you think they're seeing each other?"

Tom thought for a minute, then said, "I honestly can't tell. The Cowboy seems to save his lingering looks for the Princess. But he does watch Betty like a hawk. She flirted like crazy with me."

I let out a short, mirthless laugh. "That's our Betty. She flirts with Mr. Williams too."

Tom looked aghast. "You mean it's not my irresistible charm?"

I punched him on the arm. "Silly."

He took a sip of his drink, then said, "I'll tell you someone who not only resisted my charm but looked horrified when I showed up in her area."

"The Princess?"

"Yeah, man, she looked like I was going to attack her, drag her into the little girls' dressing room, and have my wicked way with her. Come to think of it, the only other woman I've seen behave like the Princess did was an actress I worked with. The poor girl had been, um, how should I put this?"

"Frankly," I said, leaning closer.

"Okay, she'd been used by her father in a foul way."

I closed my eyes for a moment. "I get the picture."

Tom nodded sadly. "The Princess even said for me not to come near her. In fact, now that I think about it, her exact words were, 'Don't come near me. I won't put up with you *again*.' Isn't that weird?"

"Yes." I felt a mixture of sorrow and suspicion regarding the Princess. I'd yet to talk to her and vowed to myself to correct that tomorrow.

For the next hour, while I had fun dancing and hearing Tom tell theater anecdotes, the Princess was not far from my mind.

I finally devoted my full attention to Tom. We left the Orb around eleven and stopped at a deli for a quick sandwich, since both of us were starved.

Around midnight, we cabbed it to my building, Tom paying the driver and sending him on his way. We stood under the shimmering yellow umbrella of a tree whose leaves had turned golden.

"Bebe, I'll walk down to Lexington and take the bus in a minute. I want to talk with you."

"Okay."

"You're not cold, are you?"

"No. The cool air feels good after all that dancing." I experienced an uneasy moment, feeling I should invite him up for coffee but knowing I couldn't because of Darlene. And, if I was honest with myself, I wasn't sure I wanted to be alone with attractive, funny, smart Tom. I couldn't be sure he wouldn't make a pass, one I'd have to turn down because I loved Bradley. Darn Bradley!

"I had a great time tonight, Tom. You're so much fun."

Tom leaned against the tree, appearing awkward for the first time. "I had a good time too, which is why I need to talk to you. I don't know how to say this without coming off like a jerk, and the last thing I want to do is lose your friendship. I'd like to take you out again, but . . ."

I moved closer. "Just say what's on your mind, okay?"

"The truth is, Bebe, I think you're a groovy girl. Under other circumstances, I'd be giving you the rush. But I can't do that for two reasons."

Was he blushing? I stood and waited for him to continue.

"The first is that you are a really *nice* girl, um, despite those wicked boots. The kind of girl a guy would want to settle down with and marry." He shoved his hands in his pockets. "I'm a struggling actor. I can hardly support myself, much less a wife. So the girls I date aren't like you, Bebe. I'm afraid that if I continue seeing you, maybe we'd both end up getting hurt."

"Oh, Tom . . ."

"The second reason is Bradley Williams."

I scowled.

Tom laughed. "I knew it. There's something between the two of you and it's serious. You're not exactly available, are you, Bebe?"

"Is it that obvious?"

"Yeah."

"Darn it, I—"

"Calm down. Maybe it's just plain to me because I knew we were going out and picked up the vibe between you two."

A minute passed before I realized it was my turn to say something.

"I do admire Bradley. A lot. But we're not even dating." I looked at Tom and he returned the gaze. If I were a different sort of girl, if I didn't want to marry Bradley, I knew I'd want to be with Tom. His honesty made him even more attractive.

I drew a deep breath. "I appreciate your talking to me this way, Tom. You're a fine man and I'd like to be friends with you, even after you leave Merryweathers' for your play. Do you think we could still hang out sometimes?"

Grinning, Tom pushed himself away from the tree. "I'd like that very much." He leaned toward me, his thumb running down my jaw line. "Could we be kissing friends?"

I chuckled. "That's kissing cousins."

He shrugged. "Friends, cousins, not that much difference, is there?"

Looking at his lips, I decided there wasn't. I reached an arm up and laid my hand at the back of his neck. Tom bent down and covered my lips with a sweet kiss. I kissed him back, and while I savored the feeling of

his lips on mine, I didn't feel that hot, desperate long-
ing like I did when Bradley kissed me.

Tom drew back. "Bradley Williams is one hell of a
lucky guy."

I patted Tom's shoulder. "Hey, the same goes for
the girl who wins your heart."

"I'll see you in the morning. Can I be one of your
operatives in the Case of the Dead Clown, Miss
Bond?"

"You sure can! I warn you, though, the pay is
nonexistent."

"That's okay. You can make it up to me with a kiss
now and then." He looked past my shoulder. "I've
spied something already. You've got a bum sitting on
your front stoop."

I turned around, saw Harry, then said to Tom, "It's
all right. He's cleared."

"Okay. Good night, babe."

"Thanks, Tom."

I watched for a moment as he walked toward Lexington, wondering if I'd just let go of something that
could develop into a special relationship. I comforted
myself with the certainty I felt in my bones that Tom
and I would always be friends.

"Miss Sweet Face, that's not your man. Whatcha
doing kissing him?"

"Good evening, Harry. How are you?"

"Shouldn't answer a question with a question."

In the glow of the streetlight, I could have sworn
Harry seemed more alert than usual. Even though he
was unshaven and wearing ratty clothes, he sat up
straight and did not slur his words. A spark of hope
went through me.

"The guy is a friend. It was a friendly kiss. Bradley's
the only man in my heart."

"Guess now I have to answer your question."

"I'd like that."

Harry spoke with his gaze fixed on the concrete step. "Been trying to cut back on my drinking. I get these blackouts where I wake up not knowing what happened the night before and I don't like it."

I barely refrained from doing cartwheels down the sidewalk. *Careful, Bebe, careful.* "I wouldn't like it either. I'm proud of you for drinking less." I sat beside him and opened my purse. "Mama always tells me to go out on a date with cab money in case the guy gets fresh. Here, you can have it."

Harry looked at the money and then put his head in his hands. He made a noise that sounded suspiciously like a sob. I stayed quiet, but patted him on the back. "Want to know what else Mama always tells me?"

He lifted his head, turned away from me for a moment, then looked back. "Why not?"

"She says that people should always help others. That goodwill comes back to them if they do. Sometimes, I'm not quite sure if I do it as much as I should. What I do know is that I try to be good to my friends. They're important to me. You're my friend, Harry."

"I haven't been anyone's friend in four years. I'm finding it harder and harder to take money from you and I hate myself when I do."

"Don't hate yourself! That's terrible. I'll bet you had a good job once. Am I right?"

Harry took the money from my hand. I thought he would leave me there like he usually did, without telling me anything, but then he spoke softly.

"I was a chemical engineer before drinking pickled my brain."

"Wow, my next-door neighbor back in Richmond is

a chemical engineer, or some sort of engineer. I'm impressed. Did the job get to you?"

He started to stand up.

I said, "Harry, please don't go yet. I have something else to give you."

Silently praying this was the right time, I pulled out a folded piece of paper from my purse. I'd been carrying it around for months.

Tucking the paper inside the top pocket of Harry's army jacket, I said, "Don't get mad at me. There's a name and an address for the closest place they hold AA meetings."

Harry sprang to his feet.

I jumped up and held his sleeve. "I called them. All you have to do is show up for a meeting, see how you like it. They have resources if you . . . get sick. They can help and it's free."

Harry looked me in the eye. "They can't help the pain of losing a young wife to cancer."

"Oh, Harry," I whispered. "I'm so sorry. Do you have children?"

"No, we never could have any. After she died, I figured drinking myself to death would help me join her. That is, if there's a God."

"I believe there is, Harry, but it's okay if you don't. The people at AA aren't going to preach at you. You're a good, strong man who had something cruel and terrible happen to him."

"I've gotta go."

"Will you please think about going to the meeting?"

He nodded and disappeared down the street without another word.

I hoped I'd handled talking with him the right way. There was no plaque in my room stating that I was a psychiatrist. I could only speak to him from my heart.

Chapter Eleven

"I look like a dowdy shop girl in this outfit. Heaven forbid anyone I know sees me in this square getup."

Darlene stood in my bedroom doorway dressed in a Helper's uniform.

"Those high navy heels are going to kill your feet," I said, tucking my long-sleeved white shirt into my tiny black miniskirt, making sure the charm bracelet Bradley had given me was securely latched. "Besides, it's a children's toy store, remember?"

"Is that why your outfit looks like a cross between a nun and a sexpot? I have *got* to be there when Bradley sees you. The Peter Pan collar is nothing short of inspired."

"A sexpot? Me?" I twirled around, showing off my long legs, which were clad in black-and-white-dotted tights and those killer secret agent girl boots. "Let me add a splash or five of My Sin for extra insurance."

Darlene laughed. "Insurance that you'll drive Bradley over the edge?"

"Well, I hope he'll be diverted enough that he won't flip out when he sees that you're working for the store. I need a few minutes alone with him to explain."

"What are you going to tell him?"

"This time, the truth. You know, that I need you there to help me investigate."

Darlene flung on her red trapeze-style coat. "Not a good idea, especially since Bradley turned into a fire-breathing dragon last time we investigated. How about saying that I need the extra money? He'll know I'm there to help you sleuth, but if you stay firm and add that Mallory hired me, there won't be anything he can do."

I set the perfume bottle down on my dresser. "Smart. That will be our story and we'll stick to it." I grabbed my black trench coat and we left the apartment together.

Outside, the crisp autumn air charmed me anew. "Come on, I usually walk to work."

"Walk?" Darlene uttered, amazed.

"Yes, walk. It's good exercise, plus we can stop at the store where I bought my boots and you can pick up a pair."

"In that case, let's get going."

We walked westward toward Fifth Avenue, crossing the long blocks in between.

"How was your date with Tom last night?"

I filled her in as we stayed together on the crowded streets. I ended with, "Plus he wants to be one of our operatives. He already gave me valuable information. We should tell him we're roommates and working the case. He can be trusted."

"Did he kiss you good night after y'all decided to just be friends?"

My cheeks felt warm in the cool air. "Yes, he did, and I liked it."

Red curls swung in the light breeze as Darlene turned to shoot me a smile.

Before she could say anything, I added, "But Tom doesn't make me go all funny inside my stomach like Bradley does."

Her laughter rang out, causing several admiring male heads to turn in our direction.

"So what do I need to know about these crazy characters I'm going to be spying on while I shove teddy bears into little kids' arms?"

"Let's start with the Teddy Bear. He's the store greeter and doesn't say anything, but passes white envelopes to Mallory."

"What's in the envelopes?"

"I don't know and it's driving me crazy. Then there's the Pirate. Mr. Geedunk tried to incriminate me in front of Snyder and Finelli. He keeps a parrot named Junior who started out saying 'Kill the clown' and now says 'You bet the clown's dead.'"

"Are you sure this is a toy store and not a nuthouse?"

"Oh, speaking of mental institutions, the Pirate claims the Train Conductor spent time in a mental facility. From what I've heard and what I can tell myself—and Tom confirms this—the Conductor is obsessed with his trains. Kinker delighted in messing up the displays."

"Nice guy."

"Keeper of secrets. I'm convinced one of those secrets got him killed. Next, Raggedy Ann is mad over a past romantic relationship, though she flirts with Tom and Bradley."

"If we can't find out who really murdered Kinker, we'll pin it on her. Imagine, daring to flirt with Bradley right under your nose!"

"Ha ha. Raggedy Ann is also spreading rumors that the Toymaker is a—" I pulled on Darlene's arm until

I had slowed her stride. I bent and whispered in her ear, "Homosexual."

"Leave that one to me. We're on Fifth. Now where is the shop with the boots?"

"Up ahead. The Cowboy is another one who doesn't talk much. He's the one I told you said that some people just need killing."

Darlene shrugged. "Lot of us Texans have that point of view. Is he from Texas?"

"I don't know. He seems the protective-of-women type."

"Oh my, I hope he's not the killer."

"Then there's the Princess. I plan to talk with her today. Some of the other store characters call her the Ice Princess because she doesn't date. Last night, Tom told me that when he introduced himself, the Princess freaked out and told him not to come near her, that she wouldn't put up with him *again*."

"Let me know what you find out about her, Miss Bond."

"I will, Agent Roland. Here's the shop!"

"And I plan to do some damage to my checkbook," Darlene said.

It didn't take her long.

Fifteen minutes before Merryweathers' opened for business, Darlene—boot box in tow—and I arrived.

"Good morning, Mr. Teddy Bear. I'm Darlene Roland, a new Helper," Darlene said with a smile.

The greeter merely opened the door and waved us in with his furry arm.

"Everybody always in character here?" Darlene asked me.

"Pretty much. It's a store rule that employees call each other by their character names."

Standing inside the store, I noticed the store characters watching us. "Darlene, it's going to be fun having you work here," I said in ringing tones.

She caught on quickly. "Thank you, Bebe. I know I'll enjoy it."

"I'll show you where to put your coat."

I led Darlene to the storeroom behind the employees-only door, where we left our coats.

"I didn't get a chance to ask you if you talked to Stu."

Darlene nodded. "I took your advice and called him last night. We talked for over an hour. I think he felt reassured of my affections and I hope he'll back off now."

We returned to the sales floor and stood near the escalator.

"You don't want him to back off too far," I said ruefully, thinking of Bradley.

At that moment, three things happened at once.

Mr. Mallory snuck up behind me and said, "Miss Bennett, I know that you enjoy chatting up my employees, but I am taking Darlene on a personal tour of the store this morning. You must excuse us." He whisked Darlene away.

Bradley came into the store from the street, briefcase in hand, and stared at Darlene. She ignored him. He looked at me, taking in every inch of my body. I gasped.

Tom, in Mr. Skidoo's costume, rode up on his tricycle and sang out to me, "Good morning, Sweet Lips!" Bradley heard him loud and clear.

My thoughts turned into small bright fish swimming around the murky aquarium that had taken over my brain.

"Upstairs to my office, Miss Bennett," Bradley barked. "Now."

Tom winked at me and pedaled away.

I gathered my strength and walked to the escalator, making sure I was two steps above Bradley so he could fully take in the glory of my boots. I considered resting one foot on the step above me, but decided the action might be too fast.

We rode the elevator to the third floor in a cloud of My Sin, no words exchanged. I was determined to remain in control whatever he did. Strong. Professional. Those words were my mantra.

"Good morning, Danielle," I called out when Bradley and I reached the third floor.

She turned and smiled a greeting, a smile that quickly disappeared when she saw Bradley's face.

Uh-oh. He must really be bent out of shape if his cool demeanor was ruffled. I dared not sneak a glance at him. Instead, I tried to buy time. "Shall I bring in your coffee, Bradley?" I asked, stopping in front of the coffee table.

"Yes," he ordered over his shoulder, marching to his office. I heard him slam his briefcase on what I guessed was the top of his desk.

His mug and my cup of coffee in hand, I started to follow him and stopped short. I placed my coffee back on the table, reached one hand up, and unbuttoned the first two buttons of my blouse. Okay, now I was ready.

He'd be distracted.

He'd forget to yell at me about Darlene.

He closed the door to his office behind me. In one swift blur of motion, he pinned me to the back of the door by placing his hands on either side of my shoulders. I stood helpless with the cups of coffee still in my hands, staring up into his impossible blue eyes.

"What is your roommate doing here dressed in a

Helper's uniform?" Bradley asked, voice low, breathing faster than normal.

I could barely breathe at all.

"Um, Darlene needed some money?" It came out like a question.

His gaze raked down my face, down to where my blouse opened. "You expect me to believe that a full-time stewardess cannot get by on her salary?"

"Sh-she opened a charge account at, um, Macy's and she needs to pay it off." Oh God, he was so close. I could see a tiny group of whiskers that he'd missed while shaving.

"Mallory hired her not knowing she's your room-mate. Very clever, Bebe," he said, his voice still low. His gaze snapped back to mine. "There's just one thing you overlooked."

Strong! Professional! I tried to take a deep breath but failed miserably when the scent of his lime aftershave reached my nose. "What is that, Bradley?"

"You're not a very good liar. I can go downstairs, find Mallory, and order Darlene to be dismissed. Immediately."

I silently repeated my mantra, fighting to remain calm while my heart jumped as if there were a mini trampoline in my chest. "You said there was one thing, but then said two: the part about me lying and then the part about you firing Darlene. And you won't fire her."

He raised his eyebrows, still breathing heavily. "Why the hell not? I know exactly why she's here: to help you conduct one of your amateur murder investigations. That's why you want those personnel files."

"Darlene is here to make some extra money." There, the broken-record trick.

Bradley snatched the coffee cups out of my hands

and set them on his desk, coffee sloshing over the edges. Before I had the strength to move, he had me pinned against the door once again.

"No investigating. No getting yourself in more trouble than you're already in. No getting hurt."

I raised my chin. I could have kicked myself when I realized the action put my face even closer to Bradley's. "I can take care of myself. I'm an adult."

"You certainly look like a woman in those boots and that short skirt. I don't think they are appropriate attire for the office," he said, voice thick and heavy as melting chocolate.

Strong! Profess—

His voice turned into a tight growl. "Tom called you 'Sweet Lips' downstairs. Did you let him kiss you on your damned date last night?"

My eyes widened. It really wasn't any of his business if I'd kissed Tom. I should tell him that.

"Did you kiss him? Answer me," Bradley choked out.

"Yes," I whispered.

A series of expressions flashed across his face. I could have sworn one of them was hurt. "Damn it, Bebe. You're making me do this."

His left hand went around to my lower back. His right hand came up to cup the back of my head and suddenly his lips covered mine in a heated kiss.

It had been so long since he'd kissed me. My arms came up and I clutched the back of his neck, pulling him closer and responding to his kiss with passion. My tongue darted out and licked a swipe across his lower lip and he groaned before thrusting his tongue into my willing mouth. I rubbed my tongue against his and an ache flared in my stomach, a pain I knew only Bradley could ease.

Caressing the back of his neck with one hand, I let the other fall underneath his suit jacket to rest on the side of his hip above his belt, rubbing him there. He moaned and I felt the power of making him moan, then he crushed his lips against mine, searching and demanding.

He dropped his hands to my hips and pulled me close against him, breaking the kiss to whisper, "Bebe, Bebe, I've tried not to . . . ," before his mouth found my neck. I stretched to give him easier access and he nipped my skin, making me shudder, then he licked the spot and began sucking it. I felt the sucking down to my toes and hazily thought that he must be supporting me, for surely I couldn't stand on my own.

"Mmmm, Bradley—"

Voices came from the hall. Not important.

"Bradley, I want—" Something started knocking in my head.

Not in my head. At the door.

Abruptly, Bradley guided—well, kind of dragged—me to a chair, cussing up a storm in a low whisper.

My mouth burned, along with the burning ache in my gut.

A kitten meowed. No, that was me.

Bradley dropped into his chair and slid it close to his desk. "Mallory is at the door," he hissed.

He smoothed his hair.

I could only mirror his actions. My brain cells felt as if someone had drowned them in honey, making me completely incapable of rational thought.

"Come in," Bradley called.

The store manager and Darlene walked into the office.

Neither said a word.

A short laugh, quickly covered by a cough, escaped Darlene.

"What is it, Mr. Mallory?" Bradley asked smoothly.

"Am I interrupting something?" the store manager asked. His gaze slid to the two coffee cups at the edge of the desk, then to me.

"Not at all."

"Well, that's good then. May I introduce you to Miss Darlene Roland? I hired Darlene to replace Linda. Today is her first day at Merryweathers'."

I sat up straight and poured every ounce of pleading into my eyes, silently begging Bradley not to fire Darlene.

He saw me, then his gaze dropped to my throat. He passed a hand over his eyes, then stood and held out his hand. "Welcome aboard, Miss Roland."

Relief swept through me.

Darlene leaned forward and shook Bradley's hand. She smiled at him in a knowing way. "Please, call me Darlene. Everyone I know does."

"Darlene it is. If you will all excuse me, I have several important phone calls to make. Bebe, after you went home yesterday, I left a number of assignments in your in-box. I'd appreciate it if you worked on those now."

"I'll do that," I said. Retrieving my coffee cup, I left his office on shaky legs.

Mallory was in the lead, Darlene next, then me.

Darlene dropped back a pace and whispered to me, "You've got a huge hickey on your neck. Guess he liked the boots."

She caught up to Mallory and the two headed for the elevator.

After three fumbling attempts, I buttoned my blouse.

Danielle was not around, so I was able to slide behind my desk and retrieve my compact. I opened it and gasped. My hair was a mess, my lips were red and swollen. Pushing my hair back, I stared into the mirror at a big purple and reddish bruise on the right side of my neck.

"There you are," Danielle said. "I was in the ladies' room and worried we might miss a call."

I snapped the compact closed and pulled my hair over the hickey. The problem with that was if I moved my head, everyone could see the result of . . . of . . . of Bradley's passion. Oh!

Realizing that Danielle expected a reply, I said, "If someone called, they'll call back. I've got a bunch of work in my in-box."

"Anything I can help you with, Bebe? I'm all caught up." Danielle walked over to my desk.

"Let's see what we have here." I stood, listing to one side so my hair would cover the hickey, and scooped up the contents of the in-box.

Something heavy slid onto my desk.

Danielle screamed.

In slow motion, my fingers reached for it.

A pirate's knife, exactly the same as the murder weapon, including the real blade, rested in my hand. A typewritten note attached to it said simply, chillingly: *You're asking too many questions.*

Chapter Twelve

Danielle cowered in the corner, her hand over her mouth.

Bradley burst from his office. "What's going on here . . . Bebe!"

Clutching the knife, I stretched out my arm to show it to him. "I found this in my in-box," I said, my voice trembling. "I don't know where it came from. You believe me, don't you, Bradley?"

"Of course I do. Now drop that on your desk," he commanded, standing beside me as the knife hit the desktop with a clatter. He leaned over and read the note attached to it and his lips tightened, his brows coming together. "I'm calling the police. Have you got Finelli's number?"

"I suppose we do need to let them know." I hesitated.

"Bebe, where is Finelli's number? On your Rolodex? Hand it to me and I'll make the call."

I eased myself into my chair, tearing my eyes from the pirate knife and fumbling through my Rolodex.

"Danielle, are you all right?" Bradley asked.

"I can't say I'm not upset, Mr. Williams. I'm sorry I screamed. I don't think anyone heard me other than you and Bebe."

"There's no need to apologize. Your reaction is understandable. I do need to ask you to stay here until the police arrive. Why don't I get you some coffee and you can sit at your desk. Try to take a deep breath."

"I'll get the coffee, Mr. Williams. You need to stay with Bebe and make that call."

Bradley moved to my side when I produced Finelli's number. He stretched across me and dialed the detective himself.

"Finelli? Bradley Williams here. You'd better come over to the store. Another altered pirate's knife turned up, this time in Bebe's in-box."

"Yes, she did pick it up. You know her."

I looked up at him, my mouth in an offended O.

"I see. I don't like it . . . yes, I understand. Thanks for that. I didn't think Snyder was. No, only Danielle. Just tell that jackass not to come roaring up to my store with a siren blaring. I've had enough bad publicity." Bradley slammed the phone down.

"Detective Snyder is coming instead of Finelli, isn't he?" I asked, knowing the answer.

"Finelli said that since Snyder is in charge of the case, there is no choice. Don't worry, I'll be with you when he arrives. Perhaps I should call Jim Lincoln."

"You think I need my lawyer?"

Danielle spoke up. "Bebe, you can't be too careful."

"Bebe, find Jim's phone number. Danielle, are you feeling steady enough to stand by the elevator and make sure no one comes up except Snyder? He's a heavyset fellow and wears a fedora."

"Certainly, Mr. Williams." Danielle rose and disappeared around the corner.

I handed Bradley my lawyer's number and once again he dialed and spoke into the phone. Out of nervousness, I twirled my fingers like I was playing cat's cradle with no string. The childhood game helped me calm down and think. Obviously someone in the store had done this. The knife had fallen out from in between the batch of papers Bradley had left in my in-box. I imagined the killer had stuffed it there either before the store closed last night or early this morning so the knife wouldn't be found by anyone but me. That song "Secret Agent Man" kept running through my head. Right now the line "Odds are you won't live to see tomorrow" played repeatedly.

"Bebe, did you hear me? Jim is in court this morning so I can't reach him. I left a message with his secretary," Bradley said, one hand gripping my shoulder.

Feeling the strength in his fingers, I drew in a deep breath and let it out. "Thanks for calling him. I don't see how that jerk Snyder can believe I'm a suspect after this."

The smell of a cigarette heralded Detective Snyder's arrival. "Is that so, girly?" he barked from the doorway.

Uh-oh. He'd heard me. My cheeks flamed from embarrassment. My shoulder felt cold when Bradley dropped his hand. "Hello, Detective Snyder," I said in a small voice.

Dressed in a black suit, black shirt, and silver tie, Snyder took a step closer and dramatically flung out his arms. "Ain't this cute? Williams, the pretty boy, here with you again, playing the part of minder so his whittle bittle kids' store don't get a bad rep."

Bradley let out a frustrated breath. "Why don't we tell you what happened and you can be on your way, Detective?"

But Snyder had tilted his head, staring at me, or more precisely, my neck.

"Wait a second. I may not always be right, but I'm never wrong. That would be a hickey on your neck, girly. You change lovers like you change your lipstick. First Kinker, and I wonder who you're sharing your charms with now."

My face went hot with anger. "None of your business."

At the same time, Bradley said, "That's none of your business."

Snyder cackled. "That's it, girly, go directly for the boss. Must not have been hard to reel him in since Williams is known for his way with the ladies."

I shot to my feet. "If you don't want to learn what happened here this morning, then I'll call the police station and find out who *your* boss is and tell him what an unprofessional lout you are."

Snyder took a drag from his cigarette, then addressed Bradley. "Got a temper on her. Must be wild in the sack."

In a flash, Bradley moved around the desk toward the detective and drew back a fist.

Snyder dropped cigarette ash on the floor. "Go ahead. It'll be fun to see how you handle jail. I'll visit you, though I think you'll have lots of company."

"Bradley!" I cried, following him around the desk. I didn't understand what Snyder was implying about "company." I just knew I didn't want Bradley behind bars.

Bradley snarled at Snyder. "You're a coward who hides behind his badge."

"You're gonna make me cry," Snyder said, with heavy sarcasm. Then he pinned his snake eyes on me. "Let's hear what story you have to tell me this time."

Bradley called for Danielle. She came into the office

area, staring at Snyder, eyes wide. I guessed she must have heard the detective.

Snyder rudely gave her the once-over. "Williams, you have a knack for surrounding yourself with pretty young things."

Before he could taunt Bradley any more, I put my efforts into sounding businesslike. "This is Danielle. She witnessed what happened. Detective Snyder, after returning from a meeting, I found this in my in-box." I held out the pirate knife to him. "Danielle and I were going to share the work. I picked up the assignments and the knife fell out onto my desk."

He held the end point of the knife with the tips of his fingers and read the attached note. "Anyone else touch this besides you?"

"The person who made it."

"Who's that?"

"I have no idea, but I feel safe in saying it's the killer."

"So you made it and put it in your own in-box as a way of throwing me off my game."

Bradley snorted. "That's ridiculous."

Snyder shot him a glare. "You have a problem keeping that pretty-boy mouth of yours shut, don't you? I'll bet you kiss and tell all over town."

I could see Bradley's muscles tightening as if preparing for a fight.

"Look, Detective Snyder," I said, "I didn't make this knife or the one that killed Kinker. Furthermore, that note is a warning to me—"

"What kind of questions does that note refer to?"

Bradley shot me an "I know what the questions are" look.

"Since you seem to believe I murdered Mel Kinker,

I have had to investigate the case myself, interviewing the store employees."

Snyder's eyes bulged; then he burst into laughter. "You're a clever one, I'll give you that. Nothing like stirring the pot until something you can call a clue rises to the top."

"I don't see you investigating Kinker's murder, Detective Snyder," I snapped.

"I have the murderess. I'm just waiting on the coroner's report to make an arrest. The way I see it is you typed that note on that typewriter right there, stuck it on the pirate knife you made, and put it in your inbox. Then you made a big display of being shocked— probably made sure you had that quiet girly there as a witness. Am I right, Danielle?"

"I was with Bebe when she found the knife," Danielle answered softly. "There's no way she could have put it there herself because she left early yesterday for her date with Tom."

Uh-oh.

Snyder looked at me with disgust. "Yet another man. You know about this, Williams?"

"Yes," Bradley gritted out.

"And you still called Finelli for her. Awww."

"If you don't believe me, Detective, I guess there's nothing more to be said," I told him, furious that he was trying to paint me as fast and loose.

"That's where you're wrong, girly. You're going with me to the stationhouse and have your little fingers blackened."

"You can't have her fingerprinted for no reason," Bradley said.

"I've got plenty of reason right here. Suspicion of planting evidence in a murder investigation," the detective said and nodded at the knife. He walked over to the coffee table, retrieved a napkin, then gingerly wrapped the knife loosely in the napkin and pocketed it. "Let's go, girly."

Bradley held out an arm, barring my way. "I have a call in to the company lawyer. You aren't dragging Bebe anywhere until we hear from him."

Snyder shrugged. "If that's the way you want to play it, fine. I'll call for backup and formally arrest your secretary and charge her with not cooperating with the police in a murder case. She'll be led out of here in handcuffs." He leered at me, but continued speaking to Bradley. "Maybe you'll get turned on seeing that."

Bradley's face went a dark shade of red, even bordering on that bad purple color Daddy sometimes got. "We'll follow you in a taxi, Snyder. Bebe, get your purse."

Snyder threw his cigarette to the floor, crushing it into the linoleum.

Bradley hastened to his office and retrieved his suit coat.

I turned to Danielle. "Will you be okay? Can you handle the phones while I'm gone?"

"Yes, Bebe," she replied, tears in her eyes.

"Don't worry, Danielle. Everything will turn out fine. If I could ask you not to tell anyone where I've gone or . . . why—"

"I won't."

In silence the three of us took the elevator, then the escalator downstairs until Snyder turned to me and said, "Maybe it was one of your 'jungle friends' who planted the knife. The giraffe has a long neck made for sticking his little nosy where it don't belong."

Still I said nothing until we almost reached the sales floor. On the navy-and-red carpet below lay a blue plastic truck. Remembering how Snyder's wife had left him for a trucker, I said, "Oh, look at that adorable truck. Gosh, I love trucks. They're so masculine. When I think of those big men shifting the gears of those huge rigs—"

Snyder grabbed my arm and squeezed it hard. "There you go. See what a gentleman I am, Williams, helping the *lady* off the escalator."

Riling him up was worth the pain in my arm.

I put a smile on my face so no one would think anything was out of the ordinary. The next thing I knew, we were out on the crowded lunchtime street. Snyder gave Bradley an address and marched off to his brand-new black Barracuda, double-parked in front of the store.

Bradley hailed a cab. I got in, mindful of my short skirt. Bradley followed and gave the address to the driver as we settled into the backseat.

He fired the first volley. "I knew you were playing sleuth even though I told you not to."

"I'm sorry if I don't have the Williams Seal of Approval from you, Bradley, but I am the lead suspect in Kinker's death. If I don't ask questions in order to clear my name, who will?"

"No one has charged you with anything."

"Come on! How can you be so bullheaded? You heard Snyder say he'd arrest me as soon as he got the coroner's report. What am I supposed to do, wait around for the inevitable like Marie Antoinette?"

"Finelli is investigating."

"What? How do you know?"

"He told me so on the phone. Now that you know, I want you to promise me to stop asking questions and putting yourself in danger. What I said to you earlier in my office . . . er . . . never mind that. You know how I feel."

"How you feel about kissing me or about my sleuthing?"

Bradley looked out the taxi window. "The first shouldn't have happened and the second needs to stop."

Pain blossomed in my heart like ink in water. Just like this past spring, Bradley regretted kissing me. My chin trembled. I would not cry. Strong. Professional.

I sat mute, chewing on my thumbnail.

Once we reached the police station, Snyder gave instructions to an officer and the fingerprinting went off without a hitch, except that I was left with black-ink-stained fingers. I didn't say a word to Bradley the whole time.

The silence between us continued all the way back to the store.

After Bradley paid for the cab, I said, "I'll return to the office later."

"Where are you going?"

I whirled around, exasperated. "I'm hungry! I'm going to get a hot dog."

"I'll take you to lunch, kid."

"No, thank you. I'd prefer to eat alone."

At any other time, I would have jumped at the opportunity to share a meal with him. It was a testimony to how much he'd hurt me that I turned him down flat and flounced off down Fifth Avenue, hoping other men would look at me with admiration and Bradley would see it.

Not that it would change anything.

I walked and walked until I found myself in front of the Empire State Building. Remembering the list of things I wanted to do in New York, I rode the elevator to the Observation Deck and looked out over the city, my hair blowing across my face, catching in my lip gloss.

The wind made me wish for my coat, but the view was worth every second. This was my home now and I loved it. I couldn't imagine living anywhere else. I wouldn't allow Snyder to push me around without a fight, wouldn't allow him to take my freedom away.

As for Bradley, I had to put my feelings for him aside and concentrate solely on the investigation. I was tired of not knowing where I stood with him. Damn him! His assignments could wait. I was going back to the store to question the Princess. Maybe Tom or Darlene, my operatives, would have something to report.

Taking one last glance at the shining skyscrapers, I walked to the down elevator, feeling as if the high altitude had cleared my head.

Secret Agent Girl was on the case.

Chapter Thirteen

Clutching my bottle of Tab—I hadn't been able to eat anything—I slipped into the store and hastened to the ladies' room without speaking to anyone. My fingers needed a good scrubbing so no one would suspect that I'd been fingerprinted. I cleaned almost all traces of the ink away, then went to work on my face. The wind had caused me to tear up. Yes, the wind—that was it. I applied blush, a light dusting of powder, then my Mary Quant pink lip gloss. Next I attacked my hair, first brushing it into its usual flip, then back-combing the top behind my bangs and smoothing it out. My hair partially hid the hickey, but I turned up the collar of my Peter Pan blouse in a further effort to cover it. Satisfied, I tossed my empty Tab bottle in the trash and walked onto the sales floor.

Business had improved and the store was bustling. Once the ad appeared in the *Times* tomorrow, inviting the children to come see Mr. Skidoo, we'd be back to normal.

Standing by the Jungle, I caught Tom's eye. He was in Raggedy Ann's section, Betty chattering away at him. I waved him over. He pedaled toward me on his tricycle and hopped off, then pretended to pull a flower from behind my right ear.

"Thanks for saving me from Raggedy Ann, babe. Hey, that's some hickey. Guess either those boots or my calling you 'Sweet Lips' made Williams lose control."

"Tom, I don't feel up to talking about it right now, okay?" I said, handing him back the flower.

He made a sad clown face. "Yeah. If you want a male perspective on whatever happened, I'm here to serve."

I smiled. "Deal."

"Bebe, as your operative, I need to report that our Raggedy Ann is some swingin' chick. She won't let up on me, told me I could come to her place tonight for a quiet dinner. When I asked her if she was dating anyone else, she made a horrible face and said not since her last boyfriend."

"Are you going out with her?"

"No. But I admit I kinda led her on."

"Why?"

He looked around. "Because I had a sneaky suspicion I could guess who that evil last boyfriend was, and I was right. You'll never believe—"

"Mr. Skidoo!" cried a boy holding on to a plastic airplane. "Can you make this fly?"

"Sure I can! Give me one minute with this lovely lady and we'll hit the sky."

I saw that Mallory had come out of his office and was standing near the cash registers watching us. "Tom, you'd better go before you get in trouble."

"Hang on a second. Betty was seeing Kinker— maybe she has a thing for clowns. They were hot and heavy, if you get my drift. Then he dumped her for no apparent reason. At least, that's what she said. Man, I could feel the anger coming off her in waves."

"Mr. Skidoo! You promised!" The boy sat on the clown tricycle.

I nudged Tom toward the impatient boy. "Go. We'll talk later. Fantastic job, Agent Stevens."

He grinned, then tended to his young customer.

A loud wail sounded. I looked over to see the Train Conductor, his face twisted with fury, righting the locomotive of his Lionel train set. A boy of about five years old clung to his mother's skirts and screamed again. I could see the mother's lips moving, her gestures toward the Conductor heated.

"Good afternoon, Conductor," I said cheerfully, walking over.

He scowled at me and did not return the greeting.

The mother was not so quiet. "I'm Mrs. George Dalloway and I demand an apology from the store manager for this man's behavior. Do you work here?" At the sound of his mother's voice, her son stopped crying and sucked his thumb.

Southern manners kicked in. "Yes, ma'am. May I help in any way?"

"This man"—she pointed one long red nail at the Conductor—"slapped my little Georgie's hand when he touched the train set. Is this display not intended to attract children and entice them to ask their parents for a set?"

"Yes, ma'am, you're correct."

"Do you think the Train Conductor should be allowed to discipline my child?"

Mr. Kirchhoff finally spoke. "I have to discipline him if his mother does not. This is a carefully crafted town centered around the wonderful world of trains. The town people depend upon it to carry their coal for fuel, their logs for building, their cattle . . ." He went on, looking off into the distance, seeming to forget our presence.

Mrs. George Dalloway looked at me in horror.

I needed to get Mallory—this situation was more than I could handle. Plus, if I could get Mallory away from where he stood behind the registers, I could talk to the Princess. I said sweetly, "I'm terribly sorry, Mrs. Dalloway. Please wait here while I get the store manager for you."

"Thank you, young lady," she said, looking down her nose at my boots.

I crossed the sales floor, noted that Darlene was working in Raggedy Ann's section, and explained the situation to Mallory. He pursed his lips and brushed past me, swinging his walking stick, striding to the train area with an air of importance, not sparing a thank-you for me.

Remembering that the Princess was my goal, I turned away from watching Mallory. The Princess looked on while Darlene stood behind the girls' jewelry counter. Inside the glass cabinet were silver and gold pendants, charms, rings with tiny birth-month gemstones, small bangle bracelets, and earrings, most of the latter being clip-on, though there was a small selection for pierced ears.

Darlene was talking to a girl about twelve years old. "Honey, why aren't your ears pierced? Only old ladies wear clip-ons nowadays."

The girl pouted. "I've been begging my mom to let me get them pierced, but she's a real drag. She doesn't get that all the cool girls have pierced ears."

"Laura!" A conservatively dressed woman wearing almost no makeup approached in time to hear her daughter's complaints. "What's going on here?"

Darlene propped her elbows on the glass counter.

"We were discussing your old-fashioned ideas about pierced ears."

I rolled my eyes and hurried past to reach the Princess, who was now straightening dress-up costumes in the girls' changing rooms.

"Mary?"

The Princess started, then faced me. Her beautiful full-skirted silver gown fit her tiny figure perfectly. The stones in her tiara, perched atop her long golden curls, sparkled under the store's lighting. Blue eyes and rosebud lips completed her fairy-tale appearance.

"You're Miss Bennett," she said in a shy voice, hands fidgeting with a pink tutu ballerina outfit.

"Please call me Bebe. I've been meaning to introduce myself but so much has been happening. I'm sorry."

She hung the tutu inside a white built-in clothes rack. "You don't have to apologize to me. Nothing but good has come about since your arrival, Bebe."

I eyed her closely. Was the Princess in the majority who thought I'd murdered Kinker? "That's a nice compliment, Mary. Are you talking about our birthday party?"

She moved back to the changing rooms, bent and picked up a child-size version of the dress she wore. Again, she smoothed it carefully, then slipped it on a satin hanger. "I was thinking more about what happened that night after . . . after the store closed," she said softly.

I bent to retrieve a brown suede cowgirl skirt.

The Princess placed a surprisingly strong hand on my arm. "No. Leave the skirt. It's my job to take care of it."

"Okay," I said, draping it over a chair in the fitting room. The skirt reminded me of the Cowboy. I tilted my head and saw that he was watching us, his hands polishing and repolishing a die-cast toy gun. I turned back to the Princess. "Mary, when you say good things happened the night of the birthday party, are you talking about Mr. Skidoo's death?"

She halted her motions and looked at me with what I could only figure to be hero worship. "You did the right thing, Bebe. I wish I had been strong enough to do it, but I wasn't. He wasn't even human, the way he treated everyone, especially me and Betty. But then men will be cruel to girls."

Her gaze had a faraway look. I wondered if she even knew what she was saying. "Mary, what happened between Kinker and Betty?" I wanted to confirm what Tom had told me.

"He used her, then threw her away when his . . . his manly needs had been satisfied," she whispered, chest rising and falling quickly. "I didn't let him get to me even though he tried and got angry when he failed. I'm a former Miss Connecticut. I don't deserve such treatment."

Her eyes fixed on Tom, who was in the Toymaker's section.

"Mary, you do know that the person that's playing Mr. Skidoo now is not Mr. Kinker, don't you? Tom is a nice person, a friend of mine."

She listened with bewilderment. "He is? Not many men are good. They want one thing from a girl and will even threaten to tell secrets if they don't get their way."

God, I should have known. Kinker and his secrets. What did he have on the Princess? "I promise you that Tom is one of the good ones. He won't try anything with you."

The Princess sighed. "That's nice to hear. Mr. Larabee, our Cowboy, he seems good, but it's so hard to tell. He's asked to take me to dinner, which is what a proper gentleman should do, but I told him I don't date. Are you dating anyone, Bebe?"

My hand went to my throat, where I made sure my collar covered the hickey. "Um, not really."

Mary nodded. "I knew you were wise."

From behind us came Laura's raised voice. "Even Darlene thinks I should have my ears pierced, Mom. You're living in the Dark Ages. You still think Dean Martin is the cutest guy on earth when everyone else knows it's John Lennon."

Ah, a girl with good taste. I'd better intervene before mother and daughter left the store in a huff, never to return.

I didn't know what else to say to the fragile Princess. After an awkward moment, I said, "Mary, if anyone ever bothers you, or if you need to talk with someone, I'm here. Do you have family in the city?"

Her eyes widened. "No. No. He's—that is, my father—lives in Connecticut. I have a studio apartment all to myself."

I smiled. "That's good. Remember me if you need a friend."

"I will, Bebe."

The Princess was undoubtedly a troubled young woman. She hadn't mentioned her mother, I noted as I moved to Darlene's area to try to smooth some ruffled feathers.

"Did I hear the name John Lennon?" I asked with a friendly smile, gazing from mother to daughter to Darlene.

Laura's brown eyes gleamed. "Yeah. Are you a Beatles fan?"

I placed my hands on my hips in a fake annoyed

pose. "I am, and I'll have you know that John belongs to me."

Laura laughed and began bouncing and humming "She Loves You." Then, apparently remembering she was mad, she said, "Don't you think I should have my ears pierced? Darlene says I should but my mother won't let me."

Laura's mother gazed down at my boots, disapproval apparent on her face.

"Gosh, that brings back memories of when I had my ears pierced when I turned eighteen," I said. "Tell me, Laura, are you okay with getting a shot when you go to the doctor?"

The girl's complexion turned paper-white.

Her mother stroked her hair and said, "Actually, the doctor has to make Laura lie down if he has to administer a shot. She passes out."

I bit my lip and sent the girl a look of sympathy. "Oh. You see, Laura, when you get your ears pierced, the doctor takes two needles—one for each ear—and puts them through your earlobes kind of like a shot, but the needle—"

Laura put her hands over the ears in question. "Stop! I don't wanna hear any more."

Her mother smiled at me, then comforted her daughter. "Here, sweetheart, how about those nice bluebird clip-on earrings? The clips aren't very noticeable."

I hung around until Darlene had sent Laura and her mom to the cash registers.

"That was mean, Bebe," Darlene said.

"I don't think so. It's the truth."

"Yeah, but you didn't have to tell her. Anyway, I guess since Mallory and I interrupted, you and Bradley didn't make it to the magic sofa."

I felt the heat rise to my cheeks. "Let's straighten that dollhouse so we can talk."

We sat on the floor picking up tiny pieces of furniture and carefully arranging them in the dollhouse rooms.

I smiled. "Bradley did get carried away, but so did I."

"You're driving him crazy. I keep telling you. Oops—" She broke off and quickly snatched a square foil packet from the floor, where it had fallen from her pocket.

"Darlene Roland!" I hissed. "What was *that*?"

"A girl needs to be prepared."

"At work? And I thought you were on the pill."

"I am, but I want to make absolutely certain that I don't get pregnant. I always carry a condom." She giggled. "Almost needed it today. Stu showed up unexpectedly and took me out for lunch."

"That was nice of him. I take it he took you to a restaurant and you didn't need the, um . . ."

"That's right, honey." Darlene picked up a two-inch-high baby bed and shoved it in the dollhouse nursery. "To be honest, I didn't appreciate the surprise. I've been trying to flirt with Mallory for the sake of the investigation and his seeing me going out with Stu wasn't part of my plan."

"You're being too hard on Stu again. Besides, you've told me how beneficial it is to be seen with one guy while trying to catch the attention of another."

She chuckled. "Yeah, I did say that. I told Stu about the investigation so he doesn't come to the store again. I swear, he's becoming more like Bradley, warning me off getting into trouble and putting myself in danger, like I can't take care of myself. Silly."

"Stu loves you."

"He's taking me out to dinner tomorrow night at the Rainbow Room."

"Wow, I'll help you get ready. Back to Mallory. Did you find out anything pertinent to the case?"

"Not really. He is steaming mad at you, though, because someone told him you'd been in his office alone."

I put a miniature grandfather clock in the dollhouse foyer. "Hmmm. As far as I know, only the Pirate saw me, besides the girls who run the cash register. They'd have no reason to squeal on me. I was meeting with my lawyer in Mallory's office."

"There's someone else."

"Who?"

"Our Raggedy Ann," Darlene said, glancing over to where Betty was busy with customers. "Betty and I got to talking. She was going all the way with Kinker. Wonder if she made him wear his makeup."

"You are so bad. The Princess told me pretty much the same thing, that Kinker was having an affair with Betty, then dropped her for no reason. Betty is rising on my list of likely suspects."

"She plays fast and loose, I can tell you that. And she's definitely got her eye on Bradley."

I almost broke the dollhouse china cabinet. "I wonder why the Cowboy is always watching her."

"I noticed that, but I don't think it's a romantic thing. Back to the Princess, what else did she say? She seems weird."

I relayed my conversation, finishing up with, "She says she's a former Miss Connecticut."

Darlene frowned. "She's lying. We Texas girls know a beauty pageant contestant when we see one. That girl has not been in pageants. She's not the type."

"I wonder why she'd lie about a thing like that."

"Who knows? You said Kinker was a keeper of secrets. Could he have found out she lied?"

I gasped. "Maybe. But we're not even sure. She could be telling the truth."

"Tomorrow on my lunch hour I'll go to the New York Public Library and see what I can dig up."

"That would be great, though I feel sorry for the Princess. I think she's troubled and doesn't quite see reality."

"Then we have two members of that club. That Train Conductor creeps me out."

We both looked over to where Mallory appeared to be giving the Conductor a dressing-down after his obsessive behavior with Mrs. Dalloway.

"There are too many suspects if you ask me, Bebe. I chatted with the Toymaker. The gossip about him being a homosexual is true."

"How could you possibly know?"

"Because I flirted with him and he didn't respond."

I rolled my eyes.

Darlene looked at me.

"Okay, okay, I guess you're right," I added. "You are irresistible to men."

"I know I'm right. I also pretended to be all innocent—like you—and asked him if this was a safe place to work. He said that now it was. That gave me an easy opening to express my concern over an employee being murdered. The Toymaker said that Kinker was unkind and had called him a sissy."

"He told you that?"

"Yes, but he quickly covered it by saying that Kinker had taunted him only because he was 'between girlfriends.' If you ask me, that's a motive for murder right there."

"What?"

We'd been talking quietly, but Darlene pitched her voice even lower. "Kinker knew the Toymaker's secret. If the Merryweathers had found out that they were employing a homosexual, the Toymaker might be out of a job."

"How ridiculous. I never thought of that."

"Something to consider. Listen, I thought it best to fill you in on this stuff now, but I do want to know what happened when that joke of a detective led you out of here with Bradley on your heels like a puppy in love. I want the full story tonight. Here comes Mallory."

Mallory paused near the front door and motioned to the Teddy Bear.

The Teddy Bear came inside and followed Mallory to his office, the two men standing just inside the doorway.

I tried to be invisible while I watched every move. Darlene did the same.

Sure enough, the Teddy Bear slipped Mallory a white envelope.

I had to hold myself down by my boots to keep from jumping up, running over there, and demanding to see the contents of the envelope.

Whatever they were, a flash of annoyance passed over Mallory's snobby face. He drew the Teddy Bear all the way into the office and closed the door.

"Listen," Darlene said. "They've raised their voices. Can you make out what they're saying?"

I shook my head. "Let's stand up and edge closer to the Princess's area."

We stood, but before either of us could move, the Teddy Bear marched out from Mallory's office and pushed open the front door with more force than was necessary. He stood outside the store, arms crossed.

"That's some freaked-out Teddy Bear," Darlene whispered.

"I'm going to lose my mind if I don't find out what's in those envelopes," I said through gritted teeth.

"Hey, girls, thanks for fixing my dollhouse," Raggedy Ann sang, skipping over to us. "I appreciate it, but by the time we close, it'll be a mess again."

"No problem," Darlene chirped. "That's what I'm here for."

Betty turned to me. "I saw you leave with Bradley earlier. Does he take you out to lunch every once in a while as a way of saying how much he values your work?"

I felt heat rise to my cheeks. "Um, yes."

Betty let out a sigh. "That's just the kind of thing he would do for the help."

Oh! Before I could work up a snappy comeback, Mallory was stalking back across the floor. The three of us watched as he left the store and began talking with the Teddy Bear. He pointed a finger in the Teddy Bear's face, then grabbed his furry arm. The Teddy Bear snatched his arm back and Mallory opened the front door, his cheeks red with anger.

Darlene said, "Mercy, does everyone around here have a short fuse?"

As if in answer to her question, Mallory banged his walking stick on the floor, making us all jump.

"Miss Bennett, I'd like to see you in my office immediately."

"Yes, Mr. Mallory."

Once inside, he closed the door after me, but did not offer me a chair.

"I have been informed that you used my office to conduct personal business."

"Yes, but—"

"You are never to use my office for anything. I don't care if it's business or to adjust your stockings."

"I understand, but—"

"Be sure that you do understand, Miss Bennett."

He picked up the telephone and began to dial, pausing only to look up at me as if wondering why I was still there.

Clearly dismissed, I opened the door and exited, head held high.

Was everyone in the store cuckoo? Obviously some kind of mental problem was a prerequisite for employment here. The old Skidoo was a mean-spirited keeper of secrets; the Princess had a fear of dating and might be a liar; the Train Conductor was, to say the least, obsessed with trains; the Toymaker hid his preference for men; the Pirate was fixated on his parrot; Raggedy Ann was fast and had her sights set on *my* man; the Cowboy was overly protective of women; and the Teddy Bear was mad at the high-and-mighty Mallory, a feeling the store manager returned.

Even I was held in dubious regard. Depending on the characters, I was either a saint or a sinner for supposedly doing away with the evil Kinker.

Was it just a couple of hours ago that the police had fingerprinted me?

I entered the elevator, punched the button for the third floor, and shook my head. There was a lot to sort out around this place, and I felt as if I was playing a game where I didn't know the rules.

Chapter Fourteen

"Bebe!" Danielle cried as I reached my desk. "I've been worried about you. What happened at the police station?"

Sneaking a glance toward Bradley's office, I noted with relief that his door was closed. Danielle must have brewed a fresh pot of coffee. I slid into the chair behind my desk and turned toward her. "I'm okay. Just sorry that you had to be involved in this mess. I took a taxi to the police station, they fingerprinted me, and I left. I've been on the sales floor helping out since I got back."

Danielle waved a careless hand. "First, don't worry about me. I talked to Herb—he's such a gentle, caring man—and he calmed me down. He's very supportive of me, kind of like Mr. Williams is with you."

I snorted. "Bradley? Supportive of me? Are you joking? He's madder at me than a disturbed nest of fire ants."

"And he bites too," Danielle whispered, and then covered her mouth. A giggle escaped, despite her trying to hold it in.

My hand automatically went to the hickey on my neck. "That's it. I'm wearing a turtleneck sweater tomorrow."

"I think scarves might be in your future," Danielle said, and laughed again.

"You're in a surprisingly good mood."

"Bebe, I'm in love! I'm cooking dinner tonight for Herb. You know what they say: The fastest way to a man's heart—"

"Is through his stomach. That's what Mama always told me." I pondered for a moment the fact that I'd never cooked for Bradley. I had handed him a steak once when Daddy punched him in the eye. Did that count? "What are you fixing him?"

"A pot roast with all the trimmings and his favorite coconut cake drizzled with chocolate."

"Yum!" I glanced at my watch. Just past three thirty. "Danielle, don't you think you should leave early? All that cooking will take time. When is Herb coming over?"

Danielle gripped the edge of her desk. "He'll be at my place at seven. I haven't even made the cake."

"You'd better go. You don't want to look frazzled when Herb arrives, do you?"

"Gosh, no. I finished most of the assignments in your in-box. There's some typing that needs—"

"I'll take care of it. You want to be calm and beautiful when Herb arrives, making him think that whipping up that delicious meal was child's play for you."

"Thank you, Bebe." She covered her typewriter, made quick work of organizing the papers on her desk, and left, stopping only to give me a hug.

I decided to pull out my special notebook and update it. I swung around in my chair, facing forward.

That was when I saw the note from Bradley. It read: *Talked to Jim Lincoln. You did the right thing by cooperating with Snyder.*

Written on a torn-off piece of lined white paper,

the note was signed with Bradley's initials. How romantic! Our first love letter!

I crumpled it up and threw it in the trash can.

For the next half hour I wrote, stopping periodically to nibble on the end of my pen. Two suspects rose to the top of the list: the Pirate and Raggedy Ann. The Pirate had a motive (Kinker's treatment of the beloved Junior) and an opportunity (he was in the store when the murder occurred). But wouldn't he be smarter than to use a replica of a toy from his own section to do the deed?

Raggedy Ann had a motive in spades (a love affair turned sour) and possibly the opportunity (she could have murdered Kinker, then fled the store)—and she was flirting with Bradley.

I crossed that last part out.

"Good afternoon, Miss Bennett."

Detective Finelli's voice plucked me from my thoughts and sent my pen flying. "You scared me," I said, quickly closing my steno pad.

"Nervous, are you?"

"Well, I did get fingerprinted today."

"I heard about that."

"Do you want to pull up a chair?"

"Can't stay long. I was in the area . . ."

My eyes took in the dark circles under Finelli's eyes, the crew cut that needed a trim, and his overall tired appearance. It occurred to me that he had not told Snyder about my lying to the police regarding dating Kinker. Guilt washed over me. "I'm sorry if I'm a burden to you. I mean, you must not have said anything about—"

"I haven't felt it necessary to disclose confidential information yet. That doesn't mean I won't."

"But you believe me when I tell you that I didn't kill Kinker, right?" I pleaded.

Finelli gave the smallest nod of his head.

I leapt from my chair, ran around my desk, and threw my arms around him. "Thank you!"

At that moment, Bradley came out of his office to refill his coffee cup.

Finelli quickly disengaged himself from me and took a step backward. His eyes went from my boots to Bradley. The latter stood looking at us, his jaw moving as if he were grinding his teeth.

"Williams."

"Finelli."

I smiled sweetly.

Bradley stalked back to his office and shut his office door.

"Listen, Detective, I hear you're doing some investigating of your own on Kinker's murder. I appreciate it."

Finelli didn't meet my gaze. "Doing my job no matter where it leads me. Snyder treat you any better earlier?"

I rolled my eyes. "Are you kidding? He's a drip—and a determined drip at that. He's convinced I'm the killer. I wanted to call you when I found the altered pirate knife in my in-box, but we had to deal with Snyder."

"That was correct procedure. I saw the knife in the evidence room. Identical to the one that killed the clown."

He rubbed a hand across his hair, a bad sign.

"I'm thinking that you're investigating, Miss Bennett, and that's why the killer sent you that warning."

"You know me too well, Detective."

"Christ."

I let out a frustrated sigh. "You're as bad as Bradley."

"You should listen to him." Finelli tilted his head and stared at my throat. Then, he said, "I haven't seen a hickey that big since before the wife and I had kids."

My cheeks grew warm and I readjusted my collar. "Getting back to the investigation, I have my suspicions, though it's been difficult with everyone here being a head case, and so many clues to follow you can't imagine. Why, I've had to enlist Darlene's help— did you see her downstairs?—and the help of the new Mr. Skidoo, who's really a friend of mine, and even though we did go out on a date I made him one of my operatives anyway." I took a deep breath.

"One of your operatives?"

"You'll think it sounds silly, but I love James Bond movies and the new *Man from U.N.C.L.E.* series, so I've become a secret agent girl."

"With operatives."

"Exactly."

"Miss Bennett, this isn't a movie or a TV show. This is real and you're in serious trouble. You're only enticing the killer to come after you—or one of your 'operatives'—making it a dangerous situation for everyone involved."

"Okay, you've done your duty and warned me, but I won't stop until I get to the bottom of this. I'm no quitter."

"You don't have to tell me that."

"Would you like me to tell you what I've learned?"

"That's information you should bring to Detective Snyder."

I made a face. "I won't."

He pulled his ragged notepad out of his pocket along with his pencil stub. "Shoot."

Over the next fifteen minutes I told him everything. He interrupted a few times, but mostly took notes.

When I finished, I said, "Does any of this help you with your side of the investigation?"

"Maybe."

I gasped in outrage. "You're not going to share with me what you know?"

"Nope. It's a one-way street."

"That's not fair."

"Are you living the version of life where everything is fair?"

"I guess not."

"I'll tell you this much. We expect to have the coroner's report back within the next forty-eight hours."

"Snyder is waiting for that report and then he's going to charge me with murder."

"You might want to alert your lawyer," Finelli said. "I've got to go. Watch yourself, will you?"

I nodded and he left me standing there, wondering how much time I had left before I was behind bars.

Bradley didn't emerge from his office for the rest of the afternoon. I finished all the typing and headed out the door a little after the store closed at five.

I walked up to the corner of Fifth and Forty-ninth Street, stood off to the side, and waited for Darlene. We hadn't arranged anything, so I figured if I didn't see her within the next fifteen minutes, I'd take the bus home by myself. Shirley's train would be arriving that evening and I didn't want to keep her waiting.

All of a sudden, Mary Tyler Moore walked briskly toward a waiting car. Laura Petrie in person! First I stood shocked. Then I burst out laughing, remembering the episode on *The Dick Van Dyke Show* where Laura dyes her hair blond—just as I had done as a teenager—with the same disastrous results.

About five minutes went by until I spotted Darlene's flame red hair and fell into step with her. "I just saw Mary Tyler Moore! Can you believe it? Anything can happen in New York," I told her.

Darlene smiled. "Anything encompasses a lot of territory, honey, but I'm glad you saw her. Did she look as good as she does on TV?"

"Better. She's beautiful!"

"Okay, calm down and tell me if we can catch the bus here."

"Yes," I said, still grinning.

"Good, because you were right about standing around in these heels all day."

Once we took seats on the bus, Darlene was quick to ask about the knife incident and my experience at the police station.

I filled her in on both, finishing up as we walked up Sixty-fifth Street to our building.

"At least seeing Miss Moore took your mind off that ordeal for a few minutes. Hey, your wino isn't around," Darlene said, extracting keys from her purse.

"His name is Harry and I wish you'd use it. I gave him some information about AA and a Methodist church that holds meetings. I hope that's where he is."

"Good luck."

We checked our mailbox, finding nothing but bills. Darlene took off her shoes before we began climbing the stairs to our apartment.

"Oh, and Finelli came by," I said. "He's investigating, though he wouldn't tell me anything. Unless you count the fact that Snyder expects the coroner's report within the next day or two. That's when I go to jail."

Darlene undid all four locks on our door and we entered the apartment, switching on lights. "You underestimate the Giver of Hickeys. Bradley will have you out if it comes to that."

We each went to change.

I unzipped my boots and put them in their box, wondering if I should wear them again tomorrow. Even though we were expecting Shirley, I couldn't bring myself to put on anything other than a soft cotton nightgown and my pink chenille robe with the large coffee cup pattern. Detouring into the bathroom, I looked at my hickey, feeling a shiver of pleasure run up my spine as I remembered Bradley's mouth on my neck. I forced the thoughts away, promising myself I'd think about it later. I adjusted the collar of the robe so that Shirley wouldn't think I was a hussy.

I padded into the kitchen and found Darlene wearing her purple lounging pajamas.

"How does leftover chicken cut up into a salad sound to you, Bebe?"

"Perfect," I answered, and reached around her to grab the milk. Pouring myself a glass, I asked, "Do you need any help?"

"You can chop the cucumbers."

Before long we were in the living room, stretched out on either end of the pink sectional, dinner eaten and dishes washed.

Darlene had just bought us a color television, even though our favorite show, *The Man from U.N.C.L.E.*, only aired in black and white.

"Do you want to watch TV?" Darlene asked, and yawned.

"To be honest, I'd be in bed if—"

The intercom buzzed.

"That must be Shirley," I said and went to answer it.

After buzzing her in, I ran downstairs—praying none of the neighbors would see me in my robe—to help her with her bags, feeling that no pregnant woman should have to walk up to the third floor carrying luggage.

"Hi, I'm Bebe. Let me take that."

Shirley was model tall, about two inches above my five feet seven. Her dark blond hair was cut in a bob that curled up on the sides, framing her pretty face. One curl drooped. She wore a tan raincoat and carried a blue suitcase.

"I'm Shirley Harrison, no relation to George Harrison of the Beatles, I'm afraid. Bebe, I can't tell you how nice it is to meet you . . . and be off that train," she said in a Chicago accent.

I chuckled and took her suitcase. "Come on up. My roommate and I were just hanging around."

Inside the apartment, I performed the introductions and Shirley took off her coat. She wore an expensive-looking Empire-waist navy wool dress.

"Thank you for allowing me to stay here, Darlene," Shirley said.

I shot Darlene a warning look.

"We're glad to have you. We're Southern girls, so it comes naturally to us to extend our hospitality," Darlene said, earning a big smile from me.

"Where should I put my things?"

In that instant, I realized I hadn't planned ahead. Of course she must have my bed. I couldn't condemn her to sleeping on the sectional in her condition.

Before I could speak, sounds of the newlyweds upstairs met our ears.

"I feel like an animal tonight, Lily! Gonna tie you to the bed and do things to you that will make you scream."

"Do it! Here I am, naked and ready for that hot rod of yours—and I'm not talking about a car, Willie," a female voice cried, followed by girlish laughter.

Shirley glanced at the ceiling and giggled.

"There, that cord ought to hold you, Lily. Now I can begin my feast."

Embarrassed, I led Shirley to the bedroom, placed her suitcase in the banana chair, and left her to undress. I returned with a glass of ginger ale and put it on the bedside table in case Shirley felt ill in the morning.

"Thanks, Bebe. The truth is this baby does not believe in morning sickness. I'm sick on and off all day."

"How awful. You get some rest, and I'll see you tomorrow."

I grabbed a blanket from my closet and quietly closed the door to my room.

When I was back in the living room, the bed upstairs sounded like it was rocking back and forth on the floor. I threw my blanket on the sectional and looked at Darlene. She leaned against the wall near the intercom, sipping a Coke.

"I've got an extra pillow," she said, then walked into her room and returned, tossing the pillow at me. I caught it and arranged my bed.

"Thanks. Are you mad about Shirley?" I asked, keeping my voice low.

Darlene shook her head. "Not really, but if every pregnant woman is as pale and exhausted as she looks, I sure don't want to get married and have kids."

"You'll change your mind."

"No, Bebe, I won't. I've never had a shred of maternal instinct. Let's not talk about it now. I'm going to bed. Will you be okay out here?"

I listened to the loud cries of sex coming from the apartment above. "I suppose."

Darlene went back into her room and returned

holding out a small package. "Earplugs. We have them by the dozen on the planes. Good night, honey."

I went around the apartment and turned off all the lights except the one in the bathroom, in case Shirley needed it during the night. I shrugged off my robe, laid down, and covered myself with my blanket. I popped in the earplugs and closed my eyes, certain I'd be asleep in minutes.

Wrong.

Images of Bradley and me in his office that morning flashed behind my closed eyelids. He'd been jealous of Tom, I thought, remembering how he'd demanded I tell him if Tom had kissed me. That was a good sign.

He'd moaned while kissing me, had kissed me so hard. I reached my hand up and touched my mouth. There was something he said . . . I frowned, trying to recall his words . . . something about trying not to, not to kiss me. But he'd failed. Another good sign.

My fingers made their way to my throat and I groaned with frustration, feeling all over again how his mouth had felt on my neck. He'd been out of control. A third good sign.

He'd supported me when I found the pirate's knife, protected me when that drip Snyder arrived, and almost struck a police detective. But on the heels of all that, nice Bradley had become regretful Bradley. He'd told me flat out that kissing me should not have happened.

That was *not* a good sign.

Chapter Fifteen

In the morning, I woke to the sound of Shirley being sick.

When she had washed her face and rinsed her mouth, she went back to bed, trailing the sash of her blue robe behind her. I followed.

"Shirley, will you be okay by yourself today?" I asked, digging through my closet for clothes.

"I think so. When I woke in the middle of the night, I drank that ginger ale and it stayed down. The trip took a lot out of me."

"There's plenty more ginger ale in the fridge and I have a box of saltine crackers in the cupboard. I'll leave those out on the counter for you. Try to drink as much as you can or else you'll dehydrate." I didn't want to pressure Shirley for the evidence on Drew while she was ill. Hopefully she'd be in better shape tomorrow.

I selected a pale pink turtleneck, pink-and-black-checked skirt—not quite as short as yesterday's—black tights and the boots.

Grabbing underwear out of my dresser, I told Shirley about the little grocery on Lexington and promised to leave her a set of keys to the apartment. She mumbled her thanks and went back to sleep.

I eased the door closed behind me, arms full, turned around, and ran into Darlene.

"Do you know what time it is, Bebe?" she whispered, hands on hips.

"Um, about forty-five minutes earlier than we agreed to get up on workdays?"

She took my arm and guided me into the kitchen. "More like an hour. I need my beauty sleep, and I warn you, if I don't get enough sleep, I get cranky."

"I would never have noticed."

Darlene narrowed her eyes.

"Don't do that. You'll get wrinkles. Go on back to bed and rest even if you can't sleep and I'll brew a pot of coffee for us. Come on, Shirley can't be sick the whole time she's here. The woman is pregnant and she had a long trip," I said, walking Darlene back to her room. "I'll even make you scrambled eggs with cheese."

"Toast too?" Darlene asked, still sulky.

"Mounds of toast."

I arrived at the store around eight forty-five. Darlene had declared she was too tired to walk and said she'd take a cab. The Teddy Bear greeted me with a wave and swung open the front door.

"Good morning. I think the store will be busy today."

He nodded his furry head and I wondered again why the Bear, aka Mr. Runion, had argued with both Mallory and the Pirate. He never even broke character and spoke to me. Why was that?

Upstairs, I put away my purse and started coffee.

Neither Bradley nor Danielle had arrived yet. For a minute I felt uneasy alone on the third floor, thinking of how the killer had so deftly been able to leave the knife in my in-box without being seen.

The elevator pinged and Danielle appeared, glowing like a neon light.

She held up her left hand and wiggled it. "Bebe, look! I'm engaged!"

I rushed to her side and held the fingers of her left hand. A small diamond set in a slim gold band caught the light and sparkled. "Danielle, it's beautiful," I said, throwing my arms around her and squeezing her in a big hug. Mentally I slapped myself for the sharp pang of jealousy that ran through me. "I'm happy for you. I know you love Herb and he loves you. Now, tell me everything. Did he get down on one knee when he asked you?"

"Did who get down on one knee?" Bradley said behind her. A lock of his blond hair fell forward onto his forehead, probably a victim of the windy morning. He carried his briefcase and the newspaper.

Danielle smiled. "My boyfriend asked me to marry him and I said yes." She held out her hand so Bradley could see the ring.

"Another bachelor throws away his little black book," Bradley said with a heavy sigh. "I'm kidding, Danielle. Best wishes to both of you. Er, Bebe, when you get a moment, please bring me my coffee."

He hardly glanced at me before walking down the hall to his office.

I turned to Danielle. "Go ahead and get settled. I'll take Bradley his coffee and then I want to hear all the details."

Danielle giggled.

I filled Bradley's St. Louis Cardinal's mug and carried it to his office, all the while wondering how I should behave. Friendly? I didn't know if I was capable of that. Angry because he'd said he regretted kissing me? That wouldn't get me anywhere and would be pushing him. Strong and professional. Bingo. I wanted him to view me that way, and so I had to act accordingly.

"Here's your coffee, Bradley," I said with confidence. I stood to the side of his desk so he could see the black tights and boots. "Did our ad make it into the *Times* on schedule?"

"Yes, it did," he replied, flipping pages of the newspaper. "Here it is." He slid the paper in my direction.

I placed my right hand palm-down on his desk and reviewed the ad, then turned the paper back to him and straightened, only to find him staring at me.

"Looks good," he said in a low voice.

He meant the ad, not you, Bebe, I told myself sternly.

"I'm pleased you approve," I managed to say around the lump in my throat.

He held my gaze. "Very much so." He opened his briefcase and pulled out a lined pad of notes. "More than I want to," he muttered.

I looked past him and out the window. He had given me an opening, but I wasn't going to take it. Neither would I tell him that Finelli had suggested I alert my lawyer to the likely possibility that I'd be arrested when the coroner's report came in. I'd call Jim myself. Bradley had demanded that I dole out every bit of information to him when it came to the police. I wouldn't. I refused to stay dependent on him.

"If there's nothing else . . . ," I said.

Bradley's disappointed expression stopped me cold. "Is there something more, Bradley?"

He sipped his coffee, then put the mug down carefully on his desk. His long fingers rubbed his temples and he took a deep breath. "No."

"All right."

"Wait a minute."

My hopes soared that he was ready to tell me something important, something life-changing about us. I had to hold my hands behind my back so he wouldn't see how badly I was shaking.

"I talked with Herman last night about the Merryweathers' lawsuit against us."

I held my right hand tightly in case it involuntarily flew out to smack him. "What did your uncle say?"

"The Merryweathers' lawyer convinced the couple that the sale of the store to Shires Enterprises was legal and binding. Kinker's death did not affect the transaction. Since they have no recourse they dropped the suit."

I forced a smile. "That's good news. If you'll excuse me, I'll return to my desk."

He nodded and again I sensed that he was disappointed in some way.

Or maybe it was just me who was frustrated because he didn't kiss me again, didn't take back his words of regret, hadn't asked me on a date, and hadn't confessed that seeing Danielle with her engagement ring had reminded him that he needed to pick out a ring for me.

Shut up, Bebe. Bradley isn't going to say any of those things. You're a fool.

I poured myself a cup of coffee and sat in my desk chair facing Danielle.

Normally quiet, Danielle practically bounced in her seat. "Do you still want the details, Bebe?"

"Yes!"

"I took your advice. I went home, made the coconut cake, put the roast and vegetables on a slow simmer, and then I rested for about half an hour. Then I filled the tub with scented water and relaxed. When I got out, I felt like a new woman. I applied my makeup and then put on a daring—at least for me—new dress I'd bought."

"You vixen, you."

"The dress was not only hot pink, but I shortened the hem to almost the length of some of your skirts, Bebe. After all, I see the way Bradley looks at you and I wanted Herb to look at me that way."

"How does Bradley look at me?" I asked.

Danielle laughed. "You know. All you have to do is lower the neck of your sweater and see the results for yourself."

"Never mind. How did Herb react?"

"His eyes kind of bulged and he kissed me as soon as he got in the door. Usually he waits until the end of the evening. We talked and laughed all through dinner—which he kept complimenting me on—and I sensed there was something going on. You know how you can read the emotions of the man you love."

"Maybe."

"After he helped clear the dishes away, we sat on the sofa and he got down on one knee. I tell you, Bebe, my heart was racing!"

"I'll bet."

Danielle looked at her ring. "He asked me if I'd do him the honor of becoming his wife and then he opened the ring box. I've already talked to my parents in Rochester and Herb and I are going to have a June wedding."

I sighed. "Do you think you'll quit working after you get married?"

"Oh, yes. Herb said he could support us and he wants to start a family."

Danielle and I divided up assignments and worked through the morning. My emotions flitted back and forth between happiness for Danielle and fear that any minute Snyder would show up and arrest me for murder.

At lunchtime, I grabbed my purse, intending to go outside and get some air along with my hot dog and Tab.

Descending the escalator, I saw that the store was the busiest it had been since Kinker's death. I caught Darlene's attention and she rolled her eyes at me while she hooked the clasp of a scarab bracelet around a girl's wrist.

"Do you want to grab a hot dog with me, Darlene?"

"Thanks, Bebe," she said in a false tone. "It's nice of you to think of me, but I can't leave the store at this time. Boss's orders."

"I'm sorry."

The girl ran to show her mother the bracelet.

Darlene brushed back a red curl. "I'll be fine," she whispered. "I'm only going home long enough to change clothes tonight. Stu's taking me out for a fancy dinner, remember? I just hope my mood improves by then. If not, a couple of whiskey sours should do the trick. That and a pair of earplugs tonight so I can sleep."

"A quiet dinner is exactly what you and Stu need to clear the air between you. As for Shirley—"

"There's nothing to be done about her right now."

The girl returned with her mother.

"Miss Bennett," Darlene said, "I believe you should ask Mr. Skidoo about his latest trick." She flicked her eyes in Raggedy Ann's direction.

"Thank you, Miss Roland. I will."

I searched through the crowd until I found Tom holding court near the middle of the sales floor. A large group of children surrounded him while he delighted them with juggling. I smiled, wondering who was really having the most fun, Tom or the children.

He grinned when he saw me. "Why, it's the lovely Miss Bennett, boys and girls." He stage-whispered to the children: "She's too pretty for me to squirt water at from my flower pin, don't you think?"

"No! Spray her!" a chorus of young voices answered.

I held out my arms. "Wait! I have a very important question for Mr. Skidoo. Let's see if he can answer it. If he can, I'll accept my fate. But if he can't, then I get away. Fair?"

The children grumbled.

I leaned down and whispered in Tom's ear, "I heard you have something to tell me about Raggedy Ann."

Tom leaned toward me, holding one big gloved hand to his ear in an exaggerated listening position. "What's that you say? How do you cure a headache? Let me see if I have the answer."

He whispered in my ear. "Raggedy Ann and the Cowboy are brother and sister."

I know my eyes went wide. Playing along with the game, I shook my head in the manner of one who has lost.

Tom turned to the children. "I knew it. How do you cure a headache? Put your head through a window and the pane will go away."

Everyone laughed, Tom the hardest.

I tried to scurry away, but he got me in the back with a shot of water.

The children laughed louder.

The sounds of their delight left me when the Teddy Bear closed the door behind me.

I walked up Fifth Avenue, crossed Forty-ninth Street, and stood in line at the hot-dog stand.

Now that I knew the Cowboy and Raggedy Ann were brother and sister, several questions popped into my head. Did Kinker find out they were siblings and threaten to expose their true relationship? It was against store policy for relatives to work at the store, which meant that the Cowboy and Raggedy Ann had both lied on their employment applications. If the old-fashioned Merryweathers had found out, both brother and sister would have been out of a job. Add that to Betty's affair with Kinker and Raggedy Ann had two motives to murder her former lover.

But had she acted alone? I'd seen firsthand how protective of her the Cowboy was. He had a crush on Mary the Princess and probably knew from his sister that Kinker had been coming on to the delicate Princess, not to mention what the clown had done to his sister.

Absently I paid for my hot dog and drink, added mustard and relish, and started walking back to the store.

Raggedy Ann could have lured Kinker into a conversation that kept him after the store closed. Then, when she and her brother thought everyone had left, the Cowboy might have thrust the knife into the clown's heart, killing him instantly. Then brother and sister had fled the store.

I frowned. If my thinking was on target, why had the Cowboy and Raggedy Ann chosen to alter one of the Pirate's knives? I could understand them not wanting to use a gun that would make a lot of noise, but did they have a reason to see the Pirate out of the store? If so, I couldn't think what the logic might be.

The Teddy Bear opened the door for me with his usual silent flourish, staying mutely in character. I wondered if he spoke to Darlene.

I ate at my desk listening to Danielle, who'd packed her lunch, prattle on about bridal dresses, the number of guests her parents would allow her to invite to the wedding, how good Herb would look in a pale blue tux, and whether or not she should chance having the reception outdoors.

After a while, we settled into work and the afternoon flew by. Still, my thoughts were never far from the investigation and Johnny kept singing "Secret Agent Man" in my head. If I wasn't thinking about how to prove Raggedy Ann had committed the crime, I was worrying about being arrested before I could prove anything.

Jim Lincoln returned my phone call just as the day was winding down. Danielle looked questioningly at me, but I waved her away with a smile and she left for the night.

"Thanks for calling, Jim."

"I'm sorry for getting back to you after business hours, Bebe. Long day in court."

"Well, in keeping with our policy of complete honesty, I wanted to tell you that Detective Finelli warned me that the coroner's report would be back in the next couple of days."

"When did you talk to Finelli?"

I wasn't about to tell Jim how I'd shared the information I'd learned while snooping around the store with Finelli. "He, um, was in the area and dropped in. He wanted to know if Snyder had treated me okay, which of course the detective did not. Then he said for me to warn you about the coroner's report."

"Sounds like Finelli is your friend."

Remembering how Jim Lincoln most likely thought of me as fast, I said, "I wouldn't call it a friendship. I've helped him on previous murder investigations. Maybe he feels beholden to me."

"Anything else?"

"No."

"Okay, if Snyder comes to arrest you, cooperate and tell him you will only talk with him in the presence of your lawyer. Then call me."

"Thanks, Jim."

I hung up the phone and dropped my head in my hands. Hearing Jim give instructions on what to do if I was arrested put me into a deeper state of panic.

"Daydreaming of me, girly?"

A shrill scream escaped me and I jumped out of my chair at the sound of Snyder's voice above me.

This was it! He'd gotten the coroner's report! He would lead me away in handcuffs!

Bradley sprang down the hallway.

"What's going on here?" he demanded.

"If you two were any sweeter together I might have to lay off my morning trip to the doughnut shop." Snyder came around to my side of the desk. I cringed.

"I asked you a question, Snyder," Bradley growled.

"Hey, what are you doing with my typewriter?"

Snyder had unplugged the machine and wrapped the cord around it. "See this electrical cord here, girly? They give murderers the electric chair. I'm just gathering evidence so you can meet that chair."

Trembling, I stood, unable to say a word.

Bradley suffered no such condition. "What the hell are you trying to do? Scare her to death? If you don't state your business and get out of here, I'm calling a friend who knows the mayor."

Snyder chuckled. The sound was like a pig oinking. "Keep your famous cool, pretty boy. I'm only here for the typewriter today. Ya see, I got a feeling the letter *q* might match the one in the killer's note to girly. Oh, sorry, I mean in girly's note to girly. The bottom of the *q* ain't drinking as much ink as the other letters in the note, poor fella. I'm taking him in for . . . questioning," Snyder ended and laughed at his own joke.

Relieved that I didn't have to go anywhere with the coarse detective, I found my voice. "You can't take my typewriter. How will I get any work done?"

Snyder laughed harder.

"That typewriter belongs to Shires Enterprises. You can't—"

Snyder smiled, tucking the typewriter under one arm. "Yes, I can. You two have a happy night together."

When he was out of sight, I slumped into my chair.

"Bebe, are you all right?" Bradley asked.

I looked at him like he was crazy.

"Let me get my briefcase and I'll walk you out."

I pulled my purse from the desk drawer, noting the dust around the edges where the typewriter used to sit on the table.

"Let's go. Where's your coat?" Bradley asked, suit jacket on and briefcase in hand.

"In the storeroom."

He let me take the lead on the down escalator.

"I'm going to call my contact in the mayor's office in the morning, Bebe. Something needs to be done about Snyder. He's a public servant. . . ."

I looked downstairs, shaking my head . . . and didn't hear anything else he said.

I gripped the handrail and ran down the last few steps.

In a horrible case of déjà vu, I saw Mr. Skidoo lying under the Jungle animals, not moving.

But this time, it was Tom.

Chapter Sixteen

"No!" I yelled, hurrying to Tom's side. He was lying facedown on his stomach. "They've stabbed him just like they did Kinker!"

Bradley's strong arm blocked me from getting closer. He turned, gripped my shoulders, and held my gaze with his blue eyes.

"Bebe, we don't know that. You are not to touch him, whatever the relationship is between the two of you. I don't want you implicated in the attack. Stay back and let me check on him."

He waited until I nodded before he bent at Tom's side. "He's been struck on the back of his head."

"Is he bleeding?"

"Not much."

"Tell me Tom isn't dead!" I cried.

Bradley eased Tom over, then checked for a pulse. "He's not dead."

"Oh, thank God! Wait a minute. You're not just saying that, are you?"

"Don't be ridiculous. It looks as if the head wound is the only injury. He hasn't been stabbed. We'd better call for an ambulance, Bebe. You do it. The number is taped on the phone by the cash registers. The last thing we need right now is for medical personnel to find you standing over an unconscious Mr. Skidoo.''

I completed the call and returned to Bradley's side. My gaze traveled around the floor. "I wonder what they hit him with. Do you see anything?"

"No, and if you do, *do not touch it,*" Bradley ordered.

"There!" I cried, pointing at a child-sized rocking chair. The pink chair was on its side behind one of the trees. A brownish wet substance spread over the splintered bottom of its rocker. The little rocking chairs were kept in Raggedy Ann's area. Raggedy Ann, who was currently number one on my Top Ten List of Suspects.

Bradley stepped closer to peer at the chair. "Looks like the weapon, all right. You do have an eye for details, Bebe."

Scared and miserable on behalf of Tom, I didn't even allow the compliment to sink in. If it wasn't for me playing secret agent girl and enlisting help, Tom would not have been in danger. Hadn't Detective Finelli warned me that one of my operatives could get hurt? Guilt threatened to overwhelm me.

Long minutes passed until a police officer arrived, along with an ambulance. Tom had yet to regain consciousness.

Bradley and I stood together while the medical guys checked Tom over. They pronounced that he probably had a concussion, having received a strong blow to the head.

"Will he be okay?" I asked nervously.

"Can't say, lady. We're going to transport him to the hospital so one of the docs can look him over. But the sooner he wakes up, the better, I'll tell you that much."

As they lifted Tom and put him on the stretcher, I

silently prayed for him to wake. I would have taken a cab directly to the hospital, but I had Shirley to consider. Darlene was out on her date with Stu. I'd have to go home first and check on our houseguest before I could go to the hospital.

I watched as the ambulance containing Tom drove away from the store, lights flashing.

Bradley had been talking to the dark-haired police officer, who was making out a report.

"Officer Roy, Miss Bennett," he said, and tipped his black uniform hat at me. "If I could ask you to tell me how you and Mr. Williams found the victim?"

"Didn't Bradley already explain?"

"Yes, but I'd like to hear the story from your point of view."

I reached up and twirled a piece of my hair. "There's not much to say. Bradley and I were riding the escalator down from the second floor when I spotted Tom and ran over. I didn't touch him. Bradley checked Tom's pulse, then I called for an ambulance. That's it."

"Can you think of anyone who would want to hurt Tom Stevens? Or Mr. Skidoo, the clown?"

Bradley and I exchanged glances.

"No. Tom is well liked," I said.

"Obviously not by everyone, Miss Bennett. Mr. Williams, I'll be taking this rocking chair to the police station as evidence."

"I understand."

The officer picked up the chair and left, promising he'd be in touch.

Bradley turned out the lights, leaving the sales floor in the dim light of the bulbs lining the front window. "Come on, kid, you've had a rough day. I'll take you to dinner."

Oh! Bradley wanted to take me out for a meal.

Oh! I had to go home to Shirley.

Oh.

"Thanks for the offer, but Darlene's out and I have a houseguest I don't want to leave alone," I said, watching his face closely.

His expression tightened. "A houseguest. Fine by me. I do insist on taking you home."

"Okay. I'll get my coat."

A few minutes went by before a taxi stopped for us. The deep, almost mournful sighing of the wind around the skyscrapers blew our hair. I kept sneaking glances at Bradley's dreamy face. Was it my imagination or was he peeved about the houseguest? Did he think I was hosting some man? I had to put my hand over my mouth before I laughed out loud. Then I thought of Tom, which quelled my humor.

In the cab, that familiar sense of intimacy came over me, the one that riding with Bradley in the close confines of the backseat brought on. The cab radio played "Love Potion Number 9."

"I'll be leaving the office early tomorrow. I plan to drive out of town," Bradley said, jolting me back to reality.

"Have fun," I gritted out, imagining him taking a pretty blonde to a cozy restaurant in the woods somewhere.

"Thanks." Bradley faced me. "Will you be going to the hospital to visit Tom or does your houseguest require all of your time?"

I fell into the blue of his eyes. "I don't know."

His gaze dropped to my lips. "You don't know?"

A change in subject was in order. "Who do you think wanted to hurt Tom? You know it had to be one of the store characters."

He sighed. "There's no chance of you leaving this to the police, is there?"

I smirked. "You mean to Snyder's brilliant detective abilities?"

"You know my stand on the matter. A girl your age should not be investigating crimes."

There he went again about my age. I leaned closer to him, hoping he could smell my trademark perfume. In what I thought was a sultry whisper, I said, "I know you don't want me to get hurt, Bradley. But I do wish you'd give me a little credit for being able to discern what can hurt me and what can't."

"Christ," he muttered, and put his hand around my head, moving in for a kiss.

His lips were inches from my mouth when he suddenly looked out the taxi window.

Neither of us had noticed that the cab had come to a halt in front of my building.

I groaned, then swung around to see what had stopped Bradley.

A man sat on my front stoop holding a yellow rose. At my arrival, he got up slowly. His hair was cut short and looked to be a mix of brown and gray.

Bradley withdrew to his corner of the backseat and folded his arms across his chest. "Is he your houseguest?"

Recognition hit me. "No, but I know him and I have to go. Thanks for the ride, Bradley. Hopefully we can keep the attack on Tom out of the newspapers."

I scooted out of my seat and slammed the door of the cab.

The taxi roared off.

"Harry!" I exclaimed, a big smile on my face. "If it wasn't for the army jacket, I wouldn't have known you. Your beard is gone and you've gotten your hair cut. You're a handsome man!"

He looked at the sidewalk. "That's nice of you to say, Miss Sweet Face. They've been good to me at the Methodist church. I've been going to the meetings. Hell, I'm even helping out around the grounds since they're letting me stay in a small room in the back. It's just temporary until I'm ready to look for work. Here, this flower is for you."

I clapped my hands and took it. "That's wonderful news, Harry. You didn't have to get me a flower, but it's very pretty. Thank you. I'm so happy to see you like this."

He gave me a sheepish grin. "Bet you weren't too pleased that your date saw me and didn't kiss you."

"It wasn't a date. That was, um, you know, *him*."

"The one you love." Harry shook his head. "What do you think drove me to drink? My wife leaving me . . ."

"Harry, she didn't leave you on purpose. Cancer took her."

Tears formed in his eyes but did not fall. "It was years ago. I fell into drinking because of her death, but stayed an alcoholic because of me. If it weren't for you giving me the name—"

I touched his arm. "No, Harry. *You* went to get help. I merely gave you an address."

I smiled and he smiled back.

"I need to go back there now. Next meeting is at seven."

I nodded. "Best be on time."

"I'll see you again, Bebe. In the meantime, that guy better figure out what he's got and put a ring on your finger. He's the jealous type. You should have seen the way he looked at me."

"Be safe!" I called.

I watched Harry walking steadily down Sixty-fifth Street and felt so proud of him I could burst.

My nose detected the smell of homemade chicken soup as I unlocked the door to my apartment.

Shirley came to greet me, wearing another attractive Empire-waist dress—a smart choice, as the style was popular and allowed her to almost conceal her pregnancy.

"Hello, Bebe. What a lovely rose. I went to the market and have chicken soup on the stove."

"You must be feeling better," I said, taking off my black trench coat and laying it across the back of the sectional. "And the soup smells delicious."

Shirley nodded. "I haven't been sick since this morning. Would you like a bowl of soup?"

"I'd love one."

"Come on into the kitchen and sit. I've laid out the papers regarding Drew's embezzlement."

While I sat, Shirley ladled out two bowls of hot soup, and grabbed spoons, napkins, and sodas from the fridge. Careful not to spill anything on the papers, I let the soup cool while reading through them.

Shirley explained how Drew had used the old trick of keeping two sets of books. She provided proof in the form of receipts and invoices until I gained a good grasp of the situation. Drew had ripped off Shires Enterprises to the tune of almost one hundred thousand dollars! Wait until Bradley's uncle saw this. Bradley would be named the heir. He would see that I was smart and capable. Maybe even kissable without regret.

"Bebe, are you listening? You seem to have gone away somewhere."

"I'm sorry, Shirley. I was thinking ahead."

"Ahead to what will happen when Mr. Shires finds out about this?"

"Yes," I admitted.

"Do you think you'll get a promotion? A large bonus?"

My brows came together. "I hadn't thought of that."

Shirley sighed. "Then it's true."

"What's true?"

Shirley put down her spoon, stood and retrieved the saltine crackers, and came back to the table. "Drew told me that you and Bradley Williams are having an affair."

I choked on my Tab and fell into a coughing fit.

Shirley sat calmly until I was in control of myself.

"Bradley and I are *not* having an affair, despite what Drew thinks."

"Drew told me that he'd walked in on the two of you going at it on Bradley's office sofa."

Heat suffused my face. "Bradley and I are . . . attracted to each other. A couple of times we acted on that attraction, but it never went further than kissing."

"Is he the one who gave you that huge hickey on your neck?"

My hand went to my throat. She must have seen it last night. For some reason, I didn't want to explain my feelings for Bradley to Shirley. I felt sorry for her, had taken her in, wanted the evidence she'd given me, but when it came down to it, I didn't know her well enough to tell her I was in love with Bradley.

"You don't need to answer. I understand how it is. But let me warn you so that you don't make the same mistake I did. Bradley Williams has a strong reputation as a playboy. He won't marry you because you give him these papers."

Horrified that she'd figured out my plan and feeling rather small, I said, "I'm not giving the papers to Bradley. I'm sending them to Herman Shires. I know about Bradley's man-about-town ways."

"Do you think you'll be the one to change him, Bebe?"

I felt a sharp jab of pain in my chest, as if a block of ice had formed over my heart. "Probably not," I whispered.

"Drew told me that when Bradley was around twenty years old—an important time in a young man's life—he met a girl at the University of Missouri, where he was studying business. I forget her name, but Drew said she was a beautiful blonde, outgoing, popular. She was Bradley's first love. I think Drew said it was almost a year into the relationship when Bradley found out through her parents that she was engaged to a boy at another school. Bradley was devastated."

My mouth hung open. "Are you sure about this?"

"Well, I wasn't there and Drew is the one who told me—pillow talk, you know—so I guess you'll have to draw your own conclusions. According to Drew, after that girl lied to him, Bradley said he'd never be able to tell if a woman was a liar or not. Drew thinks that's why Bradley never stays with one woman for very long. Of course, Drew doesn't either, so perhaps it's a family trait."

I sat motionless. The movie screen in my mind unfurled and replayed a scene from a memorial Bradley and I had attended during another of my investigations. I remembered what Bradley had said that day.

"I, ah, live my life the way I do because . . . well, damn it, because although I believe in marriage, I've become jaded over the past ten years. I don't know if I'll ever change."

When I'd suggested that he only needed to find the right woman, he'd paused and replied, *"Someday. Maybe."*

"Bebe! I've upset you, haven't I?" Shirley said.

I blinked and looked at her. "No, Shirley, it's all right."

"I'm sorry if I have, but I just don't want to see another girl in my situation if I can help it."

I forced myself to smile. "Don't give it another thought. Let's talk about you and the adorable baby you're going to have. Listen, do your parents know where you are?"

"No."

"How about your grandmother? Where is she?"

A wistful look came over Shirley's face. "Grandma Evelyn lives in Florida. She's the one who taught me how to make this soup. My parents told me she didn't want to speak to me."

The soup was delicious, even if I couldn't bring myself to eat much at the moment.

"What if your family is worried? Shouldn't you call someone? You said you haven't even spoken to your grandmother. Although, I should say, I did have hopes of helping you find a boyfriend here. Someone to marry."

Shirley got up and started clearing the table. "You've got to be kidding. First of all, no man wants to marry a pregnant woman. Second, I don't want to get involved with another man right now. I'm still angry and hurt over what happened with Drew. That's why I warned you about Bradley."

Well, there went all my plans for Shirley. "At least think about talking to your grandmother, okay? You can use the phone even though it's long distance."

"I'll think about it," Shirley said, washing the dishes.

I went to the wall phone. "Speaking of the phone, I need to call the hospital. A friend of mine had an accident."

Shirley didn't answer, apparently already deep in thought. I pushed "0" and dragged the receiver on its long cord into the living room.

While the operator connected me to the hospital, I sank to the floor, suddenly very tired. Hearing Shirley talk about Bradley seemed to have drained every ounce of my energy.

"Nurses' station, Nurse Janet speaking."

"Hello. My name is Bebe Bennett and I was hoping you could tell me how a patient is doing."

"Name?"

"Tom Stevens. He was taken there with a concussion, unconscious. Did he wake up yet?"

"Are you a relative?"

I crossed my fingers and made a mental note to update my confessions notebook. "I'm his cousin."

"Mr. Stevens did wake up. The doctor examined him and found him to have a mild concussion."

"That's great news. May I speak with Tom?"

"That's not possible at this time. He's sleeping naturally for the first time since the concussion. However, I don't see on his chart that the doctor has restricted visitors for tomorrow."

"Thank you. I'll come see him then."

Relief hit me. I'd never forgive myself if something worse had happened to Tom.

Shirley walked by and said she was going to lie down.

I followed her into my room and selected clothes

for tomorrow: a V-necked chocolate brown dress with
gold-colored stripes, brown pumps, and a brown, yellow, and pink paisley print scarf to cover my hickey.

Later, I washed my face and curled up on the
sectional.

Time was running out for me to find the killer.
Soon, either I would be in jail or someone else would
be hurt.

An idea suddenly burst in my brain. The personnel
files! I needed to see them. I could check on all the
store characters, find out their backgrounds, find out
if Raggedy Ann and the Cowboy had falsified their
employment applications. Those files could be a trea-
sure trove of information—information that could
clear my name.

The only snag in the plan was that Bradley was
keeping them at his house for safekeeping during the
investigation. I remembered how he'd had to bring
Kinker's file from home to show Jim Lincoln. I wondered if Bradley had the file or if Jim did. Boy, would
Kinker's file make for interesting reading.

I missed Darlene then. I wanted to talk to her about
Bradley and put the plan forming in my mind to her,
see what she thought.

Darlene and I had done our share of breaking and
entering, but Bradley's house?

He would be furious. *If* he found out.

Bradley would not be home tomorrow night. He
had told me so himself.

He was driving out of town for the evening. Probably to meet some blonde.

He'd never find out as long as Darlene and I were
careful.

Chapter Seventeen

"You're down in the dumps this morning, Darlene," I said, slipping on the brown pumps that went with my dress. "Didn't you have a good time with Stu last night?"

"Dinner was great, but the evening went downhill afterward. Are you almost ready to leave for work?"

"I just need to tie this scarf. Can you help me adjust it?"

Darlene rose from where she'd been slumped on the sectional. She chuckled but the sound was hollow. "I'm an expert at covering hickeys."

I held my hair out of the way while her fingers worked the silk around my neck.

"How did your date with Stu go wrong?"

Darlene sighed. "Look, Bebe, I don't want an argument this early in the morning, okay?"

"Hey, I'm cool. You can tell me anything."

Darlene gave the scarf a little snap, then looked at me. "Stu proposed to me and I said no."

My eyes went wide. "Stu asked you to marry him? Did he have a ring?"

"Yes and no."

"Darlene Roland! How could you have refused

him? Stu must be seriously bummed out. That man loves you to pieces and I thought you loved him."

"I knew you'd fight with me about this," Darlene said, grabbing her coat.

I picked up my black trench coat and slid my arms into the sleeves. Clearly I had to take a more gentle approach with Darlene. "Honey, could you tell me why you rejected him? Are you two even a couple anymore?"

She lowered her voice and pointed to my bedroom. "See the condition Shirley is in? I don't want children, Bebe. You're the one who wants a domestic life. It's not for me. I want to fly, I want to be free, I want a career."

We left the apartment carrying black umbrellas, since rain was washing the city clean. Outside yellow, red, and brown leaves on the sidewalk and in the trees glistened. I took a deep breath, inhaling the scent of the city I loved.

Walking toward Lexington and the nearest bus stop, I said, "What does Stu want?"

Darlene shook her red curls. "He wants to marry me."

"Right, but did you two talk about children?"

"No."

"Did you tell him your feelings about a career?"

"No."

I wanted to shake her. Controlling myself with an effort, I said, "Darlene, you're my best friend. You're a good person, loving and caring. God knows where I'd be if we hadn't met on my flight up from Richmond."

"You would have managed."

We reached the bus stop. I faced her, our umbrellas making it hard for me to get close. "Hear me out because I'm not done."

"Go ahead. I can't stop you anyway."

"You know a lot about men, but there's one thing you don't know about them."

She looked at me askance. "Bebe, I'm not insulting you, but I doubt there's something about men that you know and I don't."

The bus came and we found seats.

"Darlene, I'm not talking about sex. You don't know how to let a man love you."

Her face fell.

I reached for her hand and held it tight. "I have my daddy, and even though he can be a real pain in the you-know-where, we love each other. You didn't have that with your father. I've noticed that sometimes you have a hard time telling Stu your deepest feelings. Why don't you try talking to him about how you feel about having children? He may be relieved you'd rather not be a mother. Stu's a jet-setter. Maybe he'd love to travel the world with you."

Tears formed in Darlene's eyes.

I reached into my purse and handed her a tissue. "Come on, I didn't mean to make you cry. Goodness, you'll ruin your mascara. You don't want one of your false eyelashes to fall off, do you?"

That brought a watery chuckle. Darlene whipped out her compact and dried around her eyes. "I suppose I should talk to Stu about those things."

"You might be surprised at his answers. Plus, if you married him, you'd never be without breath mints," I joked, referring to Stu's status as the heir to the Minty-Mouth Breath Mint fortune. "By the way, did you say he didn't have a ring?"

"No, he said he figured I was the type of gal who would want to pick out her own."

"Gee, Stu seems to already know how independent you are."

"Damn you, Bebe. How come you're so wise?"

I laughed. "You've got to be kidding. If I was smart, I'd be looking for another job and getting over Bradley."

She hugged me, and then I told her what Shirley had said about Bradley the night before.

Darlene looked out the rain-streaked window before replying. "Now it's your turn to listen to me, Bebe. Even if all of what Shirley said about Bradley is true, I've seen him around you. I've told you before and I'll tell you again: Bradley views you as different from other women. He respects you, whether you know it or not. He is fighting himself where you're concerned. You have only to look in the mirror at your neck to realize that he wants you physically."

A shiver ran through me at hearing her speak those words out loud.

"And he's protective of you, which means he cares."

"What am I supposed to do, Darlene? Wait around for the next ten years until he finally trusts me? He's never spoken a word of love to me, and what's worse, he's apologized every time he's kissed me."

"Yep, he's struggling all right."

"I don't know how much longer I can stand it, but the thought of giving up is equally impossible. Of course it may all be a moot point if I'm in jail."

We got off the bus and began walking the three long blocks to Fifth Avenue.

"That reminds me," Darlene said. "I never had a chance to tell you about my trip to the library yesterday."

"Did you find out something about the Princess? Is she really a former Miss Connecticut?"

"Nope. Not unless her real name is Gail, Diana,

Florence, or Joyce and she forgot to tell us. Those are the last four girls who were Miss Connecticut. I told you the Princess wasn't a pageant girl."

I grabbed her arm as we were about to turn the corner and reach the store. "Don't look for Tom today. Someone conked him over the head with a child's rocking chair last night after closing."

"What? Oh my God!"

I nodded. "Bradley and I found him. Tom's in the hospital, but I checked on him last night and he's okay. I thought we'd go visit him at lunchtime. Can you tell Mallory you have an appointment at noon?"

"Sure. He's a private guy, but I can tell he likes me."

I snorted. "You're the only one that snob favors. We need to get into the personnel files and find out these people's backgrounds."

"Why haven't we done that before?"

"Bradley is keeping the files at his town house."

"Well, that just brings all kinds of thoughts to mind."

"I hope one of them is breaking and entering, because that's the plan for tonight. Bradley will be out of town so the coast will be clear."

"Sounds like a blast."

We resumed walking.

Just before the Teddy Bear swung the door open for us, Darlene said, "At the very least we'll find out if it's boxers or briefs for Mr. Williams."

"Darlene!" I protested.

The two of us were laughing when we parted ways on the sales floor.

Up in the executive offices, Danielle had arrived before me and made coffee.

"Aren't you the early bird?" I greeted her, smiling.

She glowed. "When I woke up this morning, I had gobs of energy. I'm so excited about my engagement." She held out her hand and admired her ring.

I laughed. "If I had an engagement ring, I'd probably be looking at it all day long."

"That reminds me. Mr. Williams is hibernating in his office—you know, the way he does."

I rolled my eyes. "I see from his calendar that he has a ten o'clock appointment with the sales rep from Mattel. Has Bradley had his coffee?"

"I thought I'd leave that to you," Danielle said and winked. "By the way, that's a pretty scarf. Remember, I predicted scarves in your future."

I laughed. "Maybe Herb will let you read tea leaves until your first child is born."

She giggled. "Hey, where's your typewriter?"

I made a face. "The police took it as 'evidence' yesterday after you left. I hope there's another one around here somewhere."

"There is. It's beside that empty desk behind me."

"Thanks. I'll get it in a minute," I said, and went to fill Bradley's St. Louis Cardinals mug.

When I knocked on his door, he said, "Come in."

"Good morning, Bradley. I brought your coffee."

"Thanks," he replied. "I called the hospital and your friend Tom is doing well."

"Yes, I know. Darlene and I are going to visit him at noon."

He sipped his coffee nonchalantly, but I caught his gaze lingering on my legs.

"That's nice of you girls. There was nothing in this morning's newspaper about this latest incident with Mr. Skidoo. I'm going to tell Mallory that Tom is out sick today. When you see him at the hospital, ask him to go along with this arrangement."

"I know he will."

"I'm certain you'll be able to convince him one way or another, Bebe."

"What do you mean by that?" I said, placing my hands on my hips.

"You're dating Tom. I'm sure he's wrapped around your little finger. Does he know about your houseguest and the guy outside your apartment?"

My temper flared. Before I let my tongue loose, I remembered how Bradley believed all women lied to him. I had to tell the truth.

"Tom and I went out on one date. We decided to be friends who hang out with each other occasionally. My houseguest is female and the guy outside my building is the wino who frequents my block. You've seen him before. I've been talking to him about getting sober and he came by to let me know how it was going."

"You don't have to explain your personal life to me," Bradley said in a tone that clearly indicated the opposite.

His phone rang before I could grab him by his light blue tie and choke him.

"Shall I answer it?"

"No. Close the door when you leave."

"Don't forget you have a meeting at ten. . . ."

He waved me off, speaking into the phone.

I shut the door without slamming it, cracking a hole in it with my shoe, or writing the word *impossible* in lipstick on its cream paint to vent my frustration.

Back at my desk, I told Danielle that Tom was out sick and got out the accounts log. I found the extra typewriter, loaded it with a fresh ribbon, and typed up a quick summary of our business with Mattel for Bradley to have in hand when he spoke to their representative.

I grabbed the report, noted that Bradley's phone line was not lit, and went down the hall toward his office.

To my surprise, he emerged from his office and met me halfway with an angry look on his face.

"Bebe, that was Jim Lincoln on the phone."

"Oh, God, has he heard anything?"

"Not that I know of, but then it seems I'm not being kept in the loop regarding the murder of Mel Kinker."

"What?"

He leaned in closer, his gaze hard. "You lied, Bebe. You lied to me."

"What on earth are you talking about?"

"You didn't tell me that Finelli gave you a heads-up about the coroner's report."

"That's not a lie! I forgot to mention it. How can you call that a lie? I did tell Jim and . . . and . . . I was going to tell you. . . ."

He stood straight and nodded his head. I had been tried and convicted. It was written all over his face.

"Bradley, you're not being reasonable."

"Excuse me. I must speak with Mallory regarding your boyfriend's absence today." He brushed past me and headed for the elevator.

I followed him. "Bradley, why do you keep me on as your executive secretary, your assistant, if you don't trust me?"

The elevator doors opened and he walked inside, arms folded across his chest.

He didn't answer.

I stomped back to his office, threw the Mattel report on his chair, and went back to my desk, shaking.

Danielle whispered, "The course of true love is never easy."

"Is there something wrong between you and Herb? Because I don't know of anyone else around here who's in love."

"I'll bet you a Tab there is."

Betting. I suddenly remembered the racing form in Mallory's office. Wasn't betting on horses kind of weird for someone as stuck-up as the store manager? I made a mental note to check Mallory's personnel record tonight.

"Bebe?"

"What exactly is the wager?"

She whispered, "I'll bet you a case of Tab that Mr. Williams is in love with you."

"You're on. Start saving your money."

In unison, we both began typing. Bradley had deposited a number of assignments in my in-box, some of which I delegated to Danielle. I didn't look up when he returned, and he walked past me without a word. I gritted my teeth. While I worked, I prayed the darn coroner's report would not come back before I could execute my plan to break into Bradley's home that night.

On the way to the hospital, I filled Darlene in on how Bradley had practically called me a liar to my face. She told me to take my own advice and talk it out with him.

The sound of female giggling met my ears as Darlene and I approached Tom's room.

". . . and there I was, onstage in front of hundreds

of people with the back of my pants ripped . . .
Bebe! Darlene!"

Tom sat like a prince propped up on pillows, three
pretty nurses surrounding his bed, an empty tray of
food off to one side.

I smiled. "Hi, Tom."

"Looks like you're in a lot of pain there, clown
boy," Darlene said.

Tom moved his hands to the top of his head. "Like
you wouldn't believe, babe. I'm surprised they haven't
wrapped my head like a mummy."

One of the nurses said, "We would have, but we
didn't want to cover your handsome face."

Tom grinned.

"Ladies, we brought the patient a couple of hot
dogs. Would you mind letting us feed him," Darlene
said, voice laced with sarcasm.

The nurses began to leave, waving as they went out
the door.

Tom called after them. "Don't forget my sponge
bath! And if you bring me some balloons from the gift
shop, I'll blow them up into some interesting shapes!"

Darlene closed the door so that the three of us
were alone.

I brought out the hot dogs. "Tom, are you still
hungry?"

"I'm always hungry, and there's nothing like hot
dogs from a New York street vendor to make a man
happy."

I laughed and arranged his food on the tray that
swung around in front of him.

I passed a hot dog and a Tab to Darlene, then said,
"Tom, you look like you're feeling good."

"And you're being treated well," Darlene added.

He spread his arms wide. "If a guy's gotta be

knocked over the head to get a bed, beautiful women waiting on him, and three square meals a day, hey, I'm there."

"Are they releasing you today?" I asked.

"Not until tomorrow morning. They're keeping me for observation, and I like the sound of that."

"Will you be able to work tomorrow?" Darlene asked.

Tom nodded. "I'm fine, other than a headache. They've got me on some wild pills, though, so I'm not feeling a thing right now."

"Did you see who hit you?" I asked.

"No, but I think it's safe to assume whoever killed Kinker was warning me off the investigation. I didn't even know what happened until the fuzz told me."

I bit my lip. "Tom, I'm sorry I got you mixed up in this. I never thought you'd get hurt."

"Babe, don't get bent. I've got a hard head," he said, knocking on it as if to prove the point. "What we need to figure out is who did it. My money's on Betty, our Raggedy Ann."

"Why her?" Darlene asked.

Tom shrugged. "Betty's been flirting with me, getting nowhere, she lets it slip that the Cowboy is her brother, and maybe later she realizes that I'm one of Miss Bond's operatives."

"I'm just glad you're okay," I said.

"What kind of man would I be if I let a kid's rocking chair take me out?" Tom asked. "Have I missed anything on the investigation?"

I threw the foil wrapping from my hot dog in the trash and took a swallow of Tab. "Not much. Tonight's the big night, though. Darlene and I are going to break into Bradley's town house."

"What!"

"Bebe, do you think it's smart to tell him? We need to keep this between us for Tom's safety. He can't rat on us if he doesn't know anything," Darlene said.

"Cat's outta the bag now," Tom said. "I'm sorry I'll miss this. How are you planning to get inside and what's in there that you're after?"

I cleared my throat. "Bradley has the personnel files. I want to get a good look at them. Believe it or not, some of the store characters have been lying about their backgrounds."

Tom laughed. "I can't believe that," he said, feigning shock.

"How are we planning to get inside, Bebe?" Darlene asked.

"Don't we have that metal cuticle thing?" I asked.

Tom put a hand to his head. "I need to sneak out of here and watch this."

"No, you don't," Darlene told him. To me she said, "Yeah, we have that, and our metal nail files."

"A butter knife," Tom interrupted.

Darlene and I looked at him.

Tom managed to look sheepish. "When I was a kid, I always carried a butter knife I stole from my friend Barry's house. My parents would lock me out if I came home late, and I'd have to break into my own house."

No one spoke.

Then I started snickering. Tom joined in.

Darlene remained unaffected. "Do we have a butter knife, Bebe?"

"Of course we do."

"Are you guys gonna dress in all black?" Tom asked. "Put stockings over your heads?"

Darlene rose. "Time for us to go, clown boy. Try not to suffer while you're here. We'll see you tomorrow."

She stood by the door waiting for me.

I leaned over and kissed Tom on the cheek. "I'll tell you everything when you come into the store. Miss Bond signing out."

"Groovy. I can't wait to hear what happens."

Chapter Eighteen

Bradley kept me snowed under with work for the rest of the day. We didn't engage in any conversation other than "Thank you" and "You're welcome." Danielle and I kept quiet and typed, filed, and answered phones until I wanted to bang my head against the file cabinet. My frustration with Bradley grew until I found myself glad to be invading his privacy that night. I might even check the contents of his fridge.

Just after four o'clock, he came bustling out of his office, briefcase in hand, and dropped an order for Mattel on my desk.

"I need that typed and in tomorrow's mail, please."

"Yes, Bradley."

He tapped his fingers on the edge of my desk. "Will Mr. Skidoo be out again tomorrow?"

"Tom will be here, but not when we first open. Though I'd guess he'll be ready for work by midday."

"Very well. Have a good evening," he said in his Mr. Strict Boss voice.

"Danielle," he called out, "thanks for your hard work today."

Her face reflected surprise at being singled out, but she managed, "Thank you, Mr. Williams."

Bradley left without thanking me. I mentally added his bathroom medicine cabinet to my list of tonight's sleuthing.

Darlene and I left the store separately, but met at the corner and managed to snag a cab for the ride home. We had a lot of preparations to make.

"I saw Bradley leave early."

"Yes."

"Did the two of you talk about how you really didn't lie to him?"

"No."

"Why not?"

"He hardly spoke to me after I got back from the hospital. I just got madder and madder at him. And now he's driven out of town with some blonde—"

Darlene raised her eyebrows. "He told you he had a date?"

"No, but why else would he drive out of the city unless it was to have a romantic evening in the woods somewhere, probably a cozy dinner by the fire? Then maybe they'll spend the night at a rustic inn. She's probably a masseuse—"

"Stop!" Darlene yelled.

The cab pulled to the curb and screeched to a halt, nearly catapulting Darlene and me into the front seat.

She apologized to the driver, who grumbled but barged right back into traffic.

I picked up my purse from where it had fallen on the floor. "Darlene, what made you do that?"

Letting out a slow breath, she said, "I was trying to stop your imagination from running wild, not the cab."

"Oh."

"Is it possible that Bradley is visiting his parents or other relatives?"

"No, Darlene. They all live in Missouri. Please stop trying to make excuses for what can only be Bradley's night of lurid passion."

She burst out laughing.

So did the driver.

I shot her the hairy eyeball and whispered, "No tip," as we got out of the cab.

Darlene tipped him anyway and we made our way up to our apartment.

Shirley heard us at the door and unlocked it for us. She wore her blue nightgown and matching robe. "Hi, girls. How was your day?"

"Fine," Darlene said.

"Okay," I replied. "You're looking better, Shirley. How are you feeling?"

As we took our coats and shoes off, Shirley said, "Actually, I have good news. Bebe, I took your suggestion and called my grandma Evelyn in Florida. I'll leave you some money for the long-distance call."

"Thank you," Darlene said.

"It's not necessary," I said. "What did your grandmother say?"

"She cried when she heard my voice. Apparently the whole family has been worried about me. Grandma Evelyn told me I could come and live with her in Florida for as long as I want. I accepted her offer."

"That's wonderful, Shirley!" I exclaimed.

"Sure is," Darlene chimed in. "When are you leaving?"

Darlene stood too far away for me to kick her, so I smiled brightly at Shirley to make up for my roommate's lack of sensitivity.

"Grandma wired money to the train station. I've

got a seat on the six o'clock train headed south tomorrow."

"I'll have to come home early from work and see you off," I said.

Shirley chuckled. "No, it's six in the morning, not afternoon."

Darlene groaned and went into the kitchen, dragging a pot out of the cabinet with more noise than I thought necessary.

Shirley continued. "Grandma even offered to fly me down, but I don't think it's a good idea for pregnant women to fly."

"You're probably right. I'm happy for you, Shirley. I thought perhaps you'd decide to stay here in New York and get a job."

"No one would hire a pregnant woman, Bebe. Besides, I'm tired of the big city. Florida will be a nice change."

"Will you tell Drew when the baby is born?"

Shirley looked at the floor. "Probably. It is his baby, whether he wants to believe it or not. If he rejects the child, I'll raise it on my own."

"That's very brave of you."

"I'm no saint, Bebe. Speaking of Drew, I noticed you didn't take the papers in to work today."

"I'll mail them tomorrow, I promise."

Darlene had her famous macaroni and cheese casserole with tomatoes ready in no time and the three of us sat down to eat. Afterward, Shirley thanked us for allowing her to stay at our apartment and went to bed, saying she needed her rest.

When she was out of earshot, Darlene said, "If she wakes me up at five in the morning to catch that train . . ."

"You'll go back to sleep. That was most likely the best time she could get out of here. Remember she's pregnant and has to sleep on a train tomorrow night."

Darlene shuddered.

"When are you going to talk to Stu?" I asked.

"I might drop by his house after we're done with our criminal activity for the evening. Breaking and entering always puts me in the mood for a romp in the hay."

"Make sure none of that hay keeps you from talking honestly with Stu."

"Yes, Ann Landers."

While we were cleaning the kitchen, I convinced Darlene that even though it would be dark, we should still wear black as Tom had suggested.

Half an hour later, we met in the living room. We both had on black slacks and black jewel-neck sweaters, staples for any girl's wardrobe, especially sleuthing girls.

"I'm taking my purse, so we can put our tools in it." I hoisted the strap over my shoulder.

"Why are you taking a purse? And such a large one?"

"I have to have something to carry my money and my notebook around in. It's too bad we don't have one of those little tape recorders that are really cameras. That way, we could photograph the files and—"

Darlene held up a hand. "I'll get the butter knife. You get the nail stuff."

After a brief discussion about coats, we decided to brave the dark, chilly evening without them. Darlene ran back inside to get a flashlight, which she threw into my purse with a loud clunk.

Bradley lived on West Seventy-fifth Street. Since that was all the way around the other side of Central

Park, we took a cab. I decided it would be safer if the driver dropped us off right in front of Bradley's town house. That way we wouldn't be seen walking down the street dressed as we were, mistaken for beatniks in this upscale part of town.

A satisfied smile crossed my face when we reached number seventy-nine and saw that the town house was dark except for a light above the door. I paid the cabbie and Darlene and I got out. It was just before eight o'clock and the street was empty.

"So this is where he lives?" Darlene asked.

"Yes, isn't it modern?"

The front door was white with an oval glass inset. The oval theme was repeated on the upstairs windows. The rest of the house was black-painted brick. On the ground, behind a black wrought iron gate, black and white marble squares led to the front steps.

"The man has taste," Darlene said. "Is there a back way in? We don't want to be standing right under that light while breaking in."

"I hadn't thought of that. We better go to the end of the block and double back through the alley."

Looking as casual as possible, we walked through the alley. I tripped only twice before digging the flashlight out of my purse.

We found the back door and crept up the steps, then I pulled out our tools.

Darlene looked at the bag and then at me. "You put our tools in a Mary Quant makeup bag?"

"We might as well be fashionable thieves."

"Hand me the butter knife."

"Shouldn't we put on our face stockings?" I asked, pulling out a wad of tissue paper that contained two of Macy's finest silk stockings.

Darlene briefly shined the flashlight on them, then

swung the light back to the door. "You can if you want to, but I'm not. I'm going to Stu's and I don't want to mess up my makeup. Think what putting that over your head will do to your lipstick."

She was right. I shoved the stockings back into my purse.

Darlene worked on the lock while I watched out for nosy neighbors.

"Let's go, Bebe," Darlene said with a huge, devilish smile. She swung the door open.

My heart jumped. We were in!

Darlene held the flashlight. I couldn't have done it, my hands were shaking so hard. This wasn't an any-day-of-the-week breaking and entering. This was *Bradley's* private domain.

I crossed over the threshold and found we were in a small kitchen.

"Come on, Bebe. This is no time for sightseeing. Where do you think he keeps the files?"

"I don't know," I said. "Can we stop for a minute so I can see what's in his fridge?"

"You can snoop to your heart's content *after* we find the files and I've gone."

"Thanks a lot," I complained, following her into the living room.

"Man, this is choice. Is that a black velvet sectional?"

"Yes. I was here once before, remember. It was just for a few minutes. The sectional is built-in, there's a bar over there"—Darlene shined the light on it—"and a hi-fi system. Look, he reads Dickens, and here's *To Kill a Mockingbird*."

"Uh-huh," Darlene said without interest.

"Did you notice we're walking on white carpet?" I asked her.

"Yeah, but what I haven't seen are any files."

I gulped. "Do you think he has them upstairs?"

"Knowing men, they're probably under his bed."

But Darlene was wrong. After going through a plain spare bedroom we arrived in Bradley's room. I grabbed the flashlight from Darlene and looked around: A raised platform bed covered in a midnight blue satin bedspread, a chair in the shape of an egg with a light inside the top, and the biggest bathroom I'd ever seen met my eye.

"Give me the flashlight," Darlene said.

I reluctantly handed it over.

"Shoot, we missed that," she said, pointing to an open window. "Hell, there's a fire escape out here. Hmmm, dresser, chest of drawers, where could he have the files?" Darlene pulled open a couple of dresser drawers. "Boxers, Bebe."

"Stop that!" I commanded, my face hot. "What about the closet?"

"That's my girl," Darlene said, dropping Bradley's underwear back in the drawer and closing it with her hip. She opened the door to a deep-set closet on the right side of the bed. Racks of clothes hung on either side with a pull-down light switch.

I took a deep breath and smelled Bradley's lime aftershave. That familiar ache started deep inside me. Great, I was like Pavlov's dog.

"Let's step inside the closet and close the door so we can turn on the light," Darlene suggested.

I followed, closed the door behind me, then blinked hard when Darlene pulled the light switch. Sure enough, in a corner beside a low row of hanging shirts was a group of manila files.

"Get out your pen and notebook, Bebe."

We sat on the floor and I held my pen poised.

Darlene picked up the first file. "Ah, here's our Princess. Mary Church. Not much here. Oh, yes, she did lie on her employment application. Miss Connecticut 1962. No work references. Graduated high school . . . there's nothing else of interest."

We agreed to write everyone's address down, so Darlene rattled it off at the beginning of each file.

"Here's Betty. Let me find the Cowboy. More liars. No indication of them being brother and sister. Both list themselves as being an only child."

"Got it. Who's next?" I asked.

"Kirchhoff, the Train Conductor. Oh, look at this. He admitted on his application that he spent five months in the Albany Sanatorium. There's a note here initialed by one of the Merryweathers okaying his employment." She squinted and read, " 'Give him a chance.' "

"That was nice of them."

Darlene shot me a look. "But do you think it's worked out?"

"Questionable. Who's next?"

"Geedunk, the Pirate." She gasped. "Oh, dear, it looks like the Merryweathers didn't find out that he had a dishonorable discharge from the navy until a month after they hired him."

"Does it say what he was discharged for?"

"No, it's just a standard government letter."

I made notes.

"Here's Mallory. He's been at the store seven months. Previously a manager in the men's department at a Boston department store. Write down his supervisor's name and number."

I tapped my pen on my steno pad. "I wonder if Kinker made it his business to look through these files when they were kept in the store."

"I wouldn't be surprised. Here's something strange.

Mr. Frederick, our Toymaker, claims to be married in his application. He really didn't want anyone to know he was a homosexual."

I wrote down his address and glanced over to see his spouse's name: Gloria.

"Kinker's file isn't here, Bebe. This last one is for Runion, the Teddy Bear who won't speak to us."

"Darn it. I'll bet Bradley still has Kinker's file in his office somewhere. He had to bring it in for my lawyer to look over."

"Runion was Mallory's first hire."

"When did he start?"

"About six months ago. It says that Runion was previously employed in Las Vegas at a casino."

"Then Runion and Kinker were hired about the same time."

"Think it means anything?"

"Mama always says there are no coincidences, but—"

I heard a door close and gasped. "Did you hear that?"

"Yes!" she hissed. "I thought you said Bradley would be out all evening."

"You think it's Bradley?!"

"Who else would it be?"

We listened.

The refrigerator door closed.

Ice rattled in a glass.

Someone turned on the TV.

Darlene and I shot to our feet.

I tripped over one of Bradley's shoes, sending us swaying into his suits.

"Oh, God!" I said.

"Sshhh, you want him to hear us?" Darlene cautioned.

"Oh, God!"

"Get off my foot, Bebe!"

She switched off the light in the closet, plunging us into darkness.

"Ouch!" Darlene said, cursing. "You shoved me into the door."

"Oh, God!"

"Stop saying that, Bebe. Let's get out of here. Have you got your purse and your steno pad?"

My teeth chattered in answer.

"Give them to me. I'm going out that fire escape and you're coming with me."

I nodded.

"Bebe? Are you coming?"

"I-I-I nodded yes."

"I can't see you in the dark!" Darlene complained.

"Is someone up there?" Bradley's voice boomed from below, loud and threatening.

Darlene pushed me back, threw open the closet door and, holding my hand, made a dash for the window.

I broke away. "Wait. We forgot the flashlight."

"Forget the flashlight!"

I dove back into the closet, fumbled around on the floor, and grasped it.

Darlene stood outside on the fire escape.

I ran toward her but the bed stopped me. I landed on satin. The flashlight popped out of my hand and hit the floor with a soft thud.

A body fell on top of me.

I heard the clatter of Darlene's shoes on the fire escape.

Oh, God.

"Don't move," Bradley growled.

Please, God, if I ever did anything right in my life—

and remember Harry—let me get away without Bradley seeing me, I prayed.

"You're a woman!"

Well, God had answered one of my prayers. For once, Bradley didn't call me a kid.

"Bebe!" Bradley shouted as the dim light from the bedside lamp came on. He rolled off me and sat up.

Certain my face was bloodred, I, too, moved into a sitting position.

Rendered momentarily speechless by the fact that he wore a pair of tight-fitting blue jeans and a white crew-neck sweater, something I'd never seen him in before, I lost my chance at the first volley.

"Bebe, what the hell are you doing here?"

"M-me? You're the one who isn't supposed to be here!"

"I live here!"

"True," I conceded, pulling a strand of hair away from my lip gloss. "But you're supposed to be out of town with some blonde shacked up at a country inn."

"Have you lost your mind? I went for a long drive, ate dinner at a greasy diner, and came back home to watch the Cardinals play the Yankees."

"You did?"

"Yes, I just explained—oh, no, you don't. I want to know what *you're* doing here in my house. How did you get in?"

"I didn't do it! Darlene picked your kitchen door lock."

He stared at me like I was a madwoman from some Alfred Hitchcock movie. "You and Darlene came here and broke into my home, looking for something."

It wasn't a question, so I didn't feel the need to answer. Instead I said, "I'll leave now."

He shot a gaze around the room and then slapped

his forehead. His blue eyes narrowed at me. "The personnel files. You've broken in here as part of your investigation!"

I started to rise from the bed, which turned out to be a mistake.

A second later, I was on my back, Bradley leaning over me. "I'm right, aren't I?"

I dared not lie, not with the look of absolute fury on his face, not with one jean-clad leg next to mine, not with his muscular arms holding me down on the bed.

"Try to understand. I'm fighting for my freedom. I could be in jail tomorrow if that coroner's report comes back—and you know it will. I had to see the files, look for any clue that could get me out of this mess."

His expression softened. "Did it ever occur to you to ask me to bring the files to the office?"

"Well . . . I tried, but—"

"What if the files had been at some other man's house and you'd broken in there and been caught? Did you think of that? Of what he might have done with you when he caught you?"

As if lightning had struck, the atmosphere turned electric.

My body relaxed, but I found it hard to breathe. I licked my lips. "No, I didn't think of that," I whispered, acutely conscious that I was in Bradley's bed. *With Bradley.* He'd get up any minute now and escort me to the door.

But he didn't.

In a husky voice he said, "That's why I don't want you investigating, snooping, sleuthing, or whatever you want to call it. I don't want anything bad to ever happen to you."

He kissed the side of my face and then looked at me with those incredible blue eyes.

I swallowed hard, concentrated on the crescent-shaped scar under his left eye, and took a risk. "Why?"

He nuzzled my neck. "Because you're beautiful, inside and out."

For a second, my heart stopped and my body grew numb. Then I was on fire, my heart beating madly, my hands gently pulling his head toward my lips until he started kissing me. I moaned and opened my mouth, inviting him in. His tongue rubbed up against mine, as we explored each other's mouths again and I thought I would never grow tired of his touch and his taste. In fact, I needed to taste more of him, so after several delicious minutes, I broke the kiss and started nibbling his throat, making him groan. The sound made me push my tongue around his ear, swirling inside, one arm around his back, the other tugging the top of his sweater down so I could kiss all the way down his neck.

"Bebe, Bebe, you're so sweet, the sweetest girl ever," he whispered, his words broken between panted breaths.

I ran my tongue back up his neck to his chin, then rested my cheek against his and whispered, "Bradley, my darling."

He sucked in a sharp breath. "Don't call me that unless you mean it."

"I do mean it. I would never say it if I didn't mean it."

In one swift motion, he rose up, pulled his sweater over his head, tossed it aside, and began kissing me with passion, cutting off my gasp at the sight of his golden chest.

My hand shook as I placed it on his bare chest. His skin was as soft as the satin beneath me until I explored high enough to touch a hard nipple.

He made a sound as if he was in pain, so I moved my hand away, only to have him move it back, place his fingers over mine, and squeeze. Then he moved his hand away, leaving mine to stroke his chest. I felt cool air on my stomach followed by Bradley's hot hand rubbing my skin, making me quiver. All the while we were kissing deeply and I couldn't get enough, the ache growing into an intense desire.

With one knee, Bradley pushed my legs apart and lay completely on top of me. I felt his need push into exactly where I wanted it the most.

Bradley's hands cupped my face as if he held something fragile, and he whispered, "Bebe, I've never wanted another woman as much as I want you right now. God, baby."

His head dropped and he sucked my neck.

Bradley Williams has a strong reputation as a playboy.

Shirley's words rang in my ears. I shut my eyes even tighter, somehow thinking the action would silence her voice.

Do you think you'll be the one to change him, Bebe?

Shirley again.

Bradley was out of control, sucking and nibbling my neck, kissing me, his hand on my stomach inching toward the waist of my pants. We were minutes from going all the way and he had not told me that he loved me, much less asked me to marry him. It was all my fault.

I must have stopped responding, because he raised his head and our gazes locked.

Damn it! "Bradley, I can't . . . I'm so sorry—you know I am."

Immediately he moved off me.

We lay side by side, our breathing the only sound in the room.

He sat up, found his sweater, and pulled it over his head.

I dragged myself up, meaning to stand, but found I couldn't.

"Please forgive me, Bradley. You must know that I—"

"There's nothing to forgive."

If he apologized, said it was a mistake—tears formed in my eyes and I forced them back—or said he regretted it, I swore to myself that I'd rip my clothes off.

"Where's your purse?"

I wanted to scream. "Darlene has it."

"Come on, I'll get you a cab and see that you get home safely."

I didn't think I could take that. "Please don't. If you could lend me cab money, I'll repay you tomorrow at the store."

He walked me down the stairs, holding my hand.

When we reached the front door, he released my hand and kissed the top of my head. I hugged him and for a moment the urge to return to his bedroom almost overcame me.

He opened the front door, holding my hand again, closed it behind us, and walked me to the corner of Columbus Avenue and Seventy-fifth Street.

I shivered, but not from the cold, and Bradley put his arm around me, his other hand in the air to hail a cab.

The taxi glided to a stop.

Bradley opened the door for me, closing it after I got in.

I focused on sitting gracefully in the back while he gave the driver my address and some money.

I even managed to return his smile, holding back my tears until the taxi took me away into the night.

Chapter Nineteen

Though I lay under a warm blanket, cozy in my nightgown, I couldn't sleep.

God, baby.

Bradley.

Bebe, Bebe, you're so sweet, the sweetest girl ever.

Bradley.

I rolled onto my stomach and started reciting the multiplication tables.

Willie and Lily were going at it upstairs, having the time of their lives. I tried to block out their sounds. Usually they were quiet by eight, but the starburst clock on the white brick wall read almost eleven. I couldn't even turn on the radio to distract myself because I didn't want to wake Shirley. To make matters worse, Bradley's lime scent clung to my hair and skin. Every time I took a breath, I smelled him.

An hour went by as my mind replayed the vision of Bradley and me on his bed together, every moment carved into my memory, his touch fresh on my body.

Finally I threw off the blanket and went into the kitchen. I pulled out the milk and a small pan and laid my head on the counter while the milk warmed on the stove.

Just as I sat down at our tiny table, glass in hand, I heard the front door locks click open.

Darlene walked into the kitchen, her black outfit reminding me of the one I wore mere hours ago when Bradley . . .

She slumped into the seat across from me. "Any more of that warm milk?"

I raised my arm and pointed to the stove.

Darlene fixed her milk and brought the bottle of Old Rose Whiskey to the table. She poured a generous dollop into my glass and handed me a spoon to stir the concoction. I saw that her milk was almost brown from whiskey and that her hands shook.

She drank, then pulled her red curls back from her forehead. She sat with her head down and her elbows on the table.

"Do you want to go first, Bebe?" Darlene asked, and then drank almost the entire contents of her glass.

"No." I followed her lead and gulped my drink.

Darlene reached for the Old Rose and topped off both our glasses. The milk was forgotten. She took a deep breath. "After I left you, I went over to Stu's town house. There was no answer when I rang the bell. I had my key, but he's changed the lock. Like the desperate girlfriend I suppose I've become, I alternated between sitting on his stoop freezing my behind off and lounging in a bar down the block drinking and fending off men. Stu never came home. I have no idea where he is or who he might be with."

"Bummer, Darlene. He'll be back, I'm sure. Stu loves you." I drank more. Why hadn't I thought of getting drunk earlier?

Darlene pushed her glass aside and drank straight out of the whiskey bottle. "For all I know, Stu could be in Rome or Paris finding a new girlfriend, one who will marry him when he asks."

I held out my glass and she poured me more whiskey. "I'm sure he didn't leave the country, Darlene. His pride took a blow when you refused his proposal. He loves you, yeah, yeah, yeah." The Beatles had lyrics for every occasion.

"Bebe, you're drunk already."

"Doesn't take much. You're not exactly sober yourself."

"What happened at Bradley's?"

I snorted. "Not what you would have done. Oh, no. I had to be Miss Virtuous, Miss No-Sex-Until-the-Wedding-Night. Miss Prude."

"So he wasn't mad."

"He was at first," I admitted.

Darlene giggled. "But not for long. There must have been *some* action. You've got a matching hickey on the left side of your throat. Were any clothes removed?"

Bradley's golden chest flashed in my mind's eye. I swayed in my seat. *I am so gone on him.* "He took off his sweater."

"Groovy. Does he have a bitchin' chest?"

The room started to spin.

"Bebe?"

"We were on his bed kissing and he called me 'sweet' and 'baby' but he never said he loved me so I stopped us from going all the way." I burst into tears.

Darlene stumbled around to my side of the table and leaned her head against mine. "We're blitzed. Let's talk about this later."

She helped me to the sectional, where I promptly passed out.

*   *   *

The next morning, I cracked my eyes open when I heard the shower running. My head pounded, my tongue tasted like Snyder's cigarette ash, and my stomach felt like I'd swallowed some of the turpentine Daddy always kept out in the backyard shed.

I shuffled into the kitchen, turned on the overhead light, which nearly blinded me, and groped for the coffee can. While the coffee percolated, I tried to decide what to wear to work but couldn't conjure a single image of any of my clothes. I thought about making some pancakes, but didn't feel up to the task. The sound of the shower stopped. When Darlene got out of the bathroom, I'd ask her if she wanted anything. I doubted she would.

Finally the coffee beckoned and I sat at the table drinking a large mug of the hot brew. I couldn't remember when I'd ever felt worse. Well, there was that time I was poisoned.

A loud thump sounded from the bedroom, followed by a cry of distress. Fully awake now, I dashed out of the kitchen, only to run smack into Darlene.

She said, "I knew that woman would wake me at the crack of dawn."

"What time is it? Are we late for work?"

"Only if we have to be at the store by six. It's just before five."

"I thought *you* were in the shower! It must have been Shirley!" I moved past Darlene and found Shirley on the floor of my bedroom crying. Her suitcase lay open next to her, clothes spilling out.

"Shirley, are you all right? What happened?"

She wiped her eyes. "I packed my suitcase, but I must not have pushed the lock in securely. When I picked it up, the top swung open and my clothes fell out."

"I'll help you repack. You're not hurt, are you?"

"No, but I don't want to miss my train. Thank you for all your help, Bebe. You're one of the sweetest people I've ever met."

"So I've been told," I muttered under my breath.

Once Shirley was gone, I had to suffer through Darlene's constant complaining. She refused to return to bed, saying she couldn't sleep now. I sliced some cucumber and we lay on our beds for half an hour with the cool slices over our eyes, not speaking.

I applied a heavier coat of makeup than normal and selected a hot pink long-sleeved dress with a black daisy pin. A black scarf covered my hickeys, and black tights and the black go-go boots completed my look.

We took a cab to the store, and by nine, when I finally walked onto the sales floor, I felt as if it was nine at night.

As I hung my coat in the storeroom, the Toymaker, Mr. Frederick, came into the room.

"Good morning," I fibbed. It was just a greeting, anyway. I'd introduced myself to Mr. Frederick, but Darlene had been in charge of questioning him.

"Hello, Bebe. I wanted to talk to you. When I saw you come in here I thought it might be a good time."

"Sure." I felt a tiny shiver of apprehension at being alone with him in the storeroom. Although I had ruled him out as the killer, I had been known to be wrong in the past.

"I guess you've figured out about me. You've been as tenacious as Kinker was, finding out everyone's secrets."

"Figured out what?"

His hands were at his sides. Could one of them be holding a pirate's knife?

"That I'm a homosexual."

Okay, he wasn't going to kill me. "It's no one's business but yours."

He let out a slow breath. "Thank you. Surely you know that not everyone here would take that view. The Merryweathers certainly wouldn't have, and they almost found out because of that clown's filthy remarks."

"I'm sorry you had to endure Kinker. He delighted in torturing everyone, didn't he?"

"Yes, but we don't have to worry about him now." The Toymaker paused. "You didn't kill him like everyone in the store thinks, did you?"

"No."

"And you're investigating his death along with your friend Darlene."

"Wow, you're observant."

"I need to be. I don't know where you are in the investigation, but I'd like to offer you this idea: When Mallory came on board, he brought in Kinker and Runion. I'm certain there was something going on between the three of them. Maybe not Kinker so much at first, but he was definitely involved before his death."

"What were Kinker and Runion involved in?" I asked.

"I don't know."

"Maybe you know something you're not telling me. How do I know I can trust you?"

"You don't," Mr. Frederick admitted.

"You might be trying to cast suspicion away from yourself."

He smiled. "True. But if I'm not mistaken, you already have your own questions regarding the three men. I thought I'd offer some clarification."

"Thank you for telling me. Don't put yourself in

any danger by looking into the matter any further, but if you can think of what they had in common, please come to me."

"I will." He turned and walked out of the room.

I stared after him for a moment. My mind slogged through the information I'd written in my steno pad last night in Bradley's closet. The Toymaker was correct insofar as the hiring dates were concerned. But did whatever the three men had going on relate to the murder? Raggedy Ann remained at the top of my suspect list. She was a woman scorned, she hid her relationship with her brother, and the rocking chair that was used as a weapon against Tom came from her area. Betty wanted a man in her life, and maybe her desperation ran too deep. She had thought she had Kinker but she didn't. She flirted like a hussy with Tom and Bradley, hoping to sink her claws into one of them.

I rode the escalator upstairs, mulling over the possible suspects. By the time I reached my desk, I had decided that the killer had to be either Raggedy Ann, the Teddy Bear, or Mallory.

"Good morning, Bebe," Danielle said.

"Hi. I'm feeling a little rough around the edges today, so don't take it personally if I'm quiet. I'll try not to be a grump."

She lowered her voice. "Don't worry about it. All girls have those days of the month when we're not ourselves."

I felt my lips trying to curve into a smile, but my smile muscles were on vacation. "You made coffee."

"Why don't you get a cup? Something hot in your tummy will help."

"Good idea. Um, I see Bradley's door is shut. Has he had his coffee yet?"

"Mr. Williams hasn't come in. Does he have a meeting outside the store this morning?"

I glanced down at the calendar on my desk blotter. "No."

"Well, I'm sure he'll be in soon. Would you like me to handle the phones?"

"Danielle, you're a godsend. Thanks."

While drinking coffee, I pulled out my investigation notebook and wrote down what the Toymaker had told me. I read over all my notes and came to the same conclusion: The killer had to be Raggedy Ann, the Teddy Bear, or Mallory.

The combination of too much coffee, no food, and the coroner's report hanging over my head like an ax had made me a bundle of nerves. Bradley had yet to appear by ten o'clock. I forced myself not to think about him and instead typed a letter to Herman Shires and enclosed it with the damning evidence Shirley had given me. Once I had the package ready, I slid it into my drawer next to my purse for safekeeping. I'd leave at four, telling Bradley that I was running company errands, and take it to the post office myself.

It was noon when Bradley walked into the office with Tom.

Tom looked angry. "And I just heard on the radio that the Yankees have fired Yogi Berra over the loss."

"That's a shame, but my Cardinals beat the Yankees, so I guess they had to do something."

I couldn't take my eyes off Bradley. He looked well rested and as handsome as ever in his slate blue suit, white shirt, and blue-and-gold tie. He held his briefcase and a box of Cracker Jack. I should have left a hickey on *his* neck!

"Hey, babe," Tom greeted me.

"Tom, are you feeling better under all that face paint?"

"I'm good and ready to rock 'n' roll with the kids today. Danielle, what's this about you being off the market?"

Tom skipped over to Danielle's desk and admired her engagement ring.

Bradley lingered at my desk. "How are you, Bebe?" he asked with a smile.

I smiled back. "Fine." Now I was fine.

He glanced at Danielle and Tom, then looked at me. "You look beautiful as always," he said in a low voice.

Gosh, it was hot all of a sudden. "Thank you."

The phone rang. Danielle answered it while Bradley and I stared at each other.

"Bebe," Danielle said, "it's Detective Finelli for you."

No more smiles.

I picked up the receiver and punched a button on the phone. "Bebe Bennett speaking."

"Finelli here. Are you going to be at the store in the next two hours or are you taking lunch?"

I closed my eyes. "I'll be at the store."

"See you soon."

"Wait—"

He'd disconnected. I stared at the phone.

"Bebe, what did Finelli say?" Bradley asked.

"Not much. He wanted to know if I'd be here in the next two hours and I told him I would. He's coming over. I guess I'll be arrested."

Tom moved toward me. "We've gotta tell those crazy fuzz that we've been investigating—"

Bradley interrupted in a stern tone. "I'll be handling

this with Bebe, Tom. You need to play your part as Mr. Skidoo."

Tom put his hands in the air. "Okay, okay. Just trying to help." He walked away.

"Is there anything I can do, Mr. Williams?" Danielle asked.

"You can take your lunch hour now so that the phones are covered when Bebe and I meet with Finelli in my office."

"If it's all the same to you, I brought my lunch and I'll eat at my desk."

"Thanks, Danielle. You're a trouper," Bradley said. "Bebe, would you come into my office, please?"

He closed the door behind us and put his briefcase on his desk. "Bebe, look at me," Bradley said softly. "That's better. Here, take these Cracker Jacks since you're not able to go out for lunch. I haven't even opened them. Do you want me to send Danielle out for a sandwich for you?"

I accepted the box. "Thanks, these will be great. I haven't had anything to eat all day."

"That's not good. You need your strength. I'm going to call Jim Lincoln. I'll be here when Finelli arrives. If the worst happens, I'll get you out of jail before you realize what color the walls are painted."

"You'll do all that for me?" Maybe now he'd say he loved me. I slid a glance at the magic sofa.

"Of course I will. Your parents are all the way down in Virginia. Maybe you should call your father and ask him to come to the city. The Big Guy can take Snyder out easy."

He wanted me to call my father? Even despite last night, I was still a kid to Bradley! I shook with rage. "Don't worry about me, Bradley. I can take care of myself, as I believe I proved in your bedroom last night when you wanted to take my virginity."

"I came home and found you in my bed!"

"Stay out of my business," I snapped at him, my voice full of contempt. I would have been just another conquest. He didn't love me and he wasn't going to marry me. Shirley was right.

Bradley's shocked expression turned to anger. "Have it your way," he gritted out. "I wash my hands of the situation, damn it."

I slammed his door on my way out.

I threw the box of Cracker Jack on my desk, startling Danielle.

Fury carried me downstairs to Raggedy Ann's area. "Betty, I'd like to talk with you in the storeroom."

"I'm with customers, Bebe. Can't we chat later?"

"No," I hissed. "Come with me now unless you want me to inform Mallory that you're the Cowboy's sister."

Her face paled beneath her painted-on freckles.

Once the door to the storeroom closed, Raggedy Ann's pleasant demeanor dropped. "So the new Mr. Skidoo is just as rotten as the last one. He told you about me and Dave."

"Is that why you smashed Tom over the head with a rocking chair?"

"I don't know what you're talking about. Even now, Tom is pedaling around on his tricycle."

"Don't lie to me, Betty. You came on to him, and when he turned you down you got mad. Or did you hit him because you let it slip that you're the Cowboy's sister? Did you think the wound would be fatal? That you could kill this Mr. Skidoo like you did the last one?"

She sputtered, bristling with indignation. "You're nuts! You killed Kinker—everyone considers you a hero—and now you're trying to place the blame on me. I guess the police have got something on you. Yeah, I lied about my brother, but it was his idea. Dave thinks women need looking after."

"His protection didn't work, though, did it? You had an affair with Kinker and he dumped you. Where was your brother then? Maybe he's the one who decided to kill the clown in defense of his sister's so-called honor."

"I'm not going to stand here and listen to your insults. I think the fact that you can't get into Bradley Williams's pants has your mind twisted. Oh, yes, we all know about your pathetic little crush on your boss—"

I raised my hand to slap her face then lowered it, unable to believe I would have struck her.

"You bitch," she snarled. "I'll be laughing when those detectives lead you away in handcuffs."

"I'm going to Mallory right now and telling him about you and your brother. You'll both be out of a job by the day's end." I moved past her.

"Wait."

I turned. "Yes?"

"If you didn't kill Kinker—"

"I most certainly did not. Tell me who did."

She shook her head, red yarn curls bouncing. "I honestly don't know. I swear it wasn't me or Dave. If I had to make a guess, I'd say it was Mallory or the Teddy Bear."

"Why?"

"I've never been able to put my finger on it."

I dug in my heels. "Why are you suspicious of Mallory and Runion?"

She sighed. "Dave and I both think Mallory, Runion, and Kinker were involved in something together."

"Like what?"

"I swear we don't know. There was just an air of conspiracy about them. If I hadn't believed that you murdered Kinker, then I'd have pointed my finger at one of them."

"Unless you wanted to place the blame on someone other than yourself."

"I didn't kill Kinker! Yes, he treated me like dirt, using me for a convenient screw then dumping me when he got tired of me, but that's the way men are. Trust me, if women went around murdering men who did them dirty, the male population would be a lot smaller."

"What about the Pirate?"

"Geedunk hasn't the stomach for murder. He comes off as a bully but can't back it up."

"Why was he given a dishonorable discharge from the navy?"

"You're thorough, I'll give you that. Geedunk went AWOL. It's not just murder he doesn't have the stomach for. He's a big baby. Look at how he treats that damn parrot like a child."

"I'll keep that in mind. You're the main suspect in my book, Betty. I want your alibi for the night Kinker was murdered and it had better be solid."

"I went straight home from the store." Her voice oozed exasperation.

"Prove it. I'm going to talk to Mallory now, but I won't tell him about you and Dave yet. That should give you enough time to convince me you're not a murderess."

I left her there and marched to Mallory's office, ignoring everyone. The Toymaker and Raggedy Ann had confirmed my suspicion that *something* was going on between Mallory, Runion, and Kinker.

The store manager's door was closed, but I wasn't going to let that stop me. I barged in without knocking, planted myself inside, and shut the door.

"Have you gone stark raving mad?" Mallory said. My mouth fell open. He'd spoken in an Irish brogue.

"Answer me!"

Evidently he hadn't noticed his slip of the tongue because his last words were spoken in his usual clipped English accent. He picked up a long silver letter opener, grasped it by the ornate handle, and tapped it on his desk.

"Maybe I *have* gone crazy," I said. "I'm about to be arrested for a murder I didn't commit. You know the one I'm talking about: your business partner, Mel Kinker."

He chuckled nastily. "I've never liked your type. You're a meddling, sexually frustrated female with too much time on her hands who likes to invent stories."

Heat suffused my face at the words *sexually frustrated*.

He wasn't finished. "You're a busy bee in my back garden, flying from employee to employee trying to pit people against their coworkers. The only reason Williams permitted you to hire your friend Tom was because he feels sorry for you, a little hayseed from somewhere south of the Mason-Dixon Line. I tolerated it *once*. However, you grow tiresome, Miss Bennett. If you don't stay out of my way, I shall put the decision before Williams. Either you leave or I will. I think once Williams hears what I'll leak to the press about his mismanagement since the sale, you'll find yourself working at a five-and-dime."

"Did you insult and threaten Kinker too? Or did

you just murder him in cold blood without preamble? Maybe your other business partner, Runion, helped out."

He sighed in a bored way and picked up the phone and dialed. "Yes, Danielle—"

Someone knocked on the door.

Mallory spoke into the phone. "Excuse me, Danielle." He hung up and called, "Come in."

Jane, one of the cashiers, stood in the doorway. "I'm sorry to bother you, Mr. Mallory. Detective Finelli is here to see Bebe."

"Thank you, Jane."

"I'm not done with you, Mallory," I promised him before shutting his door behind me.

Finelli stood in the Conductor's area, hands clasped behind his back, watching the trains.

I let out a weary sigh. My lack of sleep, combined with the fury that had caused me to confront the two people highest on my suspect list, left me feeling incompetent and powerless.

"Detective Finelli."

He turned around, his appearance even more haggard than the last time I'd seen him. "Miss Bennett. Would you like to step outside or go up to Williams's office?"

"And deprive everyone of seeing me led away in handcuffs?"

"I'm not here to arrest you."

Relief flooded through me, along with a ray of hope. "Let's go outside. I could use some fresh air."

The Teddy Bear opened the door for us.

"Walk to your right," I told Finelli.

We stopped far enough away from the Teddy Bear that he couldn't hear us. Finelli leaned against the store window.

"What have you uncovered in your investigation since the last time we spoke, Miss Bennett?"

"Is this another one-way street where I give you information and you tell me nothing?"

"No."

"Okay. I've narrowed the suspect list down to Raggedy Ann, Mr. Mallory, and that Teddy Bear behind us." I explained my reasons, and discussed the attack on Tom while Finelli took notes.

"You don't know what this business is that the men are involved in?"

"Not yet. Now, what have you got for me?"

"Why wasn't a formal police report filed regarding the assault on Tom?"

"The police were here. I don't know where the report is, but I just told you everything about it. He's back on the job today. Your turn."

Finelli rubbed his hand over his crew cut. "Snyder is furious. The coroner's report came back and showed that the altered pirate's knife was not the murder weapon."

I gasped. "What?"

"Kinker was stabbed twice in the same place. The real murder weapon was a longer blade. The shorter pirate's knife was allegedly thrust into the victim to throw off the police."

My mind flashed to Mallory's letter opener.

Finelli continued. "The killer did use your typewriter on the note attached to the pirate knife left on your desk, but he or she wore gloves. The only prints we've been able to obtain are yours."

"Can Snyder arrest me based on that evidence?"

"He can arrest you anytime he wants. He's still got you at the scene of the crime, with a witness who'll say you were holding the bloody pirate's knife, and now he's got the fingerprints from the typewriter. It's more a question of whether or not he can make the case stick now that we know the pirate knife did not kill Kinker. We need the real murder weapon and Snyder knows it."

At that moment Bradley walked out of the store, stopped, and looked at us.

I turned my head pointedly away.

Bradley retreated into the store.

Finelli looked at me. "You two have a fight?"

"I don't want to talk about it."

"I haven't said anything about the fib you told Snyder about dating Kinker."

"I know you haven't, and I can tell it's taking a toll on you."

"Worry about yourself, Miss Bennett. Keep me informed."

He pushed away from the wall and crossed the street to where his Pontiac Tempest was parked.

Just as I reached the door, Mallory exited the store. He and the Teddy Bear walked down the street together, ignoring me.

I grabbed the door handle, opened the heavy door, and went directly to Mallory's office. Jane tried to stop me.

"I'm sorry, Miss Bennett, but you can't go in there."

I clutched my charm bracelet. "Jane, I think I dropped a charm off my bracelet. I just need a few seconds to check the floor."

She was about to protest, but a customer approached with an armload of merchandise for her to ring up.

I stepped into Mallory's office, closed the door partway, and grabbed the letter opener off his desk. Standing behind the door, I tried to slip the blade into my boot, but it was too big. Quickly, I raised the hem of my dress, tucked the letter opener into the top of my tights, adjusted my dress, and left Mallory's office. I waved to Jane and went upstairs to my desk as fast as possible without tripping and stabbing myself. Danielle was away from her desk. Bradley's door was shut. In a sleight of hand that would have rivaled Tom's abilities, I retrieved the letter opener and sat down at my desk.

Bradley chose that moment to emerge from his office, so I slid the letter opener in front of my in-box tray.

I watched him from under my lashes. He refilled his coffee mug and, without looking my way, returned to his office and shut the door.

I started to regret yelling at him, but the man had me in knots.

My stomach growled, reminding me I hadn't eaten all day, but I ignored it. Mallory's slip into an Irish accent had jarred me. I decided to call his previous employer and dig for information. I retrieved the steno pad that contained the notes I'd made last night from the personnel files. Running my finger down to Mallory's name, I saw that he'd been employed in the men's department of Brown's Department Store in Boston. I had a phone number and a supervisor's name, Mr. Brian Meyers.

I picked up the phone and dialed the number.

Danielle walked by my desk carrying papers. "That's a pretty letter opener, Bebe," she said.

"Brian Meyers speaking."

I nodded at Danielle, who walked down to Bradley's office. Then I spoke into the receiver. "Yes, Mr. Meyers, this is . . . Mrs. Williams calling from New York City."

"What can I do for you, Mrs. Williams?"

He had an Irish accent like the one Mallory had let slip. "I'm calling with regard to Mr. John Mallory, who used to be in your employ. He's applied for a position here in the men's department of Macy's and listed you as a reference."

Mr. Meyers paused, then said, "Sure, he's a good man, a hard worker, always punctual. I think he'd be an asset to your store."

"You never found him engaged in business activities outside his position with you?"

"No, I can't say that I did."

"What about his character? Is he a moral man?"

"To the best of my knowledge, he is. I've never known him to be a drunkard or to have a gambling problem, nor did he have trouble with women."

"Thank you, Mr. Meyers. You've been extremely helpful."

"I'm glad I could assist you. Look after yourself, Mrs. Williams."

I disconnected the call and chewed my fingernail.

It was after four o'clock. I needed to get to the post office before it closed and mail Herman Shires his package. First I took out a white envelope, pulled my wallet from my purse, and grabbed two dollars. That seemed like more than enough to repay Bradley for my cab ride home last night. I placed the money in the envelope, sealed it, then wrote Bradley's name on the front.

Danielle had returned to her desk.

"Can you give this envelope to Bradley, Danielle? I'm leaving for the day. I have to stop by the post office and mail something for the store."

"I'll be glad to, Bebe. Will you be coming back tonight?"

"Possibly," I fibbed. I was incredibly tired, hungry, and thirsty and planned to go straight home.

Taking my purse, the box of Cracker Jack, and the package, I went downstairs to retrieve my coat.

Darlene came rushing up behind me. "Bebe, what is going on? Everyone is whispering about you and I saw you with Finelli."

"I can't talk now. I have to leave. I'll see you later at home."

She gave me a hug. "You look like hell."

"Thanks."

I noticed that Raggedy Ann was in her area with her brother. The two had their heads together.

Mallory's office door was open, but the room was dark.

The Teddy Bear opened the door for me and "accidentally" let it fall onto my shoulder. I winced in pain, wondered why he'd hurt me, and hailed a cab.

After I finished at the post office, I decided to take the bus home. Sitting down, I could no longer deny my stomach. I opened the box of Cracker Jack and popped a kernel into my mouth.

"What prize did you get, lady?"

A towheaded boy about nine years old was hanging over the seat next to me. "I don't know."

He held on to the back of the seat and jumped up and down. "You've gotta look."

Sighing, I dug my hand through the sticky confection until I reached the prize. I pulled it out and held it for the boy to see, my face falling and tears forming in my eyes.

"Oh, it's just a stupid ring," the boy said and promptly lost interest.

I opened the little container and pulled out the "gold" adjustable band ring with its cloudy "diamond." I put it on my ring finger, knowing it was the only engagement ring I'd ever get from Bradley. Our personal relationship, if you could call it that, was over.

I missed my stop and had to double back to my apartment. I threw the Cracker Jacks in a trash can but couldn't bring myself to take off the stupid ring. I stopped at Joe's grocery and bought a Coke and a ham sandwich.

I sat on my stoop eating and drinking, wondering idly if Harry might show. By the time I finished, it was almost seven o'clock. Hopefully, Harry was at an AA meeting or working at the church.

I trudged up the stairs to my apartment, intent on washing my face and going straight to bed, when I suddenly stopped short.

A teddy bear was propped up against my door. The stuffing in the center of his chest was visible from around a pirate's knife. There was no note, but the message was clear. I put my hand over my mouth so I wouldn't scream.

The Teddy Bear at the store!

Someone planned to kill him, I just knew it!

Without another thought, I clutched the bear to my chest, ran down the stairs, out of my building, and all the way to Lexington. Cab after cab passed me by until finally one stopped. I gave the store address and told the driver there would be an extra dollar in it for him if he hurried. We took off like a rocket.

My brain was too tired to think of anything more than Runion's safety. He'd probably left the store, but I had his address in my steno pad. If I had to, I'd go to where he lived and show him the bear in my hand.

I panicked when the driver jolted the cab to a stop across from Merryweathers'. An ambulance and police cars with lights flashing were parked out front. I threw the driver several bills and leapt from the taxi, then crossed the street, coming face-to-face with Snyder.

"Well, well, well, here's girly now, and look, she's even got a little teddy bear all stabbed just the way the real one was. Did you want to give us a demonstration of how you did it? Is that why you brought the bear?" He took the toy out of my cold hands.

Beyond him, Bradley, Danielle, and a man in blue overalls were staring at me.

"What a helpful broad you are, even giving us the real murder weapon in the Kinker case. Dainty Danielle identified the letter opener as yours. She saw it on your desk and complimented you on it. Poor Pretty Boy is taking it on the chin."

"I have no idea what's going on," I said. The sidewalk beneath me seemed to move. I felt light-headed.

Snyder's voice hardened. "Oh, no, you're not going to faint on me. Bebe Bennett, you are under arrest for the murders of Mel Kinker and Bob Runion."

He grabbed my arms, pulled them behind my back, and snapped a pair of handcuffs on my wrists.

I was shoved into the back of a police car just before everything went black.

Chapter Twenty

Something tickled under my nose and I couldn't push it away. The world came back into focus, but I didn't like what I saw.

"That's enough," I said, turning my head. My hands were painfully cuffed behind my back. I sat in the rear seat of the police car, which was parked in front of the police station.

"The smelling salts brought her around, Detective," the officer in the front seat said to the looming figure in black standing outside the squad car.

Snyder jerked open the back door. "Welcome to your new home, girly. I'll be your personal escort inside."

I slid across the seat before he could touch me, but had some difficulty standing and walking with my hands cuffed. Snyder held me by the cuffs, making me nauseous.

"Can you take these things off me now, Snyder?"

He pointed his cigarette at me. "That's Detective Snyder to you, girly. Once I toss you in the slammer I'll take your bracelets off you. It does my heart good to be seen parading a double murderess through the station."

"You don't have a heart."

Since I'd already been fingerprinted, the official pro-
cedures went quickly. Snyder turned me over to a female guard, saying, "I'm going out for a nice, juicy
steak to celebrate. I'll see you in court tomorrow after
I meet with the DA. He's a smart fella. I'm sure he's
gonna agree with me that you need to be held without bail."

I shot him a horrified glare. "You can't do that!"

He snickered. "Awww, it won't be so bad. I'll come
visit you."

"Don't I get a phone call?"

"Elma will take care of you. I've done my job for
the day."

I could hear him laughing as the female guard led
me away. Elma was a short woman with mousy brown
hair, a nose too big for her face, and a pointed chin.
She didn't look very sympathetic. She took me into a
small room and patted me down for weapons, even
taking off my boots, then removed my scarf. She put
it in a plastic bag marked "Bennett."

I blushed, but she seemed unaffected by the hickeys
now visible on my neck.

"Elma, may I have my scarf back? I don't want to
be seen with these, um, marks on my neck."

"Prisoners are not allowed scarves for their own
safety. Another inmate could strangle you."

"What about my boots?"

"You can have them back once you're locked up."

We walked out of the room and down a hallway.
"Do you know if I can make a phone call?"

"There's a phone ahead of the holding cell where
you'll be tonight."

"May I call my father in Virginia?"

"Local calls only."

I bit my lip and hoped Darlene was home. I would

not call Bradley no matter what. My fingers shook as I dialed my number.

"Hello."

"Thank God you're there, Darlene."

"Bebe, where are you? You just caught me. I'm going over to Stu's. I talked to him and—"

"Darlene! Listen to me. I'm in jail."

"Damn!"

"Someone killed the Teddy Bear and Snyder arrested me for his murder and Kinker's."

"One more minute," Elma informed me.

"Dear Lord—"

"Darlene, I've only got a minute," I said desperately. "I need you to call my father and tell him to get here as soon as he can. Tell him . . . everything."

"What about Bradley?"

"No! Don't call him! Just get Daddy up here."

"Okay, Bebe. I'll call Skyway and see if I can get him a flight—"

"Convince him it's safe. Come visit me—"

Elma pressed the silver tab, ending the call.

I replaced the receiver. There was nothing else I could do.

Still holding me by the cuffs, Elma said, "Let's go."

"Please, can I have a drink of water? I fainted and the police officer—"

"Right here," she said and guided me to a water fountain. She pressed down the button and water shot out in an arc. My hair got in the way, but I still managed to bend and take a drink before Elma led me to a large, square cell.

She took a ring of keys from her waist and opened the door. "Get in."

I complied and she unlocked my handcuffs and locked me in the cell.

Rubbing my wrists, I said, "Thank you."

"You've only got one drunk for company now," she said, indicating my cell mate. "But as they say, the night is young."

With those comforting words, Elma departed.

I sat on the corner of a long wooden bench. I judged the woman on the other side to be in her fifties. She had greasy gray hair down to her shoulders and wore a cheap, stained brown shirtwaist dress, minus a belt, that was several shades darker than the tan cement walls around me.

I folded my hands in my lap and fixed my gaze on them. That way I didn't have to see the iron bars.

Squeezing my hands together, I imagined the phone call between Darlene and Daddy. Daddy's face would turn that shade of purple that meant he was beyond mad. I knew I could count on him, though. Besides anger, his reaction would include fear for his daughter, a thought that made guilt rest heavy on my shoulders. He'd bring money, too. Daddy believed in keeping a large amount of cash in the fallout shelter in our backyard. Then there was Mama. She'd wring her hands, kind of like how I was doing now, and pack a suitcase and something for Daddy to eat. Mama knew that Daddy would take care of me, and I knew it too. Unfortunately, this knowledge was little consolation. Where was the strong and professional independent woman I wanted to be? In jail, that's where.

I raised my chin. My arrest was a setback, that's all, I told myself. Daddy would get me out of here and I knew exactly where I would go: Mallory's apartment. With the Teddy Bear's death, there was no doubt in my mind that Mallory was the killer and that it had something to do with the men's shared business. All I needed was proof.

Out of sheer exhaustion, I fell asleep, and awoke sometime later to the sounds of raucous laughter. A glance at the round clock on the wall told me it was after one thirty in the morning. Another drunk had been brought in while I slept. She lay on the floor snoring.

The source of all the giggling appeared and my eyes widened. Elma tossed the two women inside, and they immediately focused on me.

The first woman wore a white minidress that barely covered her behind, with a gaudy gold-colored zipper that ran from the low neck to the hem. Black boots came up to her thighs and had heels at least two inches higher than mine. Her hair was bottle blond and teased into a large beehive. She smacked her gum. "How you doin'? Don't think I've seen you around. You one of those uptown girls?"

"Um, no. My name is Bebe and I'm a secretary in midtown."

"Whoo-eee, did you hear that, Sister of Mercy?" she cooed to her friend. "Miss Scarlett O'Hara here is a *secretary*. I'm the Widow. Nice to meet you, Scarlett."

"Hello."

Sister of Mercy did not look like any nun I'd ever seen. She had on red short-shorts, a matching red elastic strapless top, black fishnet stockings, and high-heeled clear plastic shoes. She wore her hair in a beehive as well, which was a shade of bright red I'd never seen on a human before.

Sister of Mercy looked me up and down. "You got a man? By the looks of your neck, he's not taking good care of the merchandise."

My hand automatically went up to cover my hick-eys, then I dropped it back to my lap, realizing I now needed two hands to cover them. I thought of Bradley and how things stood between us. "Kind of. I'm not really sure."

The Widow sat next to me and lifted my left hand. "She ain't got no man with money, Sister. Not if this is what he calls an engagement ring. Came out of a box of Cracker Jacks or my name ain't the Widow."

The two laughed.

I felt my face grow warm.

"We can set you up with a man who'll take care of you, can't we, Sister?"

"That we can. Big Daddy would love Scarlett."

"I already have a daddy, and he'll be here tomorrow," I said. "Er, Miss Widow, can I ask you how you walk in those heels? I mean, mine are high, but I can't think how I'd manage in those."

She laughed. "I don't do a whole lot of walking!"

They both laughed. I joined in to be friendly.

Sister of Mercy said, "You want us to teach you some tricks on how to keep a man coming back for more?"

The two broke out in laughter again.

"Why not? I'm not going anywhere," I said.

I sat handcuffed again in a small courthouse meeting room, Elma standing guard. She hadn't let me take a shower or send for fresh clothes. I hadn't been allowed any visitors either, but had been told that Jim Lincoln was on his way. My insides felt like rotten jelly spread on moldy toast.

A familiar voice rang out from the hallway.

"That's my Little Magnolia you've got in there and I want to see her now. I had to fly civilian from Richmond on a tin can that would have disgraced the army."

Daddy! I sprang to my feet only to feel Elma's sturdy hand on my shoulder.

"No visitors except your lawyer," she said.

"Mr. Bennett," came Bradley's voice. "None of us have been allowed to see her."

"Well, you aren't family, boy! And if she weren't still working for a person that murder follows around like a spook, she wouldn't be in this mess!"

"I have nothing but Bebe's best interests at heart, sir. Here is Jim Lincoln, the lawyer I hired for her—"

"Good. I want to meet that man. He's on my payroll now," Daddy said. "Mr. Lincoln, Earl Bennett, World War Two veteran here. You'd better tell me right now if you're capable of getting my daughter out of this or else I'll have to find another lawyer."

"I assure you, Mr. Bennett," Jim Lincoln said, "I will do everything in my power to have Bebe released today, but I must caution you that the DA is asking for no bail."

"What the hell!" Daddy shouted.

"Mr. Bennett, how nice to see you."

Darlene. Thank God.

The door opened and then closed behind Jim Lincoln.

"My father is paying for you from now on," I burst out.

"So I understand. We have thirty minutes before the hearing. Tell me what happened."

I explained everything.

The lawyer never took his eyes off mine. Finally he nodded and made notes.

"Bebe, it's important that you remain silent during the hearing no matter what the judge decides. We are going to plead innocent on all charges."

"Well, I am innocent! How else would we plead?"

He held up a hand. "I know you've been through a lot, but you must remain calm in the courtroom."

A uniformed officer came in a door opposite the one Jim had entered through. "Judge Hedley is ready for your case, Mr. Lincoln."

Jim led the way, Elma guiding me by the handcuffs. We entered a small courtroom. I didn't have to wait long before I saw Daddy.

"Why in tarnation have they got my Little Magnolia in handcuffs? Take those off her!" At six feet one, with a military bearing and iron gray hair, Daddy cut an impressive figure.

Another uniformed officer rushed to his side and said something to Daddy that made him sit down quietly.

Practically everyone I knew had shown up for this shindig: Daddy, Darlene, Stu, Bradley—dressed in a sharp black suit—Danielle, Finelli, and, of course, Snyder. The nasty detective sat with a tall blond man at a table across from where Jim and I sat.

The black-robed judge entered the room and we all stood.

The next fifteen minutes went by in a blur. The tall blond man turned out to be the DA. He said awful things about me and insisted I not be released from jail until my trial was over.

Jim Lincoln took a calm, reasonable approach with the judge. He called forth Darlene, Stu, Danielle, and Bradley as character witnesses. Darlene, Stu, and Danielle spoke so highly of me that tears fell down my cheeks. When it was Bradley's turn, he called me "a highly skilled, responsible, intelligent young woman of faith who would never think of hurting anyone." I lowered my head so he couldn't see my tears.

The courtroom went silent as Judge Hedley considered his decision.

My heart thudded in my chest.

At last he said, "Would the defendant please rise."

Jim and I stood.

"Miss Bennett, I'm releasing you into the custody of your father, Earl Bennett. You are not to leave the state of New York. If you do so, bail will be forfeited and you will spend the remainder of the time until your trial in jail." Then he named a bail amount that made me gasp.

Elma unlocked my handcuffs.

Daddy counted out a wad of cash to the court clerk. Jim Lincoln stood next to him.

The judge, the DA, Finelli, and Snyder exited the room, Snyder flashing me a look of disgust.

Danielle hugged me and I thanked her for her testimony.

Then I was in Darlene's arms. She whispered, "There's no need to wash your face in tears. Bradley is beside himself. He called the mayor trying to get you out of jail last night."

"Really?"

"Yes, so whatever fight you two had, keep that in mind. Stu and I are talking. You can reach me at his house. I tried to convince your daddy that the two of you could stay at the apartment, but he's already checked in at the Legends Hotel."

"Okay. I'll have to go by the apartment and get some things. I'm dirty and upset and I haven't slept much for two nights."

She released me. "Get some rest and call me. We'll get you through this."

Stu stepped up and hugged me. "You know my doll and I are here for whatever you need, Bebe."

"Thanks, Stu."

After they left, Bradley walked over to me. He took my hand in his, running his thumb over my palm.

I tried to look at him, but couldn't. "Thanks for what you said about me."

"I meant every word, you know I did," he whispered. "You didn't kill anyone. I just wish you'd allow me to help you."

"You were the one who suggested I call my father," I said softly.

"Baby, I shouldn't have said that. I want to be the one—"

"You!" Daddy shouted at Bradley. "Let go of her hand."

"Mr. Bennett, I need to explain—"

But it was too late. Daddy reached us and saw the marks on my neck. His face went that bad purple color. "Williams, did you mark up my Little Magnolia's neck like that?"

"Yes, I did. As I was saying—"

Before I could move, Daddy drew back his fist and punched Bradley in the eye. When Bradley remained standing, Daddy hit him again across the jaw.

Bradley staggered back to the table.

"Stop it, Daddy!"

A uniformed officer, his hand resting on his gun, came over and addressed Bradley. "Sir, do you wish to press charges against this man? I saw him strike you."

"No," Bradley said, taking the white handkerchief out of his breast pocket and wiping blood from his mouth.

"Let's go, Bebe," Daddy said. He took my arm in a firm grasp.

"Bebe!" Bradley called. "Where are you staying?"

"Don't tell that playboy anything," Daddy ordered.

"At the Legends," I cried.

Daddy swung around. "You're not welcome at the hotel, Williams, and you can get yourself another secretary. When Bebe is cleared of these asinine charges, she is coming back to Richmond with me."

"No, Daddy."

"You'll give me your promise right now, young lady, or else I'll find that judge and tell him I can't be responsible for you. Promise me."

Bradley cared about me, I was sure of that.

But he hadn't said he loved me.

He hadn't offered marriage.

I loved him too much for just an affair.

"I promise, Daddy."

Without another word, Daddy marched me out of the courtroom.

I didn't look back at Bradley. I wouldn't have been able to see him through my tears.

Chapter Twenty-one

I opened my eyes and had to think for a moment about where I was. The brown-and-gold patterned bedspread brought everything back to me. Jail, the courtroom, Daddy, the judge, Bradley holding my hand, Daddy punching Bradley twice, my promise to return to Richmond, the Legends Hotel.

I shut my eyes after taking a peek at Daddy, who sat in a chair across the room reading the newspaper. I didn't want him to know I was awake yet. I had plans to make.

After I'd gotten out of jail, Daddy had gone with me to my apartment. He stood guard while I packed a suitcase—telling me to leave the black go-go boots behind because I wouldn't be wearing them in his presence—and then escorted me to the hotel. The Legends was a luxurious hotel, and our large room contained two plump double beds, a table with two chairs, an armchair, a dresser, and a color TV. Daddy had ordered room service after I told him I was too tired to go downstairs to eat. I finally got to take a long shower and wash my hair. I crawled into my nightgown, ate a chicken dinner, and then we called Mama. Daddy talked to her first and squealed on me about my hickeys. He said he didn't know how long it would take to straighten out the legal mess or how long we'd be in this "heathen" city, but he'd call back in a few days.

Then he handed the phone to me.

"Bebe, dear, what exactly is your relationship to Bradley Williams?"

"He's my boss, Mama. You know that. He gave me an excellent character reference in court today."

"Your father said you have love bites on your neck and that Bradley admitted giving them to you. I don't want to pry," she said, and I knew I was in for it, "but you can tell me if you made a mistake with this man."

Mistake. That covered a lot of territory. "What do you mean?"

"You haven't done *that* with him, have you?" Mama's voice shook.

Proudly I said, "No, but I do love him."

Daddy heaved a sigh as if he had the weight of the world on him.

"Has he told you that he loves you, Bebe?"

"No, Mama."

She drew in a breath. "Be careful, dear. I don't want to see you get hurt. Men will not buy the cow if they can get the milk for free."

I rolled my eyes. "I know, Mama."

She cleared her throat, a sure indicator of embarrassment. "Dear, a girl doesn't want to allow petting to get out of hand. Men, er, have a difficult, if not impossible, time stopping and it's painful for them if they are led to believe—"

"Mama, I know." I didn't think it wise to mention the sex education I'd received from Sister of Mercy and the Widow.

"I'm glad. Get some sleep and everything will be better in the morning."

"Okay, Mama."

"Give the phone back to your father."

I had fallen asleep while they were talking, and didn't even remember my dreams.

I was brought to the morning and the present by Daddy's voice.

"Are you going to lie there thinking all day, or are you going to say good morning to your father?" he asked.

I smiled. "Hi, Daddy. What time is it?"

"Almost eleven," he replied, tossing the newspaper and his reading glasses onto the table. "This city is full of crime. Some of the things I read would never happen in Richmond."

"There are a lot more people here than in Richmond, so it stands to reason there would be more crime. Have you had breakfast?"

"I have breakfast at eight every morning, Little Magnolia, you know that. You slept fifteen hours. How are you?"

Itching to break into John Mallory's apartment. "Hungry."

"Why don't you get dressed and we'll have lunch downstairs. I want to be back in the room by two o'clock when the game comes on."

I'd forgotten it was Saturday. Every Saturday and Sunday afternoon, Daddy watched whatever game was on TV. I threw back the bedcovers, already plotting how I could get away from him. Mallory would be at the store. I had his address written in the steno pad in my purse. All I needed was a butter knife and I could sneak one of those out of the restaurant.

"Put on that pretty blue suit I saw you bring. It's cold here. The high is only going to be in the fifties today."

"Yes, Daddy."

I went meekly into the bathroom, lulling him into a false sense of security.

Downstairs, I ate a hearty plate of steak and eggs while Daddy tucked into meat loaf and gravy with mashed potatoes. I urged him to have a slice of apple pie, knowing the fuller his stomach was the higher the odds of him falling asleep in front of the game.

Back in our room, Daddy took off his sport coat and shoes, turned on the TV, and propped himself up in bed in front of the game.

"I'm going to sit here and write out some thoughts," I told him, placing my purse on the table and pulling out my steno pad. My gaze dropped to the notes I'd made in Bradley's closet, bringing back memories of his bed. I hoped Daddy couldn't read my mind.

"That's a good girl. The newspaper is over there if you want something to read."

Apparently, he couldn't read my mind.

Thirty minutes later Daddy was snoring.

I tore off a piece of paper and wrote, "Had to go out for a woman's personal need. Be back soon." I left the note on the table and tiptoed out of the room, opening and closing the door with extreme care.

I was free! I took the elevator downstairs and grabbed a cab that was parked outside the hotel and told the driver, "Number Seventy-eight Pershing Street."

We took off. Mallory actually lived at Number Eighty-two Pershing Street, but I was being cautious. I donned my Jackie Kennedy shades, thankful the day was sunny, and added a pair of prim white gloves. This secret agent girl wasn't going to leave fingerprints.

I paid the driver and got out of the cab. The neigh-

borhood was affluent. I had expected nothing less.
Two men, one blond and one dark-haired, sat in
wrought iron chairs on the small porch of Number
Eighty. They were engaged in conversation and didn't
notice me.

Number Eighty-two, Mallory's building, had a doorman, but I was prepared.

Knowing very well that Mallory was at the store
and would not be returning home, I said in my haugh-
tiest tone of voice, "Mr. Mallory will be joining me
momentarily."

He opened the door and I waltzed into the foyer.

According to his employment record, Mallory's
apartment was on the tenth floor. I rode the elevator,
my palms beginning to sweat. Would I manage to
break in? There had to be something there, a major
piece of evidence that would prove the store manager
was a double murderer. Would I find it? I had to.
Daddy would never allow me to go back to work at
Merryweathers'. He'd keep me in that hotel, or worse,
find an apartment outside of my beloved Manhattan
for us to stay in for the duration of the trial.

The elevator let me out on the tenth floor. A pretty
Persian rug was spread on the dark hardwood floor.
There were only four apartments. Mallory's was apart-
ment C.

I dug the butter knife I'd snagged at lunch out of my
purse and dropped to my knees. If this didn't work, I
still had the metal nail file. Imitating what I'd seen
Darlene do with Bradley's lock, I struggled to open
the door. It didn't budge. I sent up a prayer, ex-
plaining that I knew it was wrong to break into Mallory's place, but would the good Lord please
understand my motives? Finally the lock gave way,
and with a pleased cry and a quick prayer of thanks,

I opened the door. With all the broken slivers of wood I'd left on the door, when Mallory put his key in the lock tonight he'd be sure to notice that it had been tampered with, but I simply didn't care. I closed the door behind me, locked it, and prepared to turn everything upside down until I found something incriminating.

I stared in shock at the large living room. Expecting to find expensive furniture, crystal decanters, and paintings hung in fashionable frames, I couldn't believe my eyes.

An ugly green sofa that the Salvation Army would likely refuse, a scratched coffee table—empty beer cans crushed and discarded on top—and a small black-and-white TV were the only items in the room. The walls were bare. Two big windows were open—no draperies—letting in fresh air, but the apartment still smelled like a bad cigar.

I made quick work of looking in and under the sofa, finding nothing. The rickety coffee table was covered with racing forms, scribbled notes in the margins, names of horses circled, and numbers noted. I stood very still. Suddenly, things I had thought unrelated joined together to form a picture. I remembered seeing a racing form in Mallory's desk at the store. The Pirate's parrot had said, "You bet the clown's dead." The white envelopes passed between the Teddy Bear and Mallory. Betting money? The day Kinker had been murdered, he had told Mallory he "could bet on it," as if it was a common taunt.

Was horse racing the business the three men had in common? Who exactly was John Mallory, a man who pretended to be English but hid an Irish accent? Did the men have a disagreement, perhaps over money? Was that why Mallory had killed Kinker? I thought back to the argument I'd observed Mallory having with the Teddy Bear outside the store.

I moved on to the next room. In the kitchen, a roach crawled across the dirty stove. Yesterday's paper lay on the counter, turned to the results of the races held the day before. There was no table in the room. I went through the cabinets as best I could, not being tall enough to see the upper shelves. A couple of glasses, a coffee mug, and paper plates were all I could find. The refrigerator contained a tin of coffee and a cardboard pizza box.

I wandered to the bathroom and flicked on the light. Roaches ran in every direction. I shut off the light and shuddered. If there was anything in that disgusting room, I wasn't going to find it.

The bedroom contained a mattress on the floor and a decrepit chest of drawers against one wall. I went through the latter, finding socks, underclothes, more of the white gloves Mallory wore, shoe polish and the like. The bottom drawer revealed a few photographs of a younger Mallory, standing on a beach boardwalk next to a younger man who might have been his brother.

Opening the closet, I saw the only form of wealth, the only hint of the Mallory I knew: Dozens of expensive shirts and suits hung on the rack. Shiny shoes gleamed from the floor below them.

I closed the closet door, walked slowly around the bed, my mind in turmoil. I couldn't believe the squalor in which Mallory lived. Was he spending all his money on the races? I knew he made a very good salary plus bonuses at the store. He had to be addicted to gambling and spending every cent he earned on the horses. The thought occurred to me that Mallory could leave

everything he owned behind without a second thought
and flee the city at a moment's notice. But why?

My gaze dropped to a baseball bat on the floor next
to the bed. Mallory's definition of protection, I
guessed. Absently, I picked up the bat and slapped it
in my hand while I wandered back to the living room.
I felt defeated. There was no evidence here to prove
anything other than the fact that Mallory was a sick
man, obsessed with gambling. I couldn't even find anything to link him with Kinker or Runion.

Frustrated and angry, I slapped the bat across the
palm of my left hand. It was then that I noticed the baseball bat seemed lighter than normal. Not that I was any
expert in the matter, but I had played softball in school.

Examining the bat, my heart jumped as I turned the
handle and it came off in my hand. Papers fell to the floor.
I dropped to my hands and knees, laying the hollowed-
out baseball bat beside me.

There was a rolled birth certificate from the state
of Massachusetts with the name John *O'Malley*.

Another paper turned out to be a list of men's
names and phone numbers, all with Boston area
codes. I knew since I'd just placed a call to Boston
two days ago.

A bill of sale stated that John O'Malley had transferred Boston property to a Mr. Mike Hughes for the
sum of one dollar. My brows came together. Who was
Mike Hughes? A relative? Someone Mallory—or
O'Malley—owed money to?

I peered inside the baseball bat and pried out two
social security cards with different numbers, one for
John Mallory and the other for John O'Malley.

I gathered the papers together and clutched them
in my hand.

Why would John O'Malley become John Mallory?

A person changed his identity to hide from someone else. I dismissed the idea of a wife and children he didn't want to pay support to, as I couldn't imagine coldhearted Mallory ever being married. Putting together his addiction to horse racing and the way he was living, I decided Mallory was hiding from a person he owed a great deal of money to.

"You're so predictable, Miss Bennett." O'Malley's Irish lilt sounded from the doorway.

I gasped and shot to my feet.

"Who are you and why did you kill Kinker and Runion? You were all involved in a gambling ring, weren't you?" I blurted out, relieved to see he was not holding a weapon on me.

He closed the door and locked it, shaking his head. "I tried to warn you. I told you how I felt about meddlesome women, yet you persisted."

"How did you know I was here?"

He tossed his bowler hat on the sofa. "My brother, Brian, told me a *Mrs. Williams* had called for a reference for me. The number you dialed, which I assume you got from my employment application, is Brian's apartment phone number. Brown's Department Store doesn't exist. Once I knew you were getting close to the truth, I told my well-tipped doorman that a woman I've been having an affair with might show up at my apartment. He called me as soon as you got on the elevator."

"We're not having an affair. No one will believe that."

"Oh, I'm betting they will. And we're going to have a terrible argument because I've ended it. A struggle will ensue and you'll plunge to your death out of that window," he said, pointing with his walking stick.

"You're quite the betting man, aren't you, Mr. O'Malley?"

He pressed something on the walking stick and a long blade popped out of the end. "I'm hedging my bets on this one. You can always be stabbed like the others."

My breath caught in my throat. *Odds are you won't live to see tomorrow. . . .* I swallowed hard, tension knotting in my stomach. "You used that walking stick, not the letter opener, to kill Mel Kinker. Then you tried to make it look like the Pirate had killed him."

"Now you're catching on. I meant no harm to Geedunk. He was the only one in the store that Kinker couldn't uncover an ugly secret about, thus the police would find the Pirate had no motive. I thought the murder would go unsolved."

"Kinker must have known about your secret gambling obsession."

O'Malley's face hardened. "Kinker was a fool who existed only to cause misery to others, believing he was the store's true talent. He overheard Runion and me discussing our gambling profits and wanted in on the action. When I refused, he threatened to tell the new management. I couldn't lose my position. It had been hard enough to deceive the gullible Merryweathers. The clown left me no choice but to eliminate him."

"You waited until you thought everyone had gone home the night of the store's birthday party and stabbed him with that blade." I pointed to the end of the walking stick. "Then you stuck the altered pirate's knife in the wound."

"Clever of me, wouldn't you say? I did the world a service by killing that greedy, awful man. Then you came along and found him dead, very conveniently picking up the knife the police thought had killed him. You have been of some use. If only you hadn't decided to come here . . . but you've sealed your own fate."

He lunged forward and grabbed my arm in a tight hold. "It's your choice: the window or my blade. If you make me choose the blade, I'll stab you multiple times, making you look like the victim of a deranged killer. They'll find you at the bottom of the garbage chute."

Panic rioted inside me.

"Who is Mike Hughes?" I asked with a boldness I did not feel.

His nostrils flared. "I gave him everything I had, but it wasn't enough to pay back what I owed," he spat out with contempt.

"He was your bookie in Boston. You got in over your head. You had to sign that property over to him, create a new identity for yourself, and leave Boston all because of your addiction to gambling."

"It's not that simple. Big Mike would have killed me if I stayed in the city I grew up in. The son of a bitch wouldn't cut me a break. I'll find a way to kill him for forcing me to run."

"You didn't cut Kinker a break."

"I told you, he was blackmailing me."

"And what about your partner, Runion? Why did he have to die?"

O'Malley grasped the walking stick in one hand, his other arm still gripping mine, as he used the side of his body to push me toward the window. "Curious to the bitter end, aren't you? I hired Runion because during my interview with him, he answered my casual question about horse racing with interest. I needed someone to place my bets with a bookie. Big Mike had it all over the East Coast that he was looking for me. Runion didn't know that until he and our bookie, Ralph, got chummy. A few nights ago over several beers, Ralph told Runion the story of how Big Mike in Boston had word out of a reward he was offering for information about me. Runion came to me. I tried to deny that I was the one Big Mike was looking for."

"That's why you two had an argument outside the store."

"Yes. Runion wanted a bigger cut of our earnings. He was another greedy bastard, but I took care of him and left him as a gift for you at your door. Again, Miss Bennett, you came to my rescue, although why you decided to steal my letter opener is a mystery to me."

"The coroner's report came back. The police know it wasn't the pirate's knife that killed Kinker. They know it was a longer blade."

His jaw tensed. "Damn them. It will have to be the window for you. I'll stick with my story that we've been lovers, then you came to me in a desperate attempt to enlist my help in fleeing the state. When I told you there was nothing I could do, you jumped to your death rather than spend your life in prison."

"No one will believe you! Everyone knows I'm in love with Bradley Williams."

"You forget I'm a betting man." With that, he tossed his walking stick across the room so he could use both arms to force me to the window.

Frightened out of my skin, I fought him viciously, but with no carpet underneath our feet, he half dragged, half slid me across the floor to the open window. I shot a look at the windowsill, hoping he'd have to lift me up and over, but the opening was about chest high. He had only to shove me out.

I thrust my hands underneath his suit coat and dug my nails into his back with all my might. At the same time, I tried to knee him where it would hurt the most, but he blocked me with his thigh each time.

"You hellcat," he grunted.

We were beside the window now. The sounds of horns honking met my ears. The breeze blew my hair around my face, blinding me, and I pinched his back as hard as I could.

Breaking his hold on my arms, O'Malley clenched his strong hands around my waist and bent me down sideways across the windowsill. I held tightly to his suit jacket, dragging him down with me. We both dangled out the window. If I was going to my death by God, so was he.

But he was stronger than me, and I felt the balance shifting in his favor. My breath came in strained gasps. I struggled to push him out the window, but it was no use. I was going to die.

When I closed my eyes, Bradley's face flashed in my mind. I'd never have a chance to tell him I loved him. A surge of energy jolted through me.

I released my hold on O'Malley's suit jacket, raised my hands, and grabbed his hair, pulling it with all my might.

He howled in pain, caught off guard for a split second, which was all it took.

I kneed him hard in the groin.

The action weakened him. Suddenly the balance was in my favor, and he fell out the window.

With horror, I watched his body flail in the air.

I heard his scream as he plunged ten stories to the pavement below.

His body lay sprawled on the ground, twisted in an unnatural way, people rushing over to him.

I gulped air, turned from the window, and shook uncontrollably. My legs couldn't support me and I slumped to the floor, thinking over and over how easily it could have been me lying broken on the street below. I bit my lip until it throbbed like my pulse, listening to sirens and the screeching of tires.

Then someone pounded on the door, shouting my name.

Unable to stand, I crawled to the front door and unlocked it.

"Oh, thank God, you're all right, Bebe," Bradley said, sweeping me up into his arms and holding me tighter than he ever had before.

Chapter Twenty-two

I hugged Bradley, noticing the bruising around his eye and chin from Daddy's punches. "How did you know I was here?"

Clasping me around the waist with one arm, he reached up and stroked my hair, then tilted my chin and kissed me gently on the lips. Pulling back, he said, "Your father called demanding where you were. I tracked down Finelli and we put it together."

Finelli appeared in the doorway. I released Bradley, but he stood at my side, his arm still around my waist, keeping me snugly against him.

"Miss Bennett, you have more lives than a cat and are more trouble than a houseful of them."

I tried to smile. "Even James Bond runs into difficulties every now and then."

He pulled out his notebook. "What happened?"

I told him what I'd suspected about Mallory based on my observations and the combined input from Tom and Darlene, all of which had led me to search the store manager's apartment.

"No more breaking and entering for you, baby," Bradley murmured in my ear. "Even though the last time ended in the most pleasurable—"

"Excuse me," Finelli interrupted. "I have a job to do here."

I put my arm back around Bradley's waist and continued to explain how Mallory was really O'Malley—breaking away from Bradley long enough to retrieve the evidence that had been hidden in the baseball bat. I also explained about the gambling ring and how Mallory had killed Kinker and Runion, deliberately casting suspicion on others.

Pointing to the walking stick in the corner of the room, I said, "That's the real murder weapon for the Kinker case. The letter opener belonged to Mallory. I removed it from his office after I found out that the pirate's knife was not the actual murder weapon. I had intended to give it to you, Detective Finelli, but you know where it ended up."

Finelli asked for more details and I answered as best I could.

"Now that the real killer is dead, can you drop the charges against Bebe?" Bradley asked.

"I'll speak to the DA before the day is over, but I'm sure the answer will be yes."

"Snyder seems to have it in for me. He's in charge of the case. Are you sure he won't put a spoke in the wheels?" I asked.

Finelli closed his notebook. "I guess I'll tell you now what's been going on in my investigation, but it can't go any further than this room."

Bradley and I agreed.

"There's been an internal investigation of Ed Snyder. The man has been living beyond the means of a police detective for some time now, his most recent display of wealth being his brand new Barracuda. I discovered Snyder's been providing protection for

Ralph Jones, O'Malley's bookie, who's involved in a syndicate of high-profile, unscrupulous men in the gambling world that the department has been trying to bring down for years."

"Are you saying that Snyder is crooked?" Bradley asked.

"I'm saying he's under an internal investigation. I know about Big Mike, and my department is cooperating with the Boston police. From what I've gleaned, Runion had already told Ralph that he knew where O'Malley was. It was only a matter of time before Big Mike made sure O'Malley bought the farm. So you see, Miss Bennett, you were caught up in something even bigger than you imagined, even more dangerous. I don't want you involved in any police investigation ever again. Next time, I won't keep any of your secrets either."

"Wow, that's incredible, Detective Finelli. I hope you're promoted for your work. I'm available if you need a letter of commendation."

"What secret?" Bradley asked.

Finelli made for the door. "I'll let you two discuss that alone in the hallway. The crime scene boys will be here any second." He walked us out the door. "Thanks for that offer, Bebe," he said and smiled.

I then shyly confessed to Bradley that I'd never dated Kinker and had only told the police that I had because they pressed me regarding what Kinker knew about me. "The clown had observed me, and he, uh, saw that I was attracted to you. He taunted me about it and threatened to tell everyone in the store."

Instead of being angry, Bradley turned me toward him and into his arms. He said, "Hmm, perhaps you could demonstrate that attraction with a kiss."

He didn't have to ask twice.

"How about a relaxing picnic by the lake in Central Park?" Bradley asked once the police had come and driven us outdoors into the sunshine. "Are you up for it, or do you want me to take you back to your father so you can crash?"

I smiled. "I'd love a picnic. I need to change clothes at my apartment and call Daddy though. I'm sure he's flipped by now."

A short cab ride later, we arrived on East Sixty-fifth Street. Harry stood on my stoop pressing the buzzer. Bradley helped me out of the taxi and I called out to Harry.

"There you are, Miss Sweet Face," he said, moving toward us.

I took inventory of him, finding him sober and clean. He'd even trimmed his wild eyebrows. "Have you met Bradley Williams, Harry?"

The two men shook hands, Harry eyeing Bradley up and down. He said, "We haven't been introduced, but I know who you are, Williams. I like seeing you with Bebe. You should be with her more often."

"Harry," I protested, as if I meant it.

Bradley smiled. "From now on, I intend to stick by her side. She needs someone to keep an eye on her," he teased.

I pushed him playfully and then asked Harry how he was doing.

"I'm better every day I don't take a drink. I feel like a new man, Bebe, but I know it's going to be a constant struggle. They're still keeping me on at the church doing work around the grounds until I can find a job."

"We have an opening at the store, don't we, Bradley?"

"Well, yes," he said slowly.

"How would you like to be the store greeter at Merryweathers' Toy Shoppe, Harry?" I said excitedly. "All you have to do is wear a Teddy Bear outfit and open the door for customers. I know you're capable of much more than that, but this job could be a small start to getting back into meaningful work, such as being an engineer again."

A gleam of hope flashed in Harry's eyes.

I looked at Bradley.

"Harry, if you're interested, come down to the store Monday afternoon and we'll talk," Bradley said.

Harry stared at him for a long moment. "I'd be grateful for the opportunity."

I beamed, and Bradley and I entered my building. Just before we crossed into the hallway, I looked back at Harry. He gave me the thumbs-up sign, smiled, and walked on down the street.

Upstairs, Darlene and Stu were in her bedroom talking with the door open.

Darlene zoomed toward me, Stu on her heels.

"Bebe! I'm so happy to see you!" She threw herself into my arms. "I called Jim Lincoln and he'd talked to Finelli. That bastard Mallory! Are you okay?"

"I—"

"I can see you're fine! Hi, Bradley, you remember Stu."

The two men shook hands.

Darlene's face glowed with happiness. While Stu and Bradley chatted about the Cardinals-Yankees game, Darlene pulled me aside. "Honey, are you really okay?"

"Yes," I said, then briefly filled her in on the day's events.

"Doll, are we going to tell Bebe and Bradley our

news?" Stu asked, moving to place his arm around Darlene.

Darlene had her big trademark Texas grin on her face. "Stu and I have been talking a lot. We wanted to wait until this mess about Kinker had been cleared up, and then we got the good news—"

Stu interrupted. "What my doll is trying to tell you is that we're going to fly to Las Vegas and elope!"

I shrieked in delight, grabbed Darlene, and squeezed her hard. "I'm so happy for you! And Las Vegas! That sounds like a blast! And just right for the two of you."

Darlene giggled. "We won't be leaving for a few days, honey, so you and I will have plenty of time to talk. And don't worry about the apartment. We'll work something out."

My smile faded and I looked at the floor. "Once you've moved in with Stu, we might as well give up the apartment. I've promised Daddy I would return to Richmond with him. You know I'm not the type to break a serious promise."

No one said anything.

When I raised my head, Darlene and Bradley were looking at each other.

Darlene smiled at me. "Maybe your father will change his mind and release you from that promise."

"I doubt it. Speaking of Daddy, I'd better call him."

I moved to the phone in the kitchen, Bradley at my side. He sure was behaving in a manner I'd never observed before, but maybe that was because he knew our time together was limited. Heck, for all I knew, Daddy and I could be on the train to Richmond by Monday afternoon.

"Hi, Daddy. I'm sorry I left like that—Daddy, please don't shout at me—I'm fine, honest, and the

killer is, um, in the hands of the police." No sense
telling Daddy all the horrible details.

"Yes, Daddy, please calm down. My name will be
cleared. One of the detectives told me. I guess it will
be official by Monday afternoon." Now I had to ask
permission to stay out, just like the kid Bradley always
called me. "Daddy, I have plans for the rest of the
afternoon. I hope that's all right." I blushed. "Yes,
with Bradley."

I held the phone out to Bradley and whispered, "He
wants to talk to you."

Bradley accepted the receiver. "Hello, Mr.
Bennett. . . . Yes, sir, I'll see that she eats and doesn't
get cold. . . . Very well, I'll have her back to the Legends at a decent hour. . . . Er, yes, I plan to. . . . Thank
you, Mr. Bennett." Bradley replaced the receiver.

I felt seven years old.

Bradley smiled at me. "Don't worry, baby. We've
got a hall pass for the rest of the day."

"Baby," not "kid." I loved that. It was so sexy.
Laughter bubbled up inside me and spilled out.

I changed into a soft pink fuzzy sweater, a pink-
and-black-striped skirt, and the black go-go boots.

Bradley gave me the once-over when I emerged
from my room. "Have you got a jacket?"

"Here," Darlene said and ran into her room, returning with a short, black fake-fur coat. "I haven't
even worn this yet, Bebe. It'll be choice on you."

Bradley helped me put the coat on and I thanked
Darlene.

We said our good-byes and walked out of the
apartment.

"Yoohoo!"

I looked up at the stairway leading to the fourth
floor. A couple in their sixties walked toward Bradley

and me. They were both gray-haired and on the pudgy side.

The woman said, "You must be one of the girls who lives in the apartment below us."

I gripped my purse. No, it couldn't be! "I live in three-B."

She smiled. "We're directly above you in four-B. I'm Lily and this is my husband, Willie. He's the quiet type, or at least he was until he had his heart surgery six months ago. Now he has a new lease on life. We've been married for thirty-six years," she said proudly.

"I've never been quiet," Willie said. "She just needs a hearing aid."

I couldn't believe my ears. This was the sex-crazy couple upstairs? Would wonders never cease?

"It's nice to meet you both. I'm Bebe and this is my friend Bradley."

We made small talk for a few minutes, but I finally had to break away. I felt embarrassed since I'd overheard evidence of Willie's "new lease on life." Wait until I told Darlene tomorrow!

At the Plaza, Bradley told me he had a surprise visitor staying at the hotel.

"I'll call him and ask him to come downstairs. We can chat while we wait for our picnic basket."

"Okay," I said, curious.

While Bradley gave instructions for our meal, I sat in the Piano Bar enjoying the music. Bradley returned ten minutes later with a smartly dressed older man who had to be in his seventies. His posture was straight, and he had alert blue eyes with an amused twinkle in their depths. Although he was balding, his white hair was well groomed.

"Uncle Herman, I'd like you to meet Bebe Bennett," Bradley said. "Bebe, this is Herman Shires."

I tried to cover my shock. "Mr. Shires, it's an honor to meet you."

He took my hand and gave it a gentle squeeze before releasing it. "My dear, I assure you the pleasure is all mine. Bradley has told me much about you. He didn't exaggerate your beauty, I'm happy to say."

"Heavens," I murmured, drawing a chuckle from Mr. Shires. I wondered why he was in New York. My package containing the evidence of Drew's deception could not have reached Palm Beach already.

A waiter brought three glasses of champagne.

Mr. Shires raised his glass. "I'd like to make a toast. To my nephew, Bradley Williams, the new owner of Shires Enterprises. May you enjoy every success both in business and in your personal life."

I gasped and turned to Bradley. "You didn't tell me! Congratulations!"

He smiled. "Uncle Herman arrived last night. We'd been meeting all morning and he gave me the news before I picked you up this afternoon."

Mr. Shires smiled. "Are we going to drink our champagne or talk?"

I laughed and clinked glasses with Mr. Shires, then Bradley. I held his gaze, hoping mine told him how proud I was of him. He hadn't needed my help at all in landing the coveted position of heir to Shires Enterprises. I sent up a silent prayer of thanks that I'd never made any suggestion that Mr. Shires should choose Bradley when I sent my package of evidence.

Joy spread through me as Mr. Shires explained that he had already transferred ownership of the large conglomeration of companies to Bradley before leaving Palm Beach. Mr. Shires would remain as a consultant, but basically the whole thing was Bradley's to do with as he wished. How I'd like to be the proverbial fly on the wall when Drew learned he'd been defeated.

The waiter returned with a large picnic basket. Bradley signed for it and Mr. Shires said, "I'll let you two young people head over to the park. Miss Bennett, I understand your father is in town."

"Please call me Bebe, Mr. Shires. And yes, my father is here."

"I'd be pleased if you and Mr. Bennett could join Bradley and me for brunch tomorrow at noon here at the Plaza."

Bradley said, "Please say yes, Bebe."

"I'd like to, but I need to ask Daddy first. May I call you after church tomorrow and let you know?"

"Call me, dear Bebe, if it's necessary. Somehow I don't think it will be," Mr. Shires said with a glint in his eye.

Bradley and I lay sprawled on a blanket on a carpet of red, gold, and brown leaves in Central Park just as the sun was beginning to set. I tried to push aside thoughts of how this might be my last time alone with him. I'd convince Daddy to accept Mr. Shires's invitation to brunch if it killed me, but I could only pray that Daddy would release me from my promise to leave New York. Maybe I could throw myself on Mama's mercy and get her to convince him.

"What are you thinking?" Bradley asked, brushing a strand of hair off my face and tucking it behind my ear.

"I'm very proud that your uncle didn't just make you heir. He gave you the whole company! You must be thrilled. Do you think you'll stay at Merryweathers' or take on one of the other companies?"

"I haven't made any decisions yet, though I do have an interest in architecture. Uncle Herman—I mean *I*— own an architectural firm here in New York," Bradley said, tracing a lazy finger down the side of my cheek.

I shivered at his touch.

"Are you cold?"

"No."

"We should leave soon. It's getting dark."

"Okay."

"Did you enjoy the picnic?"

I placed my hand on my stomach. "Are you joking? Cold chicken, deviled eggs, caviar on toast points, chocolate cake . . . who wouldn't relish that combination? The company was nice too."

"But something is bothering you."

"You'll probably think it sounds silly, but before I moved to New York, I made a list of things I wanted to do here. I haven't done them all yet and now I'll be leaving."

"Name something you wanted to do."

I chuckled. "Well, I wanted to sail a little boat in the lake here in Central Park."

Bradley leapt to his feet. "Wait right here."

Before I could say more, he ran off. Down by the lake I saw his tall figure bent over next to a woman and her son. Bradley pulled something out of his pocket, handed it to the woman, and came running back to me. He held a sailboat in his hand.

I stood up and he presented it to me like a little boy holding out wildflowers to his first sweetheart.

"Oh, Bradley. Did you buy that boy's toy?"

"He got a great deal on it and an invitation to come into Merryweathers' and pick out another one for free. Come on, let's get this baby in the water!"

Tears formed in my eyes, but I gave Bradley the biggest smile I could.

He kissed me, then led me to the water.

All too soon, the sun began to set. People wandered home since the park wasn't safe after dark. We returned the picnic basket to the Plaza and then Bradley hailed a cab.

When we got in, he looked at me and said, "Do you mind if we run by the store before I take you back to the Legends? It's almost seven, so everyone will be gone."

"No, I don't mind."

As the cab pulled up outside Merryweathers', I found myself minding after all. Should I go ahead and clear out my desk? Should I suggest safe, soon-to-be-married Danielle as my replacement? Should I beg Bradley not to let the day end?

He unlocked the door.

"Stay here. I'll be right back."

"Okay."

He hadn't turned on the lights on the sales floor, but did so on the second floor reading area. Despite the bad things that had happened at Merryweathers', the store still held its charm for me. I could hear the echo of children's laughter, a precious sound to me now that I was leaving it all behind.

Bradley returned as I stood near the elaborate train display. The trains reminded me of one Christmas when Santa had brought me a set. I smiled, remembering how much fun Daddy had had with that train.

Bradley moved to the other side of the display near the depot, flipped a switch, and the big engine pulling the train's cars began its way toward me.

I giggled. "Should we really be playing with this?"

Bradley assumed a mock-haughty pose. "Why not? I own it."

My laughter rang out in the quiet store.

Suddenly the train stopped.

I looked down to see what was wrong.

The open freight car stood at my fingertips. Resting on top was a small, square turquoise box tied with a matching ribbon.

My pulse pounded. Slowly I raised my eyes to Bradley.

His face was a study in anxiety. Bradley was . . . nervous!

"I've never done this before, so I hope I do it right," he whispered. His fingers shook as he picked up the box and handed it to me. "Go ahead and open it, Bebe."

My hands trembled and a lump grew in my throat. I managed to untie the bow and lift the lid. A velvet box lay nestled inside. I pulled it out and held it in my hand.

A few tears escaped and ran down my cheeks. Bradley pulled me into his arms. I rested my head on his strong chest and heard his heart pounding. "Forgive me for taking so long, sweetheart. I had to be certain of *myself* because this is forever in my heart."

He took the box from my hand and opened it.

I sucked in my breath. A brilliant, huge marquis-shaped diamond set in platinum dazzled my eyes.

"Bebe," Bradley whispered, causing me to look up at him, "I love you. Will you marry me?"

Euphoria overcame me as a warm glow filled my heart and soul.

"Yes, Bradley. I want to marry you more than anything else in the world. I fell in love with you the first time I saw you, and that love has grown every single day since."

His face burst into a smile. Taking the ring from the velvet box, he lifted my left hand and slipped the platinum band on my ring finger. It fit perfectly.

Bradley's arms drew me to him and he kissed me tenderly, then whispered in my ear, "I asked your father for permission and he said yes after only two hours of arguing."

I drew back and looked into his eyes. "When did this happen?"

"Last night in your hotel room. You're very cute when you sleep, and even prettier without any makeup."

"Oh, Bradley."

"I told him I hadn't been with any woman since the spring. I didn't mention it was since that time on my office sofa when we kissed."

"Ah, yes, your office sofa. You really haven't been dating?"

He shook his head. "Like I said, I had to be sure of myself. I knew I loved you, but I hadn't told a woman I loved her in ten years and that relationship ended badly."

"Why didn't you tell me you loved me when we were in your bed the other night?"

"Because I never wanted you to think I'd said those words so you'd go all the way with me."

I held his face between my hands. "I'll never make you regret loving me, darling."

"I know you won't. I know."

He swept me into another kiss, one that quickly turned passionate. Soon he broke away panting and said, "I want a Christmas wedding, Bebe. Will that give you enough time to plan? I just don't think I can wait longer than that."

"A Christmas wedding is perfect."

We found each other's mouths again and I ran my tongue across his lips. Pushing myself up against him, I smiled mentally when I could feel how much he wanted me. Thinking back to something Sister of Mercy had said, I made a move.

Bradley moaned.

I was merciless. And half bent over the train display. I leaned forward and licked the inside of Bradley's ear.

"Bebe, I can't take much more."

"We have unfinished business on the sofa in your office."

Another moan. "Are you sure? You don't want to wait until—God! Where did you learn to do that?"

That night, the sofa in Bradley's office truly was magical.

Epilogue

June 1965

Danielle and Herb posed with their families for the wedding photographer. Guests mingled among the rosebushes and hundreds of flowers in the backyard of Danielle's parents, where the ceremony had been held. White lawn chairs were lined up in rows before the flowered archway where the couple had made their vows. A band played popular music.

"I still can't believe that you added 'promises not to get involved in police matters' to our wedding vows, Bradley." Bradley and I had been married in a beautiful ceremony on Christmas Eve. Mama had cried. Daddy had walked his Little Magnolia down the aisle.

"Come on, baby. It had to be done. And now with our first little one on the way, I feel even better about your safety."

Bradley was more handsome than ever in a sharp Brooks Brothers suit, drawing the eyes of all the girls.

I'd grown my bangs out and wore my hair parted in the middle, flowing in a straight line down my back. Bradley liked it long.

"By the way, Bebe, I didn't learn all the details

about how Drew was being forced out of the company until yesterday during a phone conference."

Uh-oh. It embarrassed me even now to think that I'd once thought Bradley needed my help in securing his position as head of the company.

"Is that so, Bradley?" I asked innocently.

"You were the one who sent Uncle Herman the proof he needed to realize Drew had been embezzling from the company," he said in a terse voice. "Why?"

I felt heat rush to my face. Mentally, I crossed my fingers behind my back. There were some things Bradley simply did not need to know. "Because Drew interrupted us on the sofa that time in your office. I never forgave him."

Bradley looked unconvinced for a moment, then threw back his head and laughed.

Tom walked over with a young brunette—I thought I recognized her as one of the nurses from his short stay at the hospital last year—who looked at him worshipfully.

Bradley held out his hand. "Congratulations on the movie role, Tom. I guess you'll be heading out to California now."

"Thanks. Yeah, I'm trading the stage for palm trees and movie studios. Miss Jordan is coming along with me."

The brunette blushed.

"Tom, you be careful out there," I said. "I hear there are a lot of crazy people in the movie business. If you get in any trouble—"

"They have a terrific police force," Bradley finished.

Tom hugged me and promised to keep in touch.

The band struck up the Dave Clark Five's "Glad All Over."

We wandered over to Darlene and Stu, Bradley

snagging another piece of wedding cake for me. "You're eating for two."

I smiled and dug into the treat.

Stu slapped Bradley on the back and the two immediately started talking business, something they always did when we all got together. After Bradley and I had married, we'd bought the other penthouse in Stu's building. Bradley had said we needed the room. I was glad I didn't have to live in his former bachelor pad.

I smiled at Darlene. "You'll make a great aunt."

"I've already got a layette picked out for a boy or a girl."

"Mama says from the way I'm carrying, it's a boy."

"Bradley Junior?"

"Bradley Junior," I confirmed, and we laughed. I lowered my voice. "Bradley told me on the drive up that Shirley had a son two months ago. He arranged a settlement for her. She and the baby are going to be fine."

"Where is Drew?" Darlene asked.

"The last we heard he was running charter boats off the coast of Florida. Shirley is still down there, so there is still hope that the two will raise the boy together."

I looked over at Bradley. He let his gaze settle on mine.

"Bradley's calling me," I said.

"I didn't hear a word," Darlene protested.

"He didn't have to say one. Are you driving back to the city tonight?"

"Yes, are you, honey?"

"Yes. You know we both love Manhattan. I'll see you tomorrow," I said and hugged her.

Bradley took my arm and threaded it through his. He walked me under an apple tree and kissed me.

"So sweet and you just keep getting sweeter," he whispered.

We kissed again.

"Mmmm, you have a very talented tongue," he said, cupping my head in his hand. He lowered his voice. "I don't know how you turned out to be such a tigress in bed. The things you do . . ."

I smiled to myself. "You inspire me, darling."

"God, Bebe, let's go home. Now."

"Whatever you say, Bradley. Whatever you say."

ROSEMARY MARTIN
Murder A-Go-Go Mysteries

IT'S A MOD, MOD, MOD, MOD MURDER

With a degree from secretarial school, Bebe Bennett has split
Richmond, Virginia, for the whirlwind of Manhattan. Getting in on the
British invasion, her boss at Rip City Records has signed up Philip
Royal and the Beefeaters. But when Bebe and her stewardess
roommate Darlene go to meet two members of the band for a fab
night out, they find Philip dead, electrocuted with his own guitar. Even
worse, the fuzz suspect Darlene. So, it's up to Bebe to abandon her
Jackie Kennedy-inspired suits and venture into the smoky nightclubs of
Greenwich Village, delving into the dark side of the swinging city to
expose a killer.

TWIST AND SHOUT MURDER

*My fab life in New York City just keeps getting better! Dreamy Bradley
Williams has a new job at the Ryan Modeling Agency, and he's taken
me with him. Of course, I'd follow Bradley
anywhere, but a bonus and a new title—Executive Secretary—can sure
boost a girl's spirits! Now if only Bradley would figure out that the title I
really want is Mrs. Williams...*

Bebe Bennett's spent her bonus on glad rags straight from Carnaby
Street—all with miniskirts to show off her legs. But Bradley still calls
her "kid," and worse, he's totally gone on the company's top model,
Suzie Wexford. Suzie's beauty really is only skin-deep—she's scratched
her way to the top, making plenty of enemies along the way. So it's
no surprise when she winds up dead, strangled with a Pucci scarf—a
gift from Bradley!

Available wherever books are sold or at
penguin.com

The Bestselling
Blackbird Sisters Mystery Series
by
Nancy Martin

Don't miss a single adventure of the Blackbird
sisters, a trio of Philadelphia-born, hot-blooded
bluebloods with a flair for fashion—and for
solving crimes.

Available in Paperback:

How to Murder a Millionaire
Dead Girls Don't Wear Diamonds
Some Like It Lethal
Cross Your Heart and Hope to Die
Have Your Cake and Kill Him Too

**Available wherever books are sold or at
penguin.com**